An
kn
chair across from he

"You have no idea how many times I have held this conversation in my head," she said. "Of course, you were so much nicer then. But I can't blame you for not knowing your lines if I don't give them to you."

A reluctant chuckle burst from him and he quickly smothered it. He wasn't going to fall back into the habit of letting Andrea charm him like she had when they'd been kids. Not when he knew that she had a steel streak that wouldn't allow her to bend. When she was on a mission, nothing and no one got in her way—including him and their child. "How about you just say what you came to say and then we can each go on with our lives."

Though the smile on her face remained, the light in her eyes faded, and despite knowing that she didn't deserve his sympathy, he felt guilty for hurting her feelings.

"It wasn't easy for me to come here," she said softly.

"And yet here you sit."

"Yes."

Dear Reader,

Welcome back to Aspen Creek, Colorado, where love is in the air. This time it strikes Cole and Andrea. *A Reunion to Remember* has two of my favorite tropes—second-chance romance and a single father. There's something about watching two people try to regain the close relationship they once had that grabs my attention and won't let go. The single dad element just heightens the appeal.

Cole and Andrea had once been the best of friends. A brief fling the summer before their senior year in high school led to an unplanned pregnancy. When their parents pressured them to give up the baby for adoption, Andrea agreed that'd be for the best. But Cole refused to relinquish his rights and raised their daughter on his own. Now, nearly sixteen years later, Andrea comes to Aspen Creek for the summer in order to see her daughter. Will Cole and Andrea be able to put the past behind them and build a new relationship and family of three?

I hope you enjoy reading *A Reunion to Remember* as much as I enjoyed writing it.

I love hearing from my readers, so feel free to visit my website, kathydouglassbooks.com, and drop me a line.

Happy reading!

Kathy

A REUNION
TO REMEMBER

KATHY DOUGLASS

Harlequin

SPECIAL EDITION

Harlequin®
SPECIAL EDITION™

Recycling programs for this product may not exist in your area.

ISBN-13: 978-1-335-18005-6

A Reunion to Remember

 Harlequin Enterprises ULC
22 Adelaide St. West, 41st Floor
Toronto, Ontario M5H 4E3, Canada
www.Harlequin.com

Printed in Lithuania

MIX
Paper | Supporting responsible forestry
FSC® C021394

Kathy Douglass is a lawyer turned author of sweet small-town contemporary romances. She is married to her very own hero and mother to two sons, who cheer her on as she tries to get her stubborn hero and heroine to realize they are meant to be together. She loves hearing from readers that something in her books made them laugh or cry. You can learn more about Kathy or contact her at kathydouglassbooks.com.

Books by Kathy Douglass

Montana Mavericks: The Trail to Tenacity

That Maverick of Mine

Montana Mavericks: The Anniversary Gift

Starting Over with the Maverick

Harlequin Special Edition

Aspen Creek Bachelors

Valentines for the Rancher
The Rancher's Baby
Wrangling a Family
The Cowboy Who Came Home
A Reunion to Remember

Montana Mavericks: Lassoing Love

Falling for Dr. Maverick

Montana Mavericks: Brothers & Broncos

In the Ring with the Maverick

Visit the Author Profile page
at Harlequin.com for more titles.

This book is dedicated to the following:

My parents, whose love and support was unwavering.
I miss you both every day.

My aunts and my sister, who read each of my books.
Thank you for your constant support.

My siblings. You were my first friends
and our friendship is just as strong today.

My readers. Whether this is the first time you're reading
one of my books or you've read them all, I thank you.

My editor, Susan Litman. You always make my books the
best they can be. Thank you for all of your hard work.

Finally, this book is dedicated with love to my husband
and sons. The three of you are the best part of my life.

Chapter One

Andrea Taylor read the highway sign welcoming her to Aspen Creek, Colorado, and automatically eased up on the gas pedal. Her breath caught in her throat, and suddenly she found it difficult to breathe. *Her daughter lived in this town.*

The daughter she hadn't seen since the day she was born.

Andrea had surrendered her parental rights to her baby days before her thirteen hours of labor had commenced. Her eyes misted with unexpected tears, and she automatically blinked them away. She reminded herself that she'd chosen of her own free will to relinquish her rights. It had been best for both of them. There were no do-overs in life.

But now...she wanted at least a glimpse of the life her daughter had. The town itself seemed nice—a haven for great skiing and outdoor sports that several winter Olympians called home. The town was a vacation destination for the rich and famous as well as families seeking winter getaways.

Was it a good place to grow up? She hoped so. She needed to know that her little girl was happy. Then maybe she finally would be able to put the past behind her once and for all and get on with her life. Maybe then she would be able to find the peace that still eluded her.

Andrea drove until she reached downtown. She cruised up and down the streets, taking in everything. The wealthy resort town didn't have the kitschy feel of a town whose economy depended on tourism dollars. Instead, Aspen Creek had a warm feeling. A welcoming feeling. It felt like a real community. Just being here made the tension ease from her body. The boutiques and restaurants lining the pristine streets were charming and the streets bustled with activity as people strolled along, popping into the various establishments and emerging with shopping bags.

If this was a regular vacation, she would enjoy shopping and investigating this little town, straying off the beaten path and finding hidden jewels. But this wasn't a vacation. Andrea hadn't gone on a real vacation since the summer between her junior and senior years of high school.

The summer that changed her life.

Andrea's parents had been best friends with Cole Richards's parents since the four of them met at medical school. The families celebrated holidays together and regularly traveled as a group. Andrea and her two sisters had grown up with Cole and his two younger brothers in Chicago. She had always thought that Cole was handsome, but that summer she'd felt a new attraction to him. He'd become irresistible and her heart skipped a beat whenever he was around. He'd also begun to see her in a new light, and they'd started a hot romance that they'd hidden from their parents. The secrecy had made their relationship more intense and exciting. One thing led to another and on Halloween she discovered she was pregnant, and the secret was out. Almost immediately, their parents began pressuring them to give the baby up for adoption so she and Cole could continue on the path they'd planned for their lives.

Initially Cole and Andrea had formed a united front, resisting the pressure. He'd wanted to get married so they could raise their child together. Cole had said that if they each got jobs they could manage financially. He'd made it all sound so easy. Even though she had started to wonder at that point whether what she felt for him was actually love or a serious case of infatuation mingled with lust, she'd been seriously considering the possibility.

Then her parents had sat her down and confronted her with some hard facts. She had always said she wanted to be a doctor. She'd studied and worked toward that goal for years. If she gave up the idea of college and med school, what was going to go in its place? Even if finding work would be as easy as Cole said, was she really willing to give up her dream career for a job she didn't love, just to pay the bills? And did she have any idea how high those bills would be? Rent was expensive. Childcare to look after the baby while they worked was expensive. Babies themselves were expensive, when you looked at all the money that had to be spent on cribs and strollers and diapers and food and everything else. She and Cole would end up working around the clock just to make ends meet, leaving them next to no time to actually spend with the child they'd fought so hard to keep. Would that really be best for them or for the baby? Wouldn't that baby be happier given to a couple who was truly ready to start a family?

Swayed, Andrea had reluctantly agreed to surrender all rights to her daughter. Cole had never agreed. Even faced with rejection by their parents, he'd stood strong, determined to raise their daughter on his own if need be. Andrea recalled the last time she'd seen Cole. It had been in her hospital room the day she'd given birth. He'd held the tiny baby in his arms and pleaded with her to trust him. He'd promised to keep her and the baby safe. Tears rolled down his face as he'd sworn he would provide a good home for them. All she had to do was say yes.

She'd said no.

Every now and then, Andrea wondered what her life would be like if she'd had more faith in him. Would they be happily married, raising their child together? Or would the stresses of life have ruined their relationship long ago, leaving them bitter and unhappy? Not that it did any good to play "what-if." They'd each made their choices and had walked their paths separately.

Andrea shoved the memories and regrets to the recesses of her mind where they belonged as she drove to the real estate agency. She pulled into the tree-lined street, parked in front of the redbrick building and went inside. The office was airy, and sunlight streamed through the front windows. A cozy seating area was on one side of the room, and a woman was seated behind a large desk on the other. Soft music played from unseen speakers.

The woman flashed a friendly smile, stood and gracefully approached Andrea. She held out her hand. "Hello. I'm Rolanda Jensen. How may I help you?"

Andrea automatically shook the offered hand. "I'm Andrea Taylor. I've rented a cabin for the summer. I've come to finalize the paperwork and pick up the keys."

"Wonderful. I wasn't expecting you until later in the day, so please give me a minute."

Andrea had driven halfway from her Chicago home and then checked into a hotel yesterday. She'd planned to get a good night's sleep and arrive in town by the afternoon, but she'd only managed to sleep for a few hours, anxious to reach the place where her daughter lived. She'd gotten up with the sun and resumed her drive. "I hope it's not an inconvenience. I can look around town for a few hours and come back at the appointed time."

"That's not necessary. The cabin is clean and ready. I'll show you there once we've finished the paperwork."

Once they'd completed the documents, Rolanda slipped on a lavender jacket that matched her slim skirt and led the way out of the office. Andrea was surprised when the impeccably dressed agent walked past the expensive sedan and climbed into a dusty blue pickup.

Rolanda leaned out the window. "Just follow me. When we get out of town, there won't be a lot of traffic."

Andrea got into her car and followed the pickup. Her phone rang and when her best friend Dana's name popped up on the screen she put the phone on speaker.

"Are you on the road yet?"

Andrea smiled. "I'm already in Aspen Creek. I'm following the Realtor to the cabin as we speak."

"You made good time. Did you even sleep?"

"Some."

"Did you bother to look around while you were driving? You might be on a mission, but this is still your vacation."

"I kept my eyes on the road." On the way from Illinois to Colorado, she'd been focused on driving and hadn't paid attention to the scenery. Now, prodded by Dana's comment, she took it all in. The wildflowers growing on the side of the road in purple, red and orange bunches were more beautiful than the bouquets that Andrea purchased weekly. The white-peaked mountains soaring majestically in the distance were awe-inspiring. The deer and wildlife romping in the fields made her smile. She couldn't have chosen a better place for her little girl to grow up than here. "But it is pretty here."

"That should help you to relax."

Andrea sighed. "I hope so. But I'm scared of what I might find."

"What do you mean? You know Cole and Crystal live there."

"It looks nice, but is Crystal happy? What kind of father is Cole? What kind of relationship do Crystal and Cole have?"

That was information the private investigator she'd hired couldn't provide. Andrea could only learn what she truly wanted to know by observing Cole and Crystal for herself. That's what she intended to do. *From a distance.* She wouldn't intrude on their lives. They wouldn't even know she was here. When she had the answers she was seeking, she would go back home and they'd be none the wiser.

"That's what you're there to discover. But the Cole we knew in school was easygoing and kind. I doubt if his character has changed."

Andrea hoped that was the case. But he'd been so angry that last day. She'd never seen that look in his eyes before. She forced the disturbing image away.

Rolanda turned off the highway and onto a two-lane road, and Andrea did the same.

"We're nearly at the cabin. I'll call you once I'm settled."

"And every Sunday."

"Yes." They'd agreed on a weekly call plus twice

weekly texts, to keep Dana in the loop and so Andrea wouldn't get antsy being on her own for so long.

After ten minutes, they turned onto a gravel road and drove slowly under a canopy of thick trees. A minute later, the trees cleared and a small cabin appeared at the end of the driveway. Andrea parked beside Rolanda's truck and quickly got out of her car. Inhaling deeply, she breathed in a lungful of fresh mountain air and expelled the tension that built every time she thought about seeing her daughter again. Or more accurately, for the first time. When she was born, the nurse had wrapped the newborn in a blanket and offered her to Andrea who'd turned her head away. She'd known that if she even looked at the baby, it would be too hard to give her away.

Andrea raised and lowered her shoulders, gave herself a little shake, pushing herself back into the moment.

"What do you think?" Rolanda asked, a wide grin on her face, clearly anticipating a positive response. She swept her arms wide, the gesture encompassing the verdant grass, the towering fir trees and the majestic snowcapped mountains in the distance as well as the rustic cabin.

Andrea returned the other woman's smile and replied honestly. "The brochure didn't do it justice. But then, I suppose no photograph could capture the sweetness of the air or how wonderful it feels to stand in the shadow of the Rockies."

"Exactly." Rolanda climbed the three wide stairs leading to the deep porch, pausing to straighten one of the flowerpots on either side of the porch rail before she unlocked the front door. "If you like the outside, you're going to love the inside. It has everything you could dream of and more."

Andrea stepped into the cabin and looked around. The space wasn't especially large, but it was plenty of room for one person. The sunlight filtered through the tall windows at the front of the cabin, casting a warm glow over the room. A colorful rug was centered over the wide-planked oak floor. A stone fireplace dominated one wall and Andrea imagined cozy winter nights beside the fire, a cup of hot cocoa in one hand and a good book in the other. Since it was early June and she wouldn't be here when it was cold enough to need a fire, imagine was all she would be doing.

"The bedroom is this way," Rolanda said, stepping through a doorway on the right. A queen bed with a striped cream-and-green comforter was centered on the far wall between two windows that provided a view of the mountains. There was a comfortable chair beside a freestanding mirror. A small desk with a lamp was stationed against the wall beside the closet.

"This is lovely," Andrea said. Truthfully, she didn't care what the room looked like. She would be content to stay in a shack with a leaky roof and sleep on the floor if she had to.

"Wonderful. Now let's check out the kitchen."

They walked down a short hallway, stopping to peer into an elegant bathroom, before stepping into the kitchen. Though of average size, it held a table for four and had updated appliances. Like the other rooms, there was a large window with a view of nature.

"There's a nice covered porch out back," Rolanda said, sliding open the French doors so Andrea could step outside. A sitting area with wicker furniture was on one side of the porch and a hot tub was on the other.

"It's perfect," Andrea said.

"There aren't many neighbors out here, but cell service is good," Rolanda said as they went back inside. "Unfortunately, the restaurants don't deliver this far out, so you're going to have to do your own cooking or drive into town to eat."

"That won't be a problem. I actually love cooking." With her busy schedule, Andrea didn't get the chance to cook often. It would be nice to spend some extended time in the kitchen preparing her favorite meals or trying out new recipes. She'd grabbed a few items at the Walmart she'd passed on the way into town, but the fresh fruit, vegetables, bread and canned goods would need to be supplemented soon.

"That's about everything. Except to give you the keys." Rolanda handed her a silver key chain in the shape of the Rocky Mountains. She also gave Andrea a business card. "I've written my cell number on here, so if you need anything or have questions about town, please feel free to contact me."

Rolanda's invitation surprised her. Andrea was used to professional relationships ending when the business was completed. Perhaps this was the way things were done in small towns. Or maybe Rolanda was simply an especially nice person. Whatever the case, knowing that she had someone she could call made Andrea happy. It felt good to know she wasn't alone.

They walked outside and Andrea watched as the other woman climbed into her pickup, waved, made a U-turn, then drove away. Two rocking chairs were on the porch, one on either side of the stairs, and Andrea sat in the nearer one. She'd left her luggage in the trunk of her car beside the groceries, but she wasn't inclined to get up and bring the items into the cabin just yet. The day was just so beautiful it would be a crime not to sit here and enjoy it.

Though she tried to be calm, one thought repeated through her mind, making her heart thud.

She was going to see her daughter soon.

"Come on, you're making me late."

Cole shook his head at the impatience in his daughter's voice. Grinning, he nudged Crystal's shoulder with his. "It's amazing the difference a few days can make. It seems like only yesterday you were begging for five more minutes of sleep. Now you're rushing me out of the house." He pretended to think. "I can't imagine what caused this change."

Crystal laughed. "Before, I had to go to school. But now it's summer break and I don't want to miss a minute of it."

"I'm going to remind you of how early you got up this morning in September."

"Yeah? And when you're rushing me out of the house, I'm going to remind you of how slowly you're moving right now. I know you don't have a chemistry test you're dreading, so what's the holdup?"

Cole looked into his daughter's brown eyes. Although she had been his spitting image when she was born, the older she got, the more she began to resemble her mother.

Andrea.

Now, at a few weeks shy of sixteen, Crystal looked so much like her mother had at that age. As usual, just thinking of his former girlfriend and the way she'd walked away from their daughter without a second thought filled him with hurt and confusion. He just couldn't understand the choice she'd made. When he was at his most generous, he acknowledged that it hadn't been an easy thing for her. She'd agonized over the decision for months, repeatedly going back and forth as she tried to figure out the right thing to do. For a while, it seemed that she was leaning his way and was going to marry him so they could raise their baby together. In the end, she'd chosen her parents and the life they'd wanted for her: college and a lucrative career as a doctor instead of him and their child. To him, that was unfathomable.

"Well?" Crystal prodded when he only stood there lost in thought.

"Nothing. I have a schedule and I like to keep it. Besides, the yarn store isn't even open yet. And I don't like the idea of you standing alone on the street waiting for someone to let you in."

"What can possibly happen? We live in Aspen Creek, Colorado's very own Mayberry."

"What do you know about Mayberry? *The Andy Griffith Show* is decades older than you are. Heck, it's even older than I am."

"I was watching it with Mrs. Rose the other day. It's kind of funny."

Crystal had to be the only teenager who liked hanging out with senior citizens. She had grown quite close to Rose when she'd begun babysitting her grandniece a couple of years ago. Rose had hurt her hip and Alexandra, Rose's niece, had moved to Aspen Creek with her infant daughter to care for her. Although Alexandra had gotten married to local rancher Nathan Montgomery and she and her daughter had moved out, Crystal had continued to visit Rose regularly. Rose had even taught Crystal how to knit. She'd become quite good at it. It wasn't unusual to see Crystal with knitting needles in her hands, working on some project or another.

"If you say so. But that's not my point. Sure, the people who live here are great. I know most of them. But the town is filled with tourists."

"If you say stranger danger like I'm a kid, I'll scream."

"I wasn't going to say that," he said quickly. Or at least not those exact words. "But you can't count on people who are getting away from their regular lives to behave themselves. People do things on vacation that they wouldn't dream of doing at home. Not all of those things are good. We don't know them or what they're capable of."

Crystal sighed. "I know all that, Dad. You worry about me too much."

"Impossible." He'd worried about her from the second the nurse placed that unbelievably tiny bundle into his nervous arms, and he would worry about her as long as there was breath in his body.

"Anyway," Crystal said, draping the purse strap over her shoulder, a sign that she had grown tired of the conversation and was silently declaring it over, "I don't have to wait outside for the store to open. Rebecca is going to let me in. She asked me to help her get things ready for the classes and clubs. She hired me to help in the store this summer."

"Really? Way to bury the lead. Well, congratulations on joining the ranks of the gainfully employed." He gave her a quick hug.

"Thanks. It'll be good to earn my own money."

"You'll still get an allowance, though." She opened her mouth, and Cole cut her off before she could object. "Don't argue."

Crystal grinned. "I wasn't going to."

"I suppose we should get going, then. Time's a-wasting."

"That's what I've been trying to tell you."

Laughing, Cole grabbed his keys, locked the door behind them, then followed Crystal down the stairs to his pickup. When Crystal was a year old, Cole had hired on as a ranch hand on the Montgomery cattle ranch just outside of Aspen Creek. He had known nothing about ranching, but he'd been a hard worker and willing to learn. To his surprise, he'd gotten more than a job. He and Crystal had gotten a family—one that filled the gap in his heart after his parents, upset with his decision, had cut all ties. Michelle Montgomery had insisted on babysitting Crystal, solving Cole's childcare problem. The job had included ranch housing, which solved another. Cole and Crystal had spent holidays and Sunday dinners with the Montgomery family. Cole counted Nathan, Miles and Isaac, Michelle and Edward's sons, among his closest friends.

A few years ago, the opportunity to buy the feedstore had come along and Cole had jumped at it. Owning the business meant relocating from the ranch to Aspen Creek, which was something Crystal had been eager to do. Her best friends lived in town, and the move meant she'd be able to get together with them more easily. Crystal was a people person who had yet to meet a stranger, and her circle of friends had grown even larger after their move.

Crystal also liked to be busy and had a variety of interests. Living in town meant she could participate in more activities. As a single parent, the responsibility of chauffeuring her around fell on him alone. There was no partner with whom to split the task. Crystal carpooled with friends on occasion, but it was still up to him to make sure Crystal made it to her practices and lessons. It was a heck of a lot easier to drive her to her activities now that they lived in town.

Cole liked working for himself, but a part of him missed ranching and the wide-open spaces. One day he hoped to own a spread of his own. But that was a dream for another day. He needed to live in town right now.

Mrs. Harvey, one of their favorite neighbors, was out for her morning walk. She brushed a pink-and-purple ponytail over her shoulder and waved to them in one smooth motion as she continued down the block. Cole and Crystal returned the gesture. Though his life was nothing like what he'd imagined back when he was Crystal's age, Cole wouldn't change a thing. Being a teenage single dad without any support from his family had been hard at times, but he'd managed. In a way, he and Crystal had grown up together. As a result, they were friends, but they were both aware that he was the parent and she was the child.

"There's Rebecca now," Crystal said, as he turned onto the one-way street and pulled in front of the Pins and Needles Craft Store. Never in a million years would he have expected a store that specialized in yarn, sewing materials and art supplies to flourish in a tourist town in ranch country, so he'd been pleasantly surprised by the store's success. He supposed crafting was a good way to keep kids busy in between skiing, ice-skating and other winter activities.

Rebecca Summers moved to Aspen Creek three years ago. Although she was friendly, she was guarded. On the few occasions they'd talked, Cole had walked away not knowing a bit more about her than he had before the conversation. But he never pressed. Since he liked his privacy, he respected hers. Though years had passed since his family had turned their back on him and Crystal, he wasn't any more eager to discuss the details of his past than he had been when they'd moved to Colorado. All anyone knew was that he and Crystal were all the family they had. Or needed.

"Aren't you going to get out and say hi?" Crystal asked when he didn't turn off the engine. There was a hopeful look in her eyes, and he sighed. She was on her match-making kick again. Not that she was ever off for very long. When she'd started kindergarten, Crystal had asked why she didn't have a mother like all of the other kids. Not wanting to lie or make his child feel she'd been unwanted, he'd said that her mother had loved her but explained that she couldn't be with them. From then on, Crystal had tried to set him up with nearly every woman she met. Back then she'd been looking for a mother. Now he suspected that she was trying to find him a wife.

"I suppose I have a minute." He would never hear the end of it from Crystal if he didn't. His daughter was mature enough to accept it—eventually—when he told her he was sure that someone wasn't right for him, but she was adamant that he give each woman a fair chance.

Crystal hopped out of the truck and ran over to the store where Rebecca was waiting for her. Cole followed more slowly.

Rebecca was undeniably an attractive woman. In her late twenties, she was only a few years younger than Cole. Tall and model thin with clear brown skin and friendly eyes, she should have appealed to him. Yet he felt no stir of desire when he looked at her. No woman had aroused him since Andrea had broken his heart. In nearly sixteen years, he hadn't found a way to heal it. More than that, he wasn't interested in trying. He was content with his life the way it was. He didn't need a woman to complete him. He just wished he could make his daughter understand that.

"Hi, Rebecca," Crystal said, hugging the other woman while giving Cole a meaningful glance over the woman's shoulder.

"It's good to see you both," Rebecca said, smiling at them. Her eyes were warm with welcome and still…nothing. Not the tiniest spark.

"You as well," Cole said. "Thanks for letting Crystal work for you."

"She's a delight."

"She certainly is." Cole turned to his daughter who was watching the interaction with undisguised interest. "I'll see you later at the store. Call me before you leave. Or if you decide that you want me to pick you up."

He could tell Crystal didn't like his last comment—it made her seem like a child—but she limited her show of displeasure to a slight frown. "Will do."

With a final nod to Rebecca, Cole hopped back into his truck and headed down the road. Five minutes later, he was parking in his spot behind the Aspen Creek Feedstore. Gary Perkins, the man he'd bought the business from, was already inside, reading the local newspaper and sipping from a mug of the thickest black coffee known to man. Gary had started the business nearly forty years ago and run it basically on his own. Seventy years old if he was a day, he'd never married and didn't have any family to speak of. A few years ago, he'd fallen and injured his leg and back, and it had taken him months to recover. Realizing that he was unable to continue running the store, he'd initially planned to sell it to a big conglomerate and move to a warmer climate. Cole's offer to buy it and keep Gary on in whatever capacity he chose—including letting him keep living in his apartment above the store, no charge—had been quickly accepted.

"How's it going?" Cole asked, stopping to rub Rusty, Gary's aging collie.

"Randy stopped in to pick up his order. His wife is due to have her baby any day now."

"What's he doing coming to town, then? I could have dropped it off for him."

"Between you, me and the lamppost, I think he wanted to get away from his mother-in-law for a while. She arrived a week ago."

Cole shook his head. Gary had to be the town's biggest gossip. Somehow, he was always the first to know everything that was going on in town.

"Well, I'm glad you were able to help him." Cole poured half a mug of coffee, diluted it with hot water and added a spoonful of sugar before taking a swallow. It wasn't quite palatable, but it would do.

"You didn't doubt me, did you, boss?" Gary said, and then they both laughed. From the day Cole signed on the dotted line, Gary had begun referring to Cole as the boss. Gary took great pleasure in pointing out that he was no longer responsible for the store, though he was full of advice on ways to deal with the quirks and idiosyncrasies in the seventy-year-old building—and ways to deal with the longtime customers, who could be just as quirky.

"Not for a second," Cole said honestly. He'd known from the moment he'd bought the business that there would be a steep learning curve. When Gary agreed to stick around, Cole had been relieved that he'd have someone to turn to for advice. As an added bonus, being needed had reignited the fire in Gary, and he spent quite a few hours hanging around the store and engaging with customers. He also made sure that ranchers knew they could trust Cole to treat them fairly. Somehow Gary had managed to transfer the goodwill that he had earned over the years to Cole.

The bell over the door jingled as a customer entered. From that minute on, there was a steady flow of business, keeping him and Gary busy. Crystal arrived shortly after noon, carrying the takeout he'd ordered from the diner.

"What do you know that's good?" Gary asked her as he always did.

"I know that it's summer and school is out," Crystal replied, giving Gary a hug. "And that I have a paying job."

"Well, I'll know who to hit up when I need a loan," Gary joked.

Crystal laughed and the three of them walked into the break room to eat. Cole listened for the bell with one ear and kept the other tuned to the conversation at the table. As Gary and Crystal talked and kidded each other, Cole felt an unexpected ache in his heart. It was no mystery why Crystal gravitated toward the senior citizens. She felt the absence of grandparents in her life. The older generation doted on her—especially those with no grandkids of their own—and she thrived under the attention.

As a kid, Cole hadn't seen either set of grandparents very often because they lived on opposite coasts, but they'd still spoiled him and his younger brothers rotten. Cole had been confident that they loved and supported him. But both his paternal and maternal grandparents had taken sides with his parents and tried to convince him to give his child away. They'd argued that keeping the baby would change his life forever. When he'd refused to give in, they'd told him he was on his own—that they wouldn't help him or Crystal until he came to his senses and agreed to put her up for adoption. They probably thought he'd cave the first time she kept him up all night crying, or the first time he really had to struggle to get food on the table. But he hadn't caved. He hadn't reached out to them for help even once. And they'd never reached out either.

Cole realized that Crystal and Gary were staring at him, and he lifted his can of pop to his lips and took a swallow. "What?"

"Nothing," Gary said with a smirk.

"I was just telling Gary about Rebecca. I think she likes you."

Cole groaned. "Not that again. That's your imagination. She's no more interested in me than I am in her." Thank goodness.

"You could do a lot worse," Gary said. "You're getting a little long in the tooth, so you shouldn't waste more time. Otherwise, you'll end up all alone."

That from a lifelong bachelor.

"That's what I'm always telling him," Crystal added smugly. "What'll he do when I head off to college in a few years, hmm? I don't like the thought of him by himself. But that's how he'll end up if I don't find someone for him soon."

After shooting his daughter a mock glare, Cole turned back to Gary. "I'm only thirty-four."

"Almost thirty-five," Gary and Crystal said in unison. Clearly they'd had this conversation before.

"Not for several months. But that's still young."

"Not to me," Crystal said.

"I imagine not," Cole conceded. "But it is much too young to be saddled with the wrong person for the rest of my life. Besides, why waste her time when I'm not interested?"

"I can tell you need more time to think about this," Crystal said. "We don't have to talk about it now."

It wasn't the answer he was hoping for, but a reprieve was better than nothing. Cole finished his lunch and left Crystal and Gary to scheme on their own while he went back to work. When the day was done, he closed the shop and he and Crystal headed home.

As he cooked dinner, Cole couldn't shake the feeling that something truly was missing in his life. He blamed the conversation he'd had with Crystal and Gary and their insistence that he needed a woman to complete him.

He added the pasta to the boiling water and checked the sauce. He was doing just fine. He didn't need a woman. That ache he felt in his heart wouldn't last.

So why did he think he was lying to himself?

Chapter Two

Andrea woke the next morning as the sun was still making its way across the sky. She'd learned at a young age that the day started early. Her father was a surgeon who generally left the house before 5:00 a.m. when he had surgeries scheduled in order to prepare for the day ahead, and Andrea's pediatrician mother hadn't been far behind. Andrea was a pediatrician as well, and she too began her day in the early morning, making her rounds at the hospital to check on her patients before going into the office for her appointments. Even though she was on vacation, she was too used to her schedule to sleep in.

Throwing aside the sheet and thin blanket covering her, she stood and stretched. As always, she started her day with yoga to clear her mind and awaken her body. After ten minutes, she felt refreshed and ready to face the day. She put away her yoga mat, made the bed and headed to the kitchen where she brewed a mug of green tea. She had planned to go grocery shopping today, but the notion held little appeal. Right now there was a rocking chair calling her name. She grabbed her tea and a banana and went outside. The morning was crisp but not cold, and as she inhaled the mountain air, contentment settled over her.

Her decision to come to Aspen Creek hadn't been well-thought-out. Actually, she hadn't intended to come here at all. For nearly sixteen years she'd believed that she had made peace with her decision to surrender her maternal rights. Though she had often wondered how Cole and their child were faring—especially on her baby's birthday—she had never tried to find them. She'd known they'd moved away from Chicago, but she hadn't known where they'd gone. She sometimes wondered if going no contact with them had been the best thing for her, but at the time, it had felt like the only way to guarantee that she stayed on track with her plans. She couldn't chase after them if she didn't know where they were. Over time, she'd shoved aside most thoughts of them and moved on with her life. Andrea gave herself one day a year—her daughter's birthday—to dedicate serious time to thinking about what might have been. For twenty-four hours she allowed herself to dream. When midnight struck, she once more put her feelings away.

Recently, she'd decided to stop running away. It was time to confront her past. She'd begun having nightmares and been unnaturally grumpy. It hadn't taken long to realize that the past she'd tried to bury was forcing its way to the surface, giving her no choice but to deal with everything she had tried to suppress. Even so, Andrea had no intention of interacting with her daughter or Cole. She wasn't a part of their lives nor would she ever be. It would be unfair to disrupt what they had made for themselves. Once she had assured herself that all was well, Andrea planned to go back home and continue the life she'd chosen.

Reassured that she had a plan that she could stick to, Andrea leaned back in the rocking chair and closed her eyes. She was pleasantly surprised to discover that the morning wasn't as quiet as she'd expected it to be. The cabin was in the middle of nowhere—on the outskirts of the owner's cattle ranch and far away from the operation—but even so there was activity. The birds chirped in the trees, their songs a call and response although occasionally they did overlap, singing a melodic duet. Squirrels noisily chomped on nuts before darting across the lawn. There was a babbling brook within walking distance and the frogs croaked noisily. Wind chimes dangled from the eaves, and they jangled whenever the breeze blew, joining in nature's songs.

Living and working in a city as busy as Chicago, Andrea had become an expert at tuning out background noise. She barely heard traffic sounds, freight trains or jackhammers on construction sites. Now she found herself attuned to the sounds surrounding her and enjoying every one.

She lifted her mug to her lips and realized with no small amount of dismay that it was empty. Apparently, she'd mindlessly drunk her tea, something that she never did. Ordinarily Andrea was aware of every little thing she was doing. Acting without conscious thought could be dangerous, especially for a doctor. But she was on vacation, so she supposed it was okay to ease up on her discipline as long as it didn't turn into a habit.

Standing, she inhaled one last fragrant lungful of pine-scented mountain air before she went inside the cabin. On her arrival, she really hadn't done more than take a cursory glance around. Now, she took time to actually study the place that would be her home for the next three months. She had never been one of those people who cared about the "vibes" of a place, but even she had to admit that the atmosphere was soothing. The rooms had been designed for relaxation; a refuge from the cares of the world. It was as if some design magic had taken place. Andrea shook her head at the fanciful notion, wondering if being in this cottage had somehow begun to affect her thinking. She'd given up all belief in fairy tales the day her parents told her they would withdraw their financial and emotional support if she didn't do exactly as they said. Life had become incredibly real then.

If given the time and space, she might have come to the conclusion that giving up her child for adoption was the right thing without the arm-twisting, but she hadn't been given the opportunity. When Cole had refused to go along with the plan and she'd begun to have doubts, her parents had upped the pressure. She'd been young, unsure of herself, easily spooked by the picture of the harsh future her parents described for her if she didn't fall in line. And so she'd buckled.

Deciding that she'd had more than enough introspection for the day, Andrea took a quick shower and got dressed in a beige-and-white-striped sundress, and then automatically pulled her hair away from her face and into a thick ponytail that hung between her shoulders. Although she had planned on making a quick run to the store to pick up more supplies, she found herself bypassing the Walmart and continuing into Aspen Creek. It was a small town, and for a minute she worried that she might run into Cole. But once she saw the number of people walking along the streets, that fear subsided a bit. They weren't in downtown Chicago, but there were still lots of tourists bustling about. She could easily blend in with the crowd if necessary. Besides, she didn't think Cole would even recognize her now. He hadn't seen her in nearly sixteen years. Her face had matured and though she was still barely five foot four, her body had filled out some. Even though she could stand to put on a pound or two, she wasn't the gangly teenager she'd been. Even so, she smashed a floppy hat onto her head and put on her dark sunglasses.

The investigator had included photos of Cole and their daughter in the dossier. She still thought Cole was one of the most handsome men she had ever seen. In high school, he'd played both football and baseball and excelled at each, though he hadn't planned on playing either sport in college. His hours in the weight room had been productive, and he'd been quite built back then. Recent photos showed that time hadn't hurt his physique. If anything, he was even more muscular now.

Andrea knew that he had worked as a ranch hand for many years. Perhaps his work was responsible for his physique. Of course he no longer lived and worked on a ranch, so that was immaterial. As was the fact that he was still gorgeous. So why had her heart skipped a beat every time she looked at the pictures? Why had she looked at them more than once? Why had she found herself running a finger across his face or shoulders in a ridiculous attempt to feel closer to him?

She knew he wasn't married, and the private investigator didn't mention any woman who seemed to be a regular presence in his life, but that didn't mean there had never been a special someone. Andrea certainly didn't think he'd spent the past decade and a half alone. Not that his romantic life was any of her business. She had done her share of dating over the years. She'd even had a couple of serious relationships that could have ended in marriage. They'd been great men, but something held her back, making her unable to commit. She hadn't been able to give her complete heart and eventually, she'd ended things. It would have been unfair to marry either of them. They'd deserved better than a wife who'd liked them but hadn't been in love.

To date, no man had made her heart beat faster with just a look like Cole had for those few short months they'd been together. That youthful thrill had died when their relationship crashed and burned. Now there were no secret trysts or stolen kisses. Her relationships were more mature. She and her current boyfriend—a successful corporate lawyer—saw each other when their schedules allowed. They attended charity dinners, caught the occasional play at local theaters and went to museum exhibits together. When she told him that she would be going out of town for the summer, he hadn't gotten upset. Instead, he'd absently brushed a kiss on her cheek and told her to enjoy herself.

Getting out of her car, she started down the street. A warm breeze blew, and she smiled at the knowledge that she was strolling along the same streets that her daughter walked on. She spotted a man in the distance. He was tall and muscular, and there was something so familiar about him that the hairs on the back of her neck stood up. She shivered. Could it be Cole? The idea struck fear in her heart, and she almost got back into her car and drove to the cabin. And then what would she do? Would she hide out like a criminal waiting for him to break down the door and force her to leave town? Of course not. She would stick to her plan of watching from a distance.

The man kept walking, his back to her, and she turned and headed for the diner. Shaking her head, she realized she was being ridiculous. Aspen Creek might not be a thriving metropolis, but seriously, what were the odds that she would run into Cole on the street the first day she visited the town?

When she reached the Aspen Creek Diner, she opened the door and stepped inside. The aroma of frying bacon and sausage filled the air, and her stomach rumbled. This was so much better than cold cereal.

"Take any seat," said a smiling waitress carrying a tray filled with plates.

There was a vacant booth in front of the window, and Andrea quickly slid onto the bench seat. Though she always carried a book in her purse, she didn't take it out. This would be a good time to people watch. After giving her order to the waitress, Andrea leaned back and looked around. With red vinyl booths lining the walls and small tables with red vinyl chairs in the middle of the room, the restaurant had the look of exactly what it was. A diner in a small town.

As a doctor at a busy practice, Andrea had grown accustomed to grabbing meals on the go and practically swallowing her food whole. Even on her days off she found it difficult to slow down and really enjoy her meals. When the waitress set the plate with an omelet, raisin toast and fried ham in front of her, Andrea picked up the fork, determined to indulge in every bite of food.

As she savored the omelet, she glanced around the room again. No wonder the place was packed. The food was delicious. There was a buzz of conversation in the diner, and the servers were greeting regulars, serving up breakfasts, coffee and even take-out orders.

From the time she'd been a small child, she'd amused herself by making up stories about the people around her. The couple with the two toddlers who seemed to be more interested in the salt and pepper shakers than the coloring page and small box of crayons they'd been given? They were definitely tourists, taking their first vacation as a family. The women with the elaborate hairdos? They were in town for a wedding. Probably bridesmaids. That older couple holding hands as they sipped their coffee? They were definitely residents in town who were having their weekly breakfast date.

Making up stories about the other diners kept her from focusing too much on her life and the nagging sense that something was missing.

Once Andrea had finished eating, she paid her bill, left the restaurant and started down the street. Now that she was in town, she decided to do some sightseeing. Looking up, Andrea glanced at the mountains. They looked so close that she almost thought she could touch them if she reached out a hand. The thought made her giggle. Putting the hat back onto her head, she started down the street.

The streets of the town were pristine, and the air was quite fresh. As she wandered along, taking random turns and stopping into shops here and there, she was impressed by just how friendly everyone was. How content. The happiness was contagious, and she found herself smiling.

Though she was still full from breakfast, she stopped into Sweet as Pie bakery and bought a brownie for later.

"I hope I can hold out and not eat this now," Andrea joked to the woman behind the counter.

"There's no need for that. Treat yourself. Eat this one now and come back for more later. I'm open until eight. And if anyone gives you grief, tell them to come see Maggie."

"I'll do that," Andrea said as she stepped outside the shop.

Still smiling, she wasn't paying close enough attention to the other pedestrians and she bumped into someone.

"Excuse me," she said. She glanced up and her mouth

dropped open. Andrea had just bumped into the one person she had hoped to avoid. "Cole."

The photos the private investigator had provided hadn't done Cole justice. Standing here in person, she got the full effect of his aura. He was so filled with life and energy. The full force of his charisma could never be captured in a one-dimensional picture.

He'd always had a dynamic personality and gorgeous body that had made her lose all of her good sense. When he was around and directing the full power of his smile on her, she'd been willing to cast aside her goals and focus only on him. That's how her daughter had come to be. It was shocking to realize that her body still reacted to him in the same manner. Apparently, sixteen years of not seeing each other hadn't changed a thing. She could only hope that she was wiser now.

"Andrea. What are you doing here?"

Andrea couldn't talk to save her life. This couldn't be happening. She was looking into the frowning face of the father of her child. The eyes that had once glowed with amusement and affection now were cold. Her stomach sank to her toes. This wasn't going to go well.

Cole blinked as if the woman standing in front of him was an apparition that would vanish in the blink of an eye. Though he knew it was foolish and wishful thinking at its worst, he closed his eyes momentarily. When he opened them, she was still standing there, looking just as shocked as he felt. His stomach churned, and he even felt a bit lightheaded.

"Why are you here?" he repeated when she only stood there gaping at him.

"Would you believe I'm here on vacation?"

He narrowed his eyes. The last thing he wanted was to play games with her. "No. Try again. This time with the truth."

She swallowed, a sign that she was nervous. Once he would have tried to put her at ease. But not this time.

"Andrea. Come on. Tell me why you came here." His voice was louder than he'd intended, and he lowered it. He didn't want anyone passing by to overhear their conversation. They were near an alley, and he gestured for her to follow him there. They would be able to talk without drawing attention. When they were alone, he repeated his question.

She sighed deeply. Despite his annoyance, he couldn't stop his eyes from noticing the way her breasts rose and fell. Nor could he stop the way his body reacted to her nearness. "I'm actually here to see you."

"What? Why? You and I have nothing to talk about."

"Not talk. I meant that literally. I only wanted to *see* you and Crystal."

"Why now? Sixteen years ago, you could have seen Crystal. Heck, you could have been a part of her life. You could have been her mother, but you chose not to be." He looked her up and down. Her dress was simple, but he recognized quality when he saw it. And a dress like that cost a pretty penny. "I take it that you've been successful. As determined as you were, I'm betting that you didn't miss a beat."

Some emotion he couldn't name flashed in her eyes. He told himself that he didn't care enough to try to decipher it. In a moment, it was gone anyway.

"I just wanted to make sure that she was doing well. And that she's happy."

"It's sixteen years too late for that. What were you planning to do if you discovered that she wasn't happy? After all, you don't have any parental rights to her. Remember, that piece of paper that you signed?"

She wrapped her arms around her stomach. "It wasn't easy for me to come here."

"No? And yet you did. Hopefully it'll be a lot easier for you to leave."

"I don't remember you being this cruel."

"It's a learned trait. I picked it up over the years of caring for my daughter alone. I needed to be willing to do any and everything to protect her."

"I don't want to hurt her."

He huffed out an exasperated breath. "Good. Because I'm not going to let you."

"You aren't going to give me a chance, are you?"

"A chance to what? What do you want, Andrea?"

"I want to see her." The words were a cross between a plea and a demand. Neither would work with him.

"No. Not in this lifetime. My daughter is a person with feelings, not some toy you can play with now that you've decided you're interested. You made your decision when she was born. We've lived with it. Now you can do the same."

"Cole."

"I mean it. Stay away from Crystal. And stay away from me."

She was still nodding when he turned and stalked away.

He went back to the diner to pick up the lunch he'd ordered. Crystal was working at the craft store this afternoon so it was just him and Gary. He'd been thinking about the club sandwich and vegetable soup most of the morning, but running into Andrea had ruined his appetite.

Sixteen years had passed, and she still had the power to

get to him. Even worse, his attraction hadn't diminished. For years, he'd assumed that that part of his life was over. Despite all the lovely women Crystal had pushed him toward over the years, he'd never felt anything warmer than friendship. But all he had to do was lay eyes on Andrea, and his pulse had sped up. At times they'd been standing close together and her enticing scent had wafted under his nostrils, teasing his senses. It had taken all of his self-control not to get swept away. But he had Crystal to protect, and he couldn't allow himself to weaken. He had to keep Andrea at a distance.

"I'll be right with you," Barbara, the cashier, said. "Rhonda is getting your order together right now."

"Thanks."

Barbara was one of the women Crystal had tried to set him up with. She was nice and pretty, but thankfully she was no more interested in him than he was in her. According to Gary, she had a big crush on the high school football coach. Cole had never seen the two of them together, but Gary had yet to be proven wrong.

Five minutes later, Barbara placed the paper bag in front of him. He swiped his credit card, picked up the bag and walked back to the feedstore. While he went, he tried to gain control of his feelings and come up with a plan of action. Though it had been nearly sixteen years since he and Andrea had talked, he knew her well enough to know that she wouldn't leave town simply because he'd asked her to.

But he wasn't a lovesick teenager now. She wasn't going to convince him to give in. Not this time. One way or the other he was going to keep her away from his daughter.

Chapter Three

Andrea staggered down the street, the pain in her heart growing with each step. Her earlier pleasure in the day was now a distant memory. The boutiques, art gallery and candy shop no longer held the magic they had only moments before. Now she was filled with a sorrow and despair she hadn't felt in years. She dropped onto a black iron bench and closed her eyes as Cole's angry words echoed in her mind. The last thing she expected was for Cole to have become a cold and harsh man, but clearly he had. True, he'd been shocked to see her, but she couldn't attribute his behavior to surprise entirely.

Perhaps it had been a mistake not to let him know that she coming to Aspen Creek. Maybe it would have been better to contact him first and explain herself. Maybe she would have been able to convince him to see things from her perspective and realize that she meant no harm. Well, it was too late to change things now. All she could do was forge ahead.

But she wasn't ready for a fight now. She was too emotionally wounded to take on another battle. Nor was she ready to face the fact that her friendship with Cole was well and truly over. Despite the way things had ended between them and the years of silence, a part of her had believed that if they could simply talk, they would be able to resolve any problem. Now she had to face the fact that he had no interest in being friends again.

She needed something to help her clear her mind. A knitting project would do the trick. When she'd been a child, her grandmother had given her a pair of knitting needles and taught her how to use them. As she'd become busier with her extracurricular activities, she'd had little time for knitting as she'd grown up, but after she'd given away her child, she'd found herself knitting blankets and hats for a child she would never know, donating them to charity when she was done. The quiet activity filled her with an unexpected serenity and pleasure, and it was a hobby she'd kept up over the years.

She remembered passing a craft store earlier, and decided to head back to it, planning to buy enough supplies to keep her busy for a couple of days.

"Welcome," a feminine voice called as Andrea stepped inside. "Feel free to look around."

"Thank you." Andrea immediately headed for the colorful yarn. It was soft to the touch and obviously of high quality. She picked up a wicker basket and put in a bright pink skein.

"Are you buying for a special project or are your hands just feeling a bit idle?" the woman asked as she approached her.

Andrea gave her a practiced smile. She'd learned long ago how to disguise her pain. It was second nature now. "I suppose I'm in the latter category. I'm in town on vacation and need something to help fill the hours."

"I'm Rebecca, the owner of the store. You're not the first vacationer to visit my shop with that intention although I generally get more tourists in the winter."

"I imagine there is only so much skiing a person can do before boredom or the cold inevitably sets in."

Rebecca laughed. "Just between you and me, I don't get the attraction of sliding down a snowy mountain on a couple of sticks. And I'd much rather be inside with a mug of hot chocolate watching the snow fall than being in it."

"I'm with you there." She'd set enough broken bones in her practice to make her avoid activities where danger was inherent.

The door opened and several well-dressed women walked in. "I'm going to look around, so feel free to help them."

"If you need anything, my faithful assistant is over there." Rebecca pointed to a teenager. She was sorting a pile of colorful fabric squares, her back to them.

As if sensing that someone was talking about her, the girl turned until she was looking directly at them. Andrea glanced at the girl's face and goose bumps popped on her arms. A loud buzzing sound filled her ears. Her heart began to pound, and the rows of yarn and thread faded away.

She was looking at her daughter.

Apparently, her shock was not visible to others, because Rebecca patted her shoulder as she walked over and greeted the newcomers. A part of Andrea wanted to turn and run away from the intense feelings bombarding her while the other part yearned to run over and pull her daughter into her arms. Andrea realized she was holding her breath, and she forced herself to breathe. She didn't want to alarm her child by fainting.

Even without the photos the private investigator had given her, Andrea would have recognized her child. Her heart would have known her anywhere. Crystal was absolutely beautiful. She was several inches taller than Andrea, but given Cole's height, that wasn't unexpected. But she was slender like Andrea. Clearly she was a combination of her parents.

Andrea told her feet to move, but it was as if they were glued to the floor. Considering the fact that she had no idea which direction she would head—to the exit to escape or across the store to her child—that was probably for the best.

"Hi. I'm Crystal. Can I help you find something?" While Andrea had been swimming in her emotions, her daughter had walked over to her.

Andrea swallowed. Then she swallowed again. Talking seemed impossible when her sweet child was near enough to touch. It was all she could do not to burst into tears. Crystal's smile began to wilt so Andrea forced words past the lump in her throat. "Something soft. I'm knitting baby booties, hats and blankets."

"Oh, congratulations. Did you have a boy or a girl?"

"Both. Neither." She stopped and gathered her wits. "They aren't for me. I don't have a baby." Her heart ached as she said the words. Especially since she was staring at the child that she'd given birth to almost sixteen years ago. Crystal certainly wasn't a baby anymore. Her sweet little one was nearing adulthood.

"Okay." Crystal's expression was puzzled, but it didn't hold any judgment. It was almost as if she were used to people rambling incoherently.

"I'm a pediatrician. I knit clothing and blankets for the newborns at my hospital."

"Really? That is so cool. Are you here on vacation?"

"Yes. I'll be here for the summer."

Crystal glanced at Andrea's hands, and then looked

back at her face. Andrea had felt a little ridiculous walking around in her makeshift disguise and had been tempted to remove her sunglasses when she'd stepped into the shop. After all, Cole had recognized her right away. Now she was glad that she'd kept them on, to hide the way she couldn't stop herself from staring. And it wasn't only that—she wanted to keep Crystal from getting a good look at her in turn. Though Andrea saw a lot of Cole in Crystal's face, their daughter had inherited some of Andrea's features as well. Andrea didn't want to risk Crystal—or anyone else for that matter—noticing the resemblance.

"You and your husband are going to enjoy spending time here in Aspen Creek."

Andrea smiled at the not so subtle attempt to gain information. "I'm not married. This is a solo vacation."

Crystal's smile broadened. "The people in Aspen Creek are very nice and friendly. There's a crafting group that meets here a few times a week to make clothes for the needy. We have a lot of fun. You're welcome to join us."

Andrea was proud of the generous spirit her daughter possessed even though she knew she didn't have the right to be. She'd had no part in raising her. Cole deserved all of the credit. He was the one who'd influenced her from birth.

The entire moment was surreal, and Andrea felt as if she was having an out of body experience. It was as if she was looking at herself talking to her child. She knew she was coming dangerously close to losing the tenuous grip on her emotions so despite the fact that she yearned for more time with her child, Andrea decided to wrap up the conversation. "Thank you. I'll think about it."

Crystal nodded before she tilted her head to the side and tapped her chin. That gesture was all too familiar.

She'd seen it reflected in her mirror as a teenager when she'd been plotting something.

"There's a stack of flyers with the schedule near the cash register. You can look around, but let me know if you need anything." Crystal smiled again and then walked away, returning to her previous task.

Consumed with a myriad of emotions, Andrea doubted she would be able to sit still long enough to knit, but she didn't want to leave the store empty-handed. She picked up a half dozen skeins of yarn, a few knitting needles and a crochet hook, then headed for the checkout counter. Rebecca made small talk as she tallied Andrea's purchases. After sliding her credit card through the reader and grabbing a flyer, Andrea walked to the door, resisting the urge to glance over her shoulder for one more look at her child.

Andrea's legs trembled as she hurried back to her car. Her hand was shaking so badly it took three tries for her to open the car door. Once she was safely seated behind the wheel of her vehicle, she blew out a breath. Her entire body was wracked with tremors. Her vision blurred, and she realized that she was crying. She swiped at the moisture on her cheeks, but the tears continued to fall.

After all these years, she'd looked at her baby's face in person rather than in a photograph. She'd stared into her eyes. They'd shared smiles. Crystal was kind and friendly and beautiful. She had a sweet aura. She was everything Andrea ever dreamed she would be. And more.

Gulping huge amounts of air, Andrea allowed her emotions to course through her. She'd thought she'd been prepared to see her child, but she'd been wrong. She had underestimated the impact this moment would have on her. Even so, she wasn't going to push the feelings away, as she usually did with any strong emotion. She was going to feel every ounce of joy coursing through her body.

This reunion with her daughter was infinitely better than the one she'd had with Cole. *Cole*. How would he react when he learned that Andrea had met their daughter after he'd explicitly told her to stay away from her? Would he believe it had been purely coincidental? Or would he think that she'd orchestrated the whole thing? She had no idea how he would respond. The cold and bitter man she'd encountered today bore no resemblance to the boy she'd known before.

Andrea briefly considered going to the feedstore and telling him what had just happened. Then her better sense prevailed. Just thinking of seeing him again made her stomach churn. No, she was too emotional to deal with another argument. Not only that, she didn't think he would appreciate her coming to his place of work to discuss a personal matter. She didn't anticipate the conversation would be any friendlier than their earlier one.

She'd talk to him later. Right now, she was going to bask in the joy of having met her daughter.

Though she had planned to watch her daughter from a distance, Andrea wouldn't be doing that now. She couldn't. She wanted more time. The few minutes that she'd spent with Crystal would never satisfy her. She wanted to get to know her daughter. No, she *needed* to get to know her. Needed to know what things interested Crystal, what her goals and dreams were for the future. She wanted to know her favorite foods. She wanted to know big things and small things.

She wanted to know everything.

Andrea wouldn't tell Crystal who she was, of course. That part of the plan remained unchanged. It would be unfair to disrupt Crystal's life. The time when they could have been mother and daughter had come and gone. She accepted that. So she would do the next best thing. Andrea would make memories with her child that she could carry with her for the rest of her life.

"There's a new movie streaming tonight," Crystal said as she and Cole cleaned the kitchen after dinner.

It had been two days since his encounter with Andrea. During that time, he'd run the gamut of emotions. Annoyance that she would just pop into his and Crystal's lives without warning. Disbelief that she thought he would accept her presence as if she had done nothing wrong. Sorrow at the realization that the bond that he'd once thought was unbreakable had indeed broken.

And a foolish feeling of joy that she hadn't just forgotten about them. He'd felt ridiculously happy to know that she still occasionally thought about them. That feeling disturbed him. But the most troubling was the attraction he still felt for Andrea after all this time.

Even while they'd argued, he'd been acutely aware of the desire lurking just beneath the surface. The yearning to pull her into his arms and feel her soft body pressed against his once again had been a constant presence.

Thankfully he hadn't acted on the impulse. He didn't want her to know that she still had the power to turn him on. For years now, he'd thought he was well and truly over her. Now that he knew the truth, he'd do whatever it took to rid himself of those feelings once and for all.

Right now, he needed to keep things normal for Crystal. Her well-being was all that mattered.

Sunday had always been family night. It might only have been the two of them, but it had been important to

Cole that she know that she had a family. Their family of two was just as good as a family that included cousins and aunts and uncles. Grandparents. *A mother.*

He'd taught Crystal that a family wasn't limited to people who shared blood and genes. Family could also be created by people who loved and respected each other. Crystal had taken that lesson and run with it. She had created a huge family of her own, adopting aunts, uncles and cousins. She's found numerous honorary grandparents including several seniors who otherwise would be alone.

"Please tell me that it's not that romance you've been talking about," he said, determined to keep his focus where it belonged—on his daughter.

She shook her head, pausing as she put the clean plates into an upper cabinet. "No. You always whine through those. I'll watch it with Livvie when I spend the night with her next Saturday."

"That's a relief." Cole glanced at Crystal as he swiped a sponge across the counter. "And just for the record, I don't whine."

"Okay. Whimper." Crystal giggled.

He shook his head. "What can I say? I like a little more action in my entertainment."

"Which is why I know that you're going to love this movie. It's sci-fi."

"Now you're singing my song." Sci-fi was a compromise genre for them. Crystal loved musicals and romantic comedies where a happily-ever-after was guaranteed. It helped if the male lead was one of the many actors that she was crushing on. Cole would rather watch suspense or psychological thrillers. Both of them found science fiction acceptable for movie night. But when there was a movie that Crystal just had to see and she couldn't wait to watch with her friends, he endured, watching it as any good father would.

Once the kitchen was clean, they went into the living room. Cole purchased the house three years ago when they'd moved to town. The real estate agent had used words like "cozy" and "starter home," terms he supposed were code for *little*. They had two decent-sized bedrooms, one bathroom that they shared although she cluttered up his side of the sink, a half bath that Crystal had commandeered for her own purposes, a living-dining room slash dining room and kitchen. The kitchen was actually larger than he would have expected for a house this size, with enough space for a table and four chairs. There was also a screened back porch and a small patio. But the main selling point for Crystal had been the proximity to her best friend's house. Olivia lived two blocks away.

Crystal grabbed the remote and dropped onto the couch, picking up her knitting needles.

"I thought we were watching a movie."

"Mrs. Rose knits and watches TV all the time. She likes to keep her hands busy."

"If you want to watch the movie later, I'll understand." Cole kept the disappointment from his voice. He looked forward to their daddy and daughter time. Though he'd wanted to make sure Crystal knew she had a family, he needed her, too. She was the only family he had left.

"No way," she protested with a smile that looked way too much like Andrea's for his peace of mind. "We can't go against fifteen and a half years of tradition. Who knows what would happen? It might knock the earth off its axis and where would the world be then?"

"We can't have that." Cole got comfortable in his recliner and turned his attention to the movie.

The reference to the number of years behind this tradition was an uncomfortable reminder that his baby girl was growing up. Crystal had begun talking about college, and she'd made a list of schools she was interested in. She'd excelled in all of her classes, and Cole expected her to be accepted at whatever college she applied to. Biology and chemistry had been her favorite classes, and she talked a lot about being a doctor. He didn't believe that career interest was genetic, but maybe an interest in science had been passed down in a way from both sides. There were times when he wondered if he should tell her about her grandparents, but since she hadn't asked about her family since she'd been in first grade, he'd let sleeping dogs lie. His parents hadn't shown a bit of interest in her from the day she'd been born. There was no reason to think their attitudes had changed.

Unbidden, he thought of Andrea. Her presence in town could shake up his and Crystal's lives. He'd thought of her regularly in the months following Crystal's birth, but over time he'd managed to keep thoughts of her to a minimum, except around Crystal's birthday. Whenever that time of year rolled around, he'd always find himself remembering the day she was born.

He'd been sure that he could convince Andrea not to relinquish her rights to their child. He'd thought that once she'd held that warm bundle in her arms, she would fall in love with their child the same way he had. He would never know if that would have happened because Andrea had refused to hold her. In fact, she hadn't even looked at Crystal. Instead, she'd demanded that he leave her hospital room and take the baby with him.

For weeks he'd held out hope that Andrea would change her mind. It was only after she'd gone away to Northwestern University as she'd planned that he admitted they would never become a family. Now she was back, trying to wedge her way into the life she'd walked away from. Well, it was too late for her regrets.

She had walked out of their lives sixteen years ago. He wasn't about to let her walk back in.

Chapter Four

Andrea studied the flyer she'd picked up at the craft store, then placed it on the kitchen table beside her half-eaten bowl of cold cereal. She'd read it so many times that she knew it by heart. The club Crystal mentioned met on Tuesday and Thursday evenings and Wednesday and Saturday afternoons, but knitters were welcome to come in anytime and gather. Though Andrea had always knit alone, she knew that going to the club meetings would give her the opportunity to spend time with her child. That was, if they attended the same one.

Thinking about Crystal made her smile even as her heart began to race. Her physical responses were the manifestation of her mental state. Andrea was conflicted and confused. Hopeful and afraid. She wanted to get to know her child, but now that she'd had a few days to think about it, she wasn't sure making contact again was the right thing to do. Legally, did she even have the right to connect with Crystal? It wasn't as if she was trying to assert her parental rights—she knew she'd given those up—but would it be considered crossing the line for her to try to form any kind of relationship with Crystal, even just a friendly one? She'd gotten the sense that Cole wouldn't be happy with the idea if he found out about it. Perhaps the

right thing would be to work things out with Cole first…
but based on his reaction to her earlier, she was pretty sure
that if she asked, he'd say no. Frankly, Andrea couldn't
imagine any scenario where he would welcome her into
their lives even momentarily. Not after all of this time.

Maybe it would be better if she didn't ask…if she just
acted. Cole would likely find out eventually, but by the
time that happened, she'd have had a chance to prove to
him that she wasn't there to do any harm. Crystal would
never even know who she really was. Surely Cole couldn't
be too angry as long as Andrea was careful not to disrupt Crystal's life.

He'd never been the type to hold a grudge. That had
been one of the qualities that had endeared him to her.
Maybe he would be amenable to her spending time with
Crystal once he realized she wasn't going to make trouble.

She had to believe that he'd be okay with it eventually, because she knew that no matter what he said, she
couldn't just walk away. Not now.

Her stomach clenched, an unmistakable sign that she
wasn't entirely comfortable with her plan. Deception had
never set right with her, and no matter how she tried to
dress it up in her mind, she *was* planning on deceiving
Cole. She knew that secrets had a way of blowing up in
your face. When that happened, the best of intentions
never seemed to matter. The harm was done and couldn't
be undone. Just like the harm she had done by leaving
Crystal behind in the first place, nearly sixteen years ago.

The thought was followed by a deep, heartrending sorrow. Rather than try to force the feelings away, Andrea
went to the bedroom and picked up her journal. The therapist she'd been seeing for the past year had suggested
journaling as a way to work through her emotions.

A few days before Crystal's birth, Andrea said a mental goodbye to her child. She'd wanted to keep her distance from the child growing inside her, so she hadn't given her baby a name. Instead, she'd referred to the babe as Little One. She'd sat on the corner of her bed, rubbing her pregnant belly and telling her daughter how much she loved her and how desperately she would miss her. She'd promised her Little One that she would never forget her.

And she hadn't.

Each year on her daughter's birthday, Andrea had bought a birthday card, written a long letter that she had started with My Dearest Little One, donated a toy to charity in her daughter's name, bought a cupcake, and celebrated her child's life. She'd longed to know how her baby was doing, but she'd never tried to find out. Instead, she had imagined only good things. At a quarter to midnight, she'd put the card and letter into a photo album and tuck it into her nightstand while she tucked away her feelings, as well.

Since she knew that she would be in Aspen Creek for Crystal's birthday, she'd brought the album with her. Her heart held a sliver of hope that she would be able to spend Crystal's birthday with her, but she forced herself to crush it. Why would a teenager invite a stranger to help her celebrate her sweet sixteen?

She picked up her pen and began to write. Journaling was still challenging for her—she'd spent so many years trying to keep her emotions repressed so they wouldn't overwhelm her. But she thought she was starting to get better at it. When her therapist first gave her the assignment, she'd agonize over how to start, so worried about doing it wrong that she barely managed to write anything at all. But finally, she'd learned not to try to organize her feelings. Instead, she simply let the feelings flow onto the page as randomly as they came to her. She wrote for nearly twenty minutes, not stopping until all of her emotions had spilled out of her and onto the page. When she was done, she closed the journal, no longer stressed.

With her mind now clear, she could give some thought to the resemblance she and Crystal shared. Though she could do nothing about the facial features, she could alter her hair. She and Crystal each had long, thick black hair. They both wore it blown dried straight and bumped at the ends. Since Andrea didn't intend to wear a hat all the time, she needed to change her hairstyle.

Off and on over the years, she'd thought about cutting her hair, but had never followed through. She was busy and long hair was convenient. Pulling her hair into a ponytail on workdays was so easy, and she could style it into her natural curls when she wanted to look sexy on date nights or at a club. Besides, she liked the length. But desperate times called for desperate measures.

She hopped into the car and drove to town. She'd seen a salon while sightseeing earlier. After parking, she headed to the salon. The streets of town were pristine, and the air was quite fresh. It was as if nature was telling her it was time for a new start.

After taking a deep breath, she stepped inside and looked around. There was a reception area off to the right complete with a plush burgundy sofa and chairs, and side tables with glass lamps. A rack held a variety of magazines and books. A beverage center was nearby with sweets and drinks. A woman sat in a chair, sipping a cup of tea and flipping through a magazine.

Six stations with pink swivel chairs in front of enormous mirrors were on either side of the room. Four of the chairs were occupied. Laughter and conversation filled the air and Andrea immediately felt at home. Although the decor was different, this salon felt like the one she went to in Chicago.

"Can I help you?" a woman seated at the mirrored front desk asked.

Andrea nodded. "I was hoping to get a haircut. That is, if one of the stylists has an opening."

"You're in luck. Melanie had a cancellation."

The woman at the checkout tapped her credit card on the reader. "Melanie is my stylist. She's the best."

"I don't know about that," the woman flipping through the magazine said. "Cheyenne always makes me look fantastic."

"Both of you look great," Andrea said honestly.

A curvy woman joined the group. "I'm Melanie."

"Nice to meet you," Andrea said, and then introduced herself. "I'm looking for something different."

"Your hair is gorgeous," Melanie said as she led Andrea to a chair and draped a smock over her torso. "What kind of style are you looking for?"

"I don't know. Something easy to manage. And long enough to pull back into a ponytail." She didn't want it in the way when she returned to work at the end of summer.

Melanie handed Andrea a few hair magazines. "Look through here and make a note of anything you like."

"Okay."

"Do you have a regular stylist? Someone who'll be able to help you maintain the style? Because I can tell you now it's going to be fire."

Andrea nodded. "Yes. And that's what I want to hear."

After skimming the magazines, Andrea found two styles she liked. "What do you think about one of these?"

Melanie looked at the pictures, and then studied Andrea's face, using a manicured finger to turn her head in different directions so she could view her face from every angle. Then she tapped on a picture. "This one will work best with your face. It's different from the way you wear your hair now, but you won't get a shock every time you look in the mirror."

Andrea nodded. "I do like that one a little bit better."

"Then let's get started."

Melanie ran her fingers through Andrea's hair, and then asked her a few questions about her hair-care routine. Satisfied with the answers, Melanie led Andrea to the sink and wet her hair. The shampoo smelled wonderful, and Andrea closed her eyes as Melanie gently massaged her scalp. A deep conditioning followed and before long Andrea was sitting in the stylist's chair.

Melanie held up her scissors. "Last chance. Speak now or forever hold your peace."

Andrea smiled. "I'm good."

While Melanie cut Andrea's hair, she told her about the places that she might be interested in visiting while she was in town. Most of them were the touristy places she'd passed while sightseeing, but a couple were off the beaten path. Andrea didn't know if she would go to any of them—the risk of running into Cole was too great—but the dude ranch sounded interesting. And since Cole had worked on a ranch for years, he'd have no reason to want to try out the lifestyle as a paying guest, so the odds that he would show up there were minimal.

When Melanie was finished styling Andrea's hair, she spun the chair around so Andrea faced the mirror. Andrea took one glance at her reflection and gasped. Her hair had been cut to frame her face, accentuating her cheekbones and playing up her eyes. It was sexy enough for a night at the club, but it was still long enough to pull back into a ponytail for work. Best of all, the style minimized her resemblance to Crystal. "I love it."

Melanie clapped her hands in obvious delight. "That's the reaction I was aiming for."

Andrea admired herself for several long moments before tipping Melanie, and then going to the checkout and paying the bill. She felt lighter and practically skipped down the street. She wandered through town with no particular destination in mind. Before she knew it, she was standing in front of the craft store, as if she'd been drawn there by an invisible force. She had no intention of going inside and was walking away when the door opened and Crystal stepped outside.

"Hi. I remember you," Crystal said, a smile in her voice. "But I forgot to ask your name."

"I remember you, too." As if she could ever forget her sweet Little One. "It's Andrea."

"I like your haircut. It's really pretty. And it's definitely a step above the hat you had on." Crystal's eyes widened and she clapped a hand over her mouth. "Sorry. That was so rude. I should have stopped talking after the compliment."

Andrea laughed. "Don't worry about it. I hope it looks better or I just wasted my time and money."

"I'm going to have lunch with my father. He owns the feedstore a few blocks from here. Do you want to join us?"

The invitation caught Andrea off guard and for a moment she couldn't speak. She inhaled deeply, and then shook her head. She could only imagine what Cole would say if she waltzed into his business beside Crystal. His head just might explode. "I want to do a bit of sightseeing.

I heard there was an art display at the park, and I thought I'd go see it. But thanks for the invitation."

Crystal gave Andrea a long look that had her wondering if her new haircut was a good enough disguise. Maybe she hadn't changed her appearance as much as she'd hoped. Perhaps she should return to the hat and sunglasses. "There's something about you. I just can't put my finger on it. Call me goofy, but I think you and my dad would really like each other."

Somehow Andrea managed to keep from choking. The last words Cole spoke to her had been filled with bitterness. No way they would hit it off. But Crystal was waiting for a reply, and Andrea knew she had to say something. "Sure. Maybe some other time."

As Crystal walked away, Andrea knew there was trouble up ahead. She'd seen the gleam in her daughter's eyes and got the sense that Crystal had matchmaking in mind. Luckily Cole was no more interested in seeing her again than she was in seeing.him.

"What made you decide to come to the park today?" Cole asked Crystal. "This morning you told me you had a taste for a burger and a shake."

Crystal shrugged as she looked around. "I don't know. I feel like getting some fresh air. And maybe I was feeling a little sentimental. Remember how much fun we used to have here when I was little?"

Cole nodded. In the early days, money had been tight and every week after running errands, they'd come to the playground. Crystal had enjoyed going down the twisting slide on her stomach. Though he had done it himself as a kid, watching his sweet child sail face-first toward the ground had wrecked his nerves. He'd much preferred pushing her on the swing where he could protect her better. Even then, she'd begged him to push her harder so she could go higher.

"I thought we could look at the art, and then grab something from one of the food trucks."

That worked for him. Though he wasn't much for art, there was something compelling about these sculptures. Hopefully they would hold his attention enough to keep him from thinking about Andrea. He nearly laughed at the thought. To date, nothing he'd tried had worked. And he had given every kind of diversion known to man a try. He'd started with reading, but the latest release by his favorite author hadn't held his attention. When he realized he'd been absently turning the pages, he closed the book before he could spoil the mystery for himself. Watching television, listening to music and working out had been just as unsuccessful.

He'd even dreamed of Andrea last night. He'd been holding her around the waist and spinning her in circles. Her laughter had surrounded them both and his had joined hers. Then he'd lowered her to the ground and leaned over, capturing her lips in a hot kiss. He'd pressed her soft body against his, giving free rein to the passion inside him. It had seemed so real that he'd reached for her this morning when he woke up. His disappointment at being alone had been as shocking as it was overwhelming. Though he'd known it was ridiculous, he could almost taste her sweetness. She'd never been in his house, but since running into her, he'd felt her presence in every room. It was as if there was an unbreakable connection between the two of them that neither time nor distance could sever.

He was starting to see her everywhere he looked.

Like the woman currently checking out the oversize

metal butterfly sculpture. His heart skipped a beat as he caught a glimpse of her before a man stepped in front of him, blocking his view. But it couldn't have been Andrea. The hair was all wrong. Andrea had always had long, straight hair and this woman's curly hair barely brushed against her shoulders. When the man stepped aside, the woman was gone. Even so, he'd felt a frisson of…something…when he'd looked at her.

He shook his head. This was ridiculous. He was getting obsessed. If he wasn't careful, he would start to see her everywhere he went.

"Crystal and her stupid romantic comedies," he muttered to himself.

"What did you say?" Crystal asked.

"Nothing. I was talking to myself."

"Why? I'm right here."

"I know. Sorry."

"You know, if you had a girlfriend, you could talk to her."

"Please tell me you aren't trying to set me up with Rebecca again. I told you, there's no possibility of that happening."

"Nope. I've talked to her about it too, and we agreed that there was no chemistry."

"Hold on a minute. What exactly do you know about chemistry? And I'm not talking about the science class you complained about all year."

"It started too early, but that's beside the point. I know *all* about it. You would too if you would bother to watch the right movies or read the right books. Honestly, you are so unromantic I don't know how I came to be."

Cole laughed. He didn't know many fathers and daughters who had these kind of conversations, but since he was a single father it couldn't be avoided. Crystal didn't have a mother to explain the facts of life to her. The birds and the bees talk had fallen to him as well as the biology lessons. Since he wanted her to be open with him about her life, he knew it had to go both ways. To a point.

"Let's just say my focus shifted."

"Well, I think it's time to shift it back."

Cole followed. "We've had this conversation too many times to count."

"But this time I know I've found the right woman for you. I'm sure she's your soulmate."

He knew better than to believe in soulmates. He'd made that mistake with Andrea. He blew out a breath, glanced at the clear blue sky and silently counted to ten. "I know you mean well, but, no."

"Don't let your stubbornness get in the way of true love."

"True love?" He shook his head. "You have no idea how happy I'll be when you outgrow this phase."

"Not nearly as happy as I'll be when you have someone else in your life to love."

He paused. "I wish you would stop worrying about me. You are the child. You're not responsible for my happiness."

"I know. I just…"

"You just what?"

Crystal's demeanor changed from playful to serious. "You're the best dad in the world, and I want you to be happy."

"What do you I have to do to convince you that I am happy?"

She looked past him, and then smiled. "Never mind. Let's grab something from the taco truck."

He didn't know what had caused this abrupt change of subject from his stubborn daughter who usually never let things drop, but he wouldn't jinx it by asking. "Now you're singing my song."

The words were barely out of his mouth when Crystal grabbed his hand and began to pull him behind her. "Wow, Crystal, you must really be hungry."

Crystal nodded, but he didn't think she was paying attention to him. She was acting like she was suddenly on a mission. When they reached the taco truck, she veered to the right toward the tables. He was about to ask her what was going on when she turned to him, a triumphant look on her face.

"Here is my friend. I just know the two of you will hit it off."

He looked where she pointed. The woman he'd spotted from a distance was sitting there, her back to him. She turned slowly. When their eyes met, his heart nearly stopped.

It was Andrea.

Chapter Five

"Andrea, this is my father, Cole. Dad, this is my friend, Andrea." Crystal smiled brightly, clearly proud of herself.

Cole couldn't believe his eyes. Or his ears. Had Crystal just referred to Andrea as her friend? He had been clear that he didn't want Andrea anywhere near Crystal. Obviously, she had ignored his wishes and done what she'd wanted. Why was he surprised? Hadn't Andrea always done what was best for Andrea?

Crystal was looking between the two of them. Since he didn't want her to become suspicious, he forced himself to smile and speak warmly. His eyes, though, told another story. "Andrea. It's nice to meet you."

Andrea's chest rose and fell as she sighed with relief. Then she smiled and extended her hand. "It's nice to meet you, Cole."

"Dad, I'm going to grab some food. I'll get your usual. Save me a seat. Do you want something more, Andrea?"

Cole looked at Andrea's plate. It was obvious that she hadn't taken more than one bite of her food. Great. Apparently, they were going to have lunch together.

Andrea shook her head. "No. Thanks."

Cole managed to keep his temper under control until Crystal had sashayed happily over to the food truck. She glanced over at her shoulder once, and Cole nodded and smiled. Then he looked at Andrea, not bothering to disguise his anger. "What game are you playing?"

"I'm not playing any game."

"I told you not to go anywhere near Crystal, yet somehow she knows you. Do you care to explain how that happened?" He kept his voice low so that the people nearby couldn't hear him. He had no intention of becoming the topic of local gossip.

"It wasn't intentional." She frowned. "And stop looming over me. I'm getting a crick in my neck. Sit down."

There were a thousand things he could have said in reply, but since he wanted this conversation over and done with before Crystal returned, he dropped into the chair across from Andrea. "Talk fast."

"Really? I had planned to meander about, never getting to the point." She rolled her eyes.

"Andrea," he warned. A person walking behind her glanced at him, and he realized he'd spoken louder than he'd intended. He leaned in closer to her and she did the same.

"After we talked, I planned to go back to the cabin I'm renting. Before I left, I went into the craft store to get some yarn because I thought a new knitting project would clear my head. And before you ask, no I didn't know she worked there. The private investigator I hired to find you didn't mention it. I wouldn't have gone there otherwise."

"She only started working there recently."

"Good. So you know I'm telling you the truth."

"Why didn't you leave when you saw her?"

She shook her head slowly and looked at her hands. When she looked back at him, he saw the deep sorrow in her eyes. "I don't expect you to understand this, but I couldn't move. For the first time in my life, I was in the same room as my sweet baby."

"Second."

She blinked. "What?"

"That was the second time you were with her. Don't forget the day you rejected her."

Andrea flinched as if he'd struck her. He felt a pang of remorse, but he tried to push it aside. It was Crystal's feelings he needed to protect in all of this, not Andrea's.

"You're right, Cole. Does hearing that make you feel better?" Her voice broke and it was like a punch to the gut.

"Nothing about this situation could make me feel better," he admitted, sounding as tired as he felt. "I just want things to go back to the way they belong. The way they were before you dropped in."

"I'm not trying to mess up things. I just want to get to know her."

"Why now? It's been nearly sixteen years."

"I can't explain why."

"Or you won't."

She shrugged. "Does it matter which it is?"

"No. Because I want you to stay away from Crystal. I mean it."

Andrea smiled brightly.

Confused by her reaction, Cole opened his mouth. Before he could speak, a plate filled with his favorite torta de chorizo appeared in front of him. Crystal was back. She set a plate of tacos in front of a vacant chair, then pulled two cans of soda from her pants pockets, gave him one, popped the top on the other and sat down. From the smile on her face, it was clear that she hadn't noticed the tension between them.

"Andrea is going to spend the summer in Aspen Creek.

She doesn't know many people. I think we're her first friends. She can hang around us."

"I don't want to intrude," Andrea said.

"Spending time with friends is never intrusive. Right, Dad?"

Cole sighed, knowing the only answer he could give if he didn't want to disappoint his daughter. "Right."

Andrea tried not to be dismayed by Cole's dry tone, but she wasn't quite successful. She knew that he found her presence in their lives very intrusive. If he had his way, she would pack up the cabin, load up her car and be on the highway on her way back to Chicago without any delay. But he wasn't going to get his way this time. Not yet. Not now that she had barely met her child. There were still two months left in her vacation, and she was going to do her best to enjoy them. She just had to find a way to win over Cole. There had to be a way to convince him that she was not a danger to him or the life he and Crystal had built here.

She'd figure that out later. For now, she was sharing an unexpected lunch with her daughter, and she intended to enjoy it. If she could let herself ignore the tension between her and Cole, she could almost pretend that they were a regular family enjoying a day in the park.

Once Andrea made up her mind to relax and have fun, she was able to carry her side of the conversation. She already knew that Crystal was kind and smart, but spending time with her and Cole showed her just how wonderful she was. Andrea also got to see how close Cole and Crystal were. Their relationship was remarkable. The old Cole she knew poked through his armor as he teased and joked with Crystal.

Time flew and before long, they'd finished eating lunch and Cole stood. "It's time for me to get back to work. You coming, Crystal?"

"I told Rebecca that I would help her this afternoon." She stood beside Cole. The facial resemblance between the two marked them as family. "It was so good to see you again, Andrea. I hope you can come to some of the meetings of the knitting club."

Cole glared at Andrea and she sighed. There had to be a way to convince him that she meant well. "I'll do my best."

Even though Andrea had been perfectly happy wandering around the park alone and had planned to eat lunch on her own, now that Crystal and Cole were gone, her previous happiness evaporated. Now that she knew how good it felt to share their company, being alone suddenly felt lonely. But hadn't she always known on some level that this would happen? That's why she hadn't wanted to see her child or hold her all those years ago. You couldn't miss what you'd never had.

But she had just had the best time of her life. It was as if she were Dorothy in *The Wizard of Oz*, stepping from the black and white world into a life overflowing with color. She wasn't sure she could go back to the life she'd known before. Somehow she had to convince Cole to let her share his and Crystal's bright world. She just wished she knew how.

It took nearly a week to figure it out. She spent those days wandering around the vast acres surrounding the cabin. As she did, it became apparent why Cole had settled in this area. It was perfectly serene. Puffy white clouds dotted the azure skies and a cool breeze blew most of the day, cooling her hot skin. She'd grown used to seeing the wildlife, but her pleasure at watching the rabbits scurry across the green grass and the squirrels chase each other up and down the trees didn't diminish. There was something about the solitude that gave her clarity of mind and calmed her spirit.

She'd deliberately stayed away from the craft store, unwilling to risk running into Crystal. No matter how innocent any encounter could be, she knew it would only upset Cole and harden his position. But her alone time had allowed her time to formulate a plan. If she was going to convince Cole, she was going to have to use everything that she knew about him. Sure, some things about him had likely changed with age, but she doubted that his core personality had changed. His likes were probably the same.

Which was why she had put on a purple fitted top—Cole's favorite color—and a pair of lavender shorts that hit her midthigh and beige heeled sandals. Then she'd spent an inordinate amount of time on her makeup and hair. With every passing day, she liked the cut even better. Her loose curls framed her face and accentuated her cheekbones, making her look younger and carefree.

Pleased with her appearance, she jumped into her car and headed down the familiar highway to town. It was amazing how quickly she had begun to feel at home here. She'd visited Sweet as Pie bakery twice, treating herself to the best baked goods she'd ever tasted in her life. Cole had always had a sweet tooth, so she decided to arm herself with treats before she headed to the feedstore. He might be able to resist her—after all, he hadn't given her a second look at the park the other day—but he had never been able to resist chocolate chip cookies.

As expected, there were several other patrons studying the goodies in the glass cases. Though she had come for a dozen chocolate chip cookies, Andrea was tempted by the variety of sweets. Due to her work schedule, she often ate her meals on the fly, sometimes skipping them altogether. As a result, her weight hovered at slightly below normal for her height. The baked goods here could help remedy that.

"Well, if it isn't my new friend, Andrea," Maggie said when Andrea stepped up to the counter. The greeting was unexpected, and Andrea was surprised by how good it felt to be called a friend. Even though she spoke to Dana on the phone every week and texted in between, she was basically alone in town. Sure, Rolanda told Andrea to call if she needed anything, but Andrea doubted she was talking about meeting for drinks. "How did you like the sweet potato pie?"

Andrea laughed. "You already know it was delicious. It reminded me of the ones my grandmother used to make at Thanksgiving."

"It's my grandmother's recipe. Are you here for another slice?"

"No. I want to try that blueberry tart. And a dozen of those chocolate chip cookies. The cookies are for a friend so do you mind wrapping them up pretty?" Not that Cole would care how the box looked. Hopefully he would see the treat as the peace offering that it was.

"Of course." Maggie put the cookies in a gold box and wrapped it with a red ribbon that she tied in a bow. "Let me know how you like the tart."

"Will do."

As Andrea walked down the street, she rehearsed her speech. This was too important to mess up by saying the wrong thing and upsetting Cole. Andrea had never been confrontational, and she doubted at thirty-four that she would be making major changes in her personality.

When she reached the feedstore, she stopped and looked at the building. She had no idea what a feedstore was supposed to look like, but the redbrick building wasn't what she'd imagined. There wasn't even a fingerprint on the plate glass window with gold lettering spelling out *Aspen Creek Feedstore* in large letters. The sidewalk in front had been swept clear of any debris.

Squaring her shoulders, she opened the door and stepped inside. A bell tinkled, announcing her arrival. It was too late to back out now.

Cole was standing behind a counter that spanned the width of the building, staring at a computer screen. When the bell over the door jingled, he looked up. The welcoming look on his face vanished the moment he realized who had entered his store. Clearly he wasn't happy to see her. He blew out an exasperated breath. "What do you want, Andrea?"

"To talk. And I hope you will at least listen." She held up a box as if to entice him. "I brought cookies."

Cole looked at the woman standing in front of him. Despite his annoyance that she'd barged into his business, he couldn't help but notice just how pretty she looked today. Her face was more mature than it had been as a teenager, but as an adult himself, he found it more interesting. She'd always possessed slender curves, and that hadn't changed. Time had been good to her and he was just as attracted to her as ever. It had been a struggle to hide that fact at the park the other day. It was even harder today with her looking sexy in that purple top that clung to her perky breasts and shorts that showed off her shapely legs.

He glanced around the store. Apart from Gary who was talking with one of their regular customers, the store was empty. "Gary, I'll be in the break room for a few minutes."

Gary glanced over. He took one look at Andrea who looked back at him, standing as regal as a queen, and smiled. "Take your time, boss."

Cole could easily guess what the older man was thinking. Once Cole finished with Andrea, he was going to straighten out his friend. He didn't need Aspen Creek's biggest gossip getting the wrong idea and mentioning Andrea's appearance at the store to anyone—especially Crystal.

"Follow me," Cole said, opening the swinging gate in the counter that separated the customers from the employees.

"Sure," she murmured. When she passed him, Cole got a whiff of her floral perfume. It was subtle yet it packed a wallop. He hadn't cared much about fragrances when they'd been teenagers. He'd just known that he liked the way she smelled. Now though, her scent, although different, was doing things to his body that weren't good for his peace of mind. Steeling himself against reacting, he led her to the break room.

"Coffee?" he asked, more in an effort to regain his control than to be polite.

"That would be nice," Andrea said. She stood by the table as if waiting for an invitation to sit down. Clearly she intended to stand on formality. He should have welcomed the distance it placed between them, yet somehow, it rubbed him the wrong way, especially since they'd once been close enough to create a child. But he wasn't the one who had caused the problem so he wasn't responsible for setting things right.

"Have a seat," he forced himself to say. Being polite shouldn't be so hard, but just being around Andrea stirred up memories he preferred to keep buried. The way she had walked away from him and Crystal still rubbed his feelings raw. She'd put him in the rearview mirror and had never once looked back. Now she was popping up out of the blue because she needed to see Crystal. Did she really expect him to be okay with letting her hang around?

"Thank you." She untied the ribbon on the bakery box, and then lifted the lid, revealing a dozen freshly baked chocolate chip cookies. His favorites, as Andrea well knew. "I got these for you."

"A bribe?" He tried to stay strong as he resisted the urge to grab one from the box.

"A peace offering," she countered with a smile before she shrugged and continued. "Maybe it's a little bit of both. I thought it might soften you up a bit."

"I always found it best to live my life so I don't have to soften up people in order for them to want to be around me."

She looked stung—but it didn't take her more than a second to snap out a comeback. "I forgot how perfect you've always been."

"I never claimed to be perfect."

"Just better than me."

He set a mug of the thick sludge Gary called coffee in front of her, then pushed the sugar and cream across the table. He could have diluted the brew as he did his, but he wasn't feeling especially charitable at the moment. "You said it, not me."

"It's not hard to guess what you're thinking. You don't have to say a word. Your attitude gives you away."

"Then you don't need me to be here for this conversation. So why don't you talk to yourself and let me know what we discussed."

Andrea actually laughed. The sweet sound nearly knocked him over. He pulled out the chair across from her and sat down.

"You have no idea how many times I've actually played out this conversation in my head. You were nicer in my imagination. Of course, I can't blame you for not knowing your lines when I haven't given them to you."

A reluctant chuckle burst from him and he quickly smothered it. He wasn't going to let Andrea charm him like she had when they'd been kids. Not when he knew what was at stake. He wasn't going to let her hurt Crystal like she'd hurt him. "How about you just say what you came to say. I've got work to do."

Though the smile on her face remained, the light in her eyes faded. He knew she didn't deserve his sympathy, but he felt guilty for hurting her feelings anyway.

"It wasn't easy for me to come here after all the things you said the other day," she said softly.

"And yet here you sit."

"Yes." She took a sip of her coffee, coughed, then stirred in more sugar. "It's not the worst that I've had, but it is definitely in the top two."

"It'll put hair on your chest."

"That's not the selling feature you think it is." Nevertheless, Andrea took another big swallow, then pointed to the box of cookies. "Come on. I know you want one. There's no need to pretend in front of me. I won't misinterpret you eating one or two as a sign that we're friends again. Nor will I look at it as a sign of weakness."

"If you insist."

"I do." She took a cookie from the box, bit it, picked up a napkin, and then set the cookie on it. "Delicious."

Cole followed suit, and then stared into Andrea's eyes. It would be so easy to be drawn into her orbit if he was willing. But he wasn't. He had Crystal to think about. Even though his daughter had the outrageous notion that he and Andrea were soulmates, he knew better. "So, what do you want, Andrea?"

"I want to spend time with Crystal."

"No."

"What do you mean no? Can't we at least talk about it?"

"There's nothing more to say. I don't want you around her."

"But you saw us together at the park. Things went well. She was happy. We had a great time." She paused. "I was hoping to do it again."

Was she including him in that invitation? Did he want to spend more time with Andrea? No way. He was having a hard enough time keeping himself under control now. He wouldn't set himself up for failure by spending more time with her. And he didn't trust her enough to be comfortable with the idea of her alone with Crystal. "I don't care what you were hoping. There are no do-overs in life. You have to live with the choices that you made just as Crystal and I did."

"I did what I thought was best."

"For you. And how did that work out?" He knew it had worked out just as she'd planned. He'd followed Andrea's life at first. He'd known when she'd graduated from college and medical school. A part of him had hoped that after she'd achieved the goals she'd set for herself that she would come searching for him and Crystal. He would have welcomed her into their lives at that point. Crystal had needed a mother's love and affection back then. But Andrea hadn't sought them out. Instead, she'd built her practice in Chicago, proving that she had put them behind her.

And now, after all these years, she wanted to be a part of their lives? Now when Crystal didn't need a mother's guidance and he didn't need a partner. They'd muddled through on their own.

She stared into her coffee cup for a long moment as if the strong brew held the answers. Finally she looked at him, an unreadable expression on her face. Then one corner of her full lips lifted in what he supposed was her attempt at a smile. "It's a mixed bag. I became a doctor and started a practice with two of my classmates. And I love what I do."

"You didn't join your mother's practice?"

"No. I—I couldn't. Not after everything that happened. Don't get me wrong, my parents didn't shut me out of their lives, nor did I exclude them from mine. But I couldn't get past what happened. I don't think they could either. I don't hold it against her that she pressured me to give up Crystal. I know she had my best interests at heart. But I'm not sure anymore that she was right. And whether she was or not, the fact that she threatened to cut off her support unless I fell in line meant that I was never able to trust her in the same way again. Over time, we drifted apart. I don't go to their house very often. And we don't talk much either." She shrugged as if the distance was no big deal, but he knew better. She'd adored her parents. And she'd idolized her mother.

Sympathy stirred inside him. He squelched it. She'd chosen her parents over him and Crystal. If things hadn't worked out the way that she'd hoped, well, life was rough.

You learned to adapt. He had. "So what does that have to do with me and Crystal?"

"For a while, I was able to focus on my goals. After everything that I'd given up… I had to make it worth it."

"Was it?"

She gave a one-shoulder shrug that meant absolutely nothing to him. "Who knows? I guess the answer depends on the day."

He decided not to probe that. He didn't want to be drawn too deeply into Andrea's world. Even after all this time she had a way of pulling him into her orbit. Now he knew there was nothing good there. At least not for him. "It sounds as if you're having a midlife crisis a few years early. Whatever is going on with you has nothing to do with Crystal."

"It has everything to do with her. She's my child."

"Wrong. She's my child. *Mine.* You signed away your parental rights years ago. I begged you not to, but you insisted that you didn't want to be a mother yet. You didn't want to put your dreams on hold. I told you I'd help you do both, but you didn't believe in me. In us. Now you have to live with that decision."

"Crystal is almost sixteen. She's old enough to choose her own friends."

"She's a child. And I'm her parent. Show some respect for that."

"I just want to know that she is happy."

"Of course she is. You have a lot of nerve coming here after all this time to question my parenting."

"I wasn't criticizing your parenting," Andrea said, spreading her hands out. "I'm just trying to explain why I showed up here after all this time."

"You don't have to explain because I don't care. Your

reasons don't matter to me now." He realized that he was getting loud, and he took a cleansing breath. He'd never had much of a temper, but Andrea had a knack for bringing things out of him that no one else could touch.

"I said the wrong thing. It's not that I don't trust you. I do. You have done a wonderful job with Crystal. She's bright and friendly and sweet as she can be."

"Agreed. So there is nothing more to discuss."

"But the fact that I walked away from her all those years ago when I was nothing more than a scared kid myself doesn't mean I stopped caring about her. Just because I wasn't a part of your lives didn't keep me from wondering how you guys were doing." He opened his mouth to speak, but she cut him off. Clearly there was more that she wanted to say, and now that she was on a roll there was no stopping her. "And I know if you had given in to our parents and given Crystal up for adoption, I would have had an even harder time finding her. But I would have tried anyway. I didn't even know that you had named her after my grandmother until I read the investigator's report."

"It was the first name that came to mind," he said begrudgingly. He would ever admit to choosing the name because he knew how close Andrea had been to her grandmother who'd died when Andrea was fifteen.

"Okay." She sounded disappointed, but she soldiered on. "After I got the report from the private investigator, I tried to let it go. But reading his report only left me with more questions. The only way to get the answers I wanted was to come here. So I took a leave from my practice and here I am."

"Why do you intend to stay here for the entire summer?"

"At first I didn't think that I would speak to either of

you. I thought I would need that much time to get a feel of the town as well as watch the two of you from a distance."

"Like a stalker."

"It sounds creepier when you say it out loud."

"I don't think it's a good idea for you to pop into her life for a couple months, and then vanish again. Not only for Crystal, but for you, too."

"I don't plan to tell her who I am. In fact, as far as she knows I'm just someone visiting town. Another tourist. When I go back home she won't give me a second thought."

"You don't know Crystal at all if you believe that."

Andrea looked into his eyes. He saw the desperation there. "Please, Cole. I'm begging. Please let me get to know her."

"And if I say no, what will you do? Will you walk away and leave town like you know I want you to, or will you find a way to go behind my back and see her anyway?"

"I wish I could tell you that I'll just walk away from her, but I can't. It's too important to me to spend time with her. But I don't want to be sneaky either."

Cole appreciated her honesty even though he hated what she was saying. "Don't tell her who you are. Don't even hint at it."

"I won't."

"I'm trusting you. Don't make me regret it."

Her eyes were filled with hope Cole couldn't ignore. She used a finger and crossed her heart. "I won't. I promise."

Cole frowned. He might regret this later but… "Okay. You can spend time with Crystal."

Chapter Six

Andrea couldn't believe her ears. Cole had actually agreed to let her spend time with Crystal. Of course, she wouldn't be able to tell Crystal that she was her mother, but as painful as that was, hiding her identity had always been the plan. Learning the truth would only hurt and confuse Crystal. Besides, Andrea wasn't moving to town. Her visit and her time with Crystal was limited. She had a full and happy life in Chicago, and it was clear that Cole didn't think there was any place for her here in Aspen Creek. She wouldn't stay and become a nuisance or a wedge between the father and daughter who were so close.

"There are a few rules," Cole said, before she could get too far ahead of herself. She should have known she wouldn't have free rein. But then, since Cole had agreed to her request, she couldn't complain.

"Like what?" Andrea mentally crossed her fingers, hoping they wouldn't be too onerous.

"I don't know where you're staying, but Crystal is not allowed to visit you there."

Andrea nodded. "Of course. That never crossed my mind. And I can give you my address."

"That's not necessary."

"It's no problem. I want to be completely transparent."

She grabbed a pen from her purse and scribbled the address on an unused napkin. After a moment, she added her cell phone number, then slid it across the table to him.

Cole glanced at it, folded it neatly, then shoved it into his shirt pocket. "Thank you."

She nodded. "What else?"

One corner of Cole's mouth lifted in a half smile. Could it be that he had expected her to put up more of a fight? Or could it be that he was remembering a time when the two of them used to negotiate about everything? Even before that fateful summer, Andrea and Cole had spent lots of time debating every topic under the sun—most especially how they would spend their time. She'd want to swim and he would want to sail. Or he wanted to go to the pizza place and she'd wanted ribs. Somehow, they had worked it out so they both were happy. Those had been the best days. She had yet to meet anyone else who'd made planning the event as much fun as the event itself. "You have to make all of your interactions appear organic. You don't want her to get suspicious."

"I wasn't planning on suddenly showing up everywhere she went. She told me about a knitting group at the craft store. I was thinking about joining."

"You mentioned that the other day. You really meant it—it wasn't just an excuse to spy on Crystal? You actually know how to knit?"

"Why do you sound so surprised?"

"Because you were always so active. I can't recall ever seeing you willingly sit still for more than five minutes. Knitting is a bit...sedate...for you."

"I'm older now. I was bound to slow down at some point."

"We're the same age. You seem to be in great shape. I

don't believe for a minute that you are a step slower now than you once were."

"I could say the same about you." She let her eyes travel over his well-developed torso, taking her time to study every muscle before meeting his gaze. She wouldn't say that Cole's body hadn't changed since they'd been teenagers. Of course it had. Now he had the build of a man. A sexy man whose clothes could not disguise his physique. It would probably be wiser for her to ignore how attractive he was—it would certainly be better for whatever type of relationship they were going to have while she was living in the same town as he was—but apparently she wasn't that smart.

Apart from that glorious yet reckless summer and start of her senior year of high school when she and Cole had been secretly dating, she had always stuck to the plan. Now, at thirty-four, she was going to allow herself to be reckless. After all, she was on vacation. Time to let down her hair and live a little.

He smiled. "But we aren't talking about me."

"Point taken. We should be talking about Crystal."

"The bottom line is I don't want her to be hurt. I can't cover every eventuality, though. Let's just play it by ear."

"I can do that."

"I think it would be best if you and I avoid each other. I don't want to be seen around town with you. Aspen Creek is a small town, and I don't want anyone to speculate about us."

That hurt. Andrea knew that Cole was being logical and that it made perfect sense for them to act as if they were strangers, but hearing him say the words was a blow.

She tried to hide her response, forcing a smile. "I can do that."

"Thanks." He looked at his watch. "I need to get back to work. And you should go."

He opened the box of cookies and took out another before offering the rest to her.

"You don't want them? I bought them for you."

"I wouldn't say I don't want them. They're still my favorite. I just don't know how I would explain having a box of cookies to Crystal without lying to her."

"Just say they were from a friend."

He laughed. "None of my friends give me cookies. That's not something that men normally do."

"Good point." Andrea reached for the box. Their hands brushed briefly and her fingers tingled at the contact. A slight shiver danced down her spine, and she told herself to ignore it. Attraction would only complicate an already complicated situation. She had enough land mines to navigate with Crystal and the secret she and Cole were keeping without adding more. "I guess I should get going."

He stared at her for a long moment. "Thank you."

"For leaving?"

"For not sneaking around behind my back. I appreciate your honesty."

"You're welcome." She took a step, and then turned back. "That man who works here. He won't say anything, will he?"

"Nah. You're good."

Cole and Andrea stood facing each, neither one moving, their gazes locked. Sexual tension arced between them and Andrea struggled to break free. *No land mines, remember?* Inhaling deeply, she took a step back then another. Turning, she hurried from the break room and through the feedstore. When she was outside, she released a pent-up breath. Though she was loath to admit it, she and Cole still shared a connection. A bond that had some-how survived angry words and accusations.

If the connection was simply a renewing of their friend-ship, it wouldn't be a problem. After all, they'd been friends a good part of their lives. But right now it felt like more than that. There was an attraction there. An at-traction that she needed to ignore at all costs.

Now that she had Cole's permission to spend time with Crystal, she was anxious to be around her. The craft store was not far away, so she headed over. A group of women were sitting around a corner table, knitting needles fly-ing as they talked.

"Hi, Andrea," Crystal said, as she walked over. Her smile looked so much like Cole's that Andrea couldn't help but return it. Andrea noticed characteristics that she shared with her daughter, but that was because she was looking for them. If Crystal's friends and neighbors no-ticed similarities between them, they would more than likely assume it was a coincidence. At least that was what she hoped.

"Hi yourself." She held up the cookies. "Everyone was so nice the other day that I thought I would bring some cookies to share. I confess to eating a couple."

"Thanks. Maggie's cookies are so delicious."

"I found that out."

Crystal took the box and set it on the counter beside the cash register. "The class is just starting. Do you want to join in? It's an intermediary group so you might be too advanced."

"Maybe. But it might be fun. What are they work-ing on?"

"They're making sweaters. We have a list with everything you need to make one. I'm helping to teach the class. Well, I'm more of an assistant."

"Sounds good. I'm in."

Crystal handed Andrea a list that she quickly skimmed. As they gathered the supplies Andrea would need, they talked. "What made you start knitting?" Andrea asked. "Most girls your age aren't big fans of it. At least in my experience."

"I like it. I learned to knit when I was babysitting a little girl named Chloe. Her great-aunt taught me. That's Mrs. Rose. She's here already. She doesn't need to take the class, but she says she likes the company. I made my dad a couple of scarves for Christmas. Last year I made him mittens. He wears them all the time. This year I'm going to make him a sweater."

"I'm sure he'll love it."

"He says that everything I make is his favorite." Crystal grinned. "I bet he's saying that just to make me feel good."

"I don't know. But even if he is, that just shows how much he loves you."

"He really is the best dad." Crystal gave her a long look. "I know you said you don't have kids or a husband, but do you have a boyfriend?"

"Why do you ask?" Andrea said cautiously even though it was obvious what Crystal was thinking. She'd already tried to set up Cole and Andrea at the park.

"Answer first, and then I'll tell you."

Andrea considered lying and saying that she was seriously involved with someone so that she could put the entire subject to rest, but she instantly thought of Cole and the relationship he shared with Crystal. They were close because—current situation aside—they were honest with each other. Andrea also wanted a close relationship with her daughter even if it only lasted for the summer. One that was based in truth even though she was keeping her identity a secret. "There's a man I'm seeing, but it's pretty casual. Now, tell me why."

"I was thinking that you might like my dad. And that he would like you."

"I don't know. I don't think he was too thrilled about you trying to set us up at the park."

"That was a coincidence."

Andrea gave Crystal a long look, and she caved almost immediately.

"Okay. I'm not admitting anything, but if I had been trying to set you up, he didn't know it."

Andrea couldn't tell her that Cole was aware of Crystal's machination without admitting that they had talked earlier. The deception was starting already. And she didn't like it.

"Besides," Crystal continued. "I try to fix him up with people all the time."

"And how does he react?" Andrea tried to keep her tone neutral, but she wasn't sure she'd successfully disguised her interest.

"Oh, you know how dads can be. He acts as if he doesn't like it, but I think he does. Besides, if I don't set him up with women, he won't have any dates."

"So there's nobody special in his life?" The minute the words escaped Andrea's lips, she wanted to yank them back. Sadly there was no way to unsay them. And Crystal had definitely heard them.

Crystal's eyes sparkled with amusement. "Not yet. But I think the two of you would like each other."

"And I think that your dad would probably like to find his own dates."

"I wish." Crystal looked around as if making sure that what she said next wouldn't be overheard. Clearly it was private. "I think he's still in love with my mom."

Andrea's heart skipped a beat, and then began thudding. Could it be that Cole was still in love with her? The idea that he hadn't moved on with his life was quite a sad one. Especially since she wasn't sure if she'd been in love with him back then or if she'd just been infatuated. And she certainly wasn't in love with him now. So why did she feel a little thrill at the thought of it? "Why do you think that? Has he said anything like that?"

"No." Crystal shook her head. "He never mentions her at all. There is not one picture of her anywhere in the house. I think she died, and just seeing her face is too painful for him."

"Did he tell you that?" Andrea was aghast. Surely Cole would never have said that. Especially when he was so insistent that they be honest with Crystal.

"No. But I can't think of another reason that he wouldn't talk about her. Can you?"

"I'm sure he has his reasons."

"That's one of the reasons I have to help him find someone new to love. To help him get over her."

"What's the other?"

"College. I'll be gone soon, and I don't want my dad to be all alone."

"As long as the two of you love each other, he'll never be alone no matter where you're living."

"That sounds exactly like something he would say. That just proves that the two of you belong together."

Andrea rolled her eyes. She should be flattered but knowing she was simply one in a line of women that Crystal paraded in front of her father dampened that feeling.

She had no doubt that after she left, Crystal would introduce another woman to Cole. And even if none of those worked out, she was sure there would come a time when Cole would meet the right woman and fall in love. Just because she had yet to find someone she wanted to spend the rest of her life with didn't mean he should be alone. And she had no right to feel a little resentful of that unknown woman who would get to have a life with Cole. Andrea had made her choice years ago. There were no do-overs. Not that she wanted one. Of course not. She didn't think of him that way.

Frankly, she was just glad that he was willing to give her a chance to connect with Crystal. She had no expectation of being able to rebuild some of her old bond with Cole. What they'd shared was truly over. Never again would he be her safe place. The one person she could relax around. Back in the day, it had been such a relief to be with him since she hadn't felt the need to compete with him the way she had with everyone else. Andrea had always felt the need to be perfect. She'd needed to excel at everything. If anyone could do something, then she believed she had the ability to excel at it, too. All she had to do was work at it.

Cole had been different. He'd believed that he could be good at something. The best even. But he'd never felt compelled to work himself to the bone to actually be the best at everything. He didn't have to be perfect in order to love himself. He had accepted himself, warts and all, and had tried to convince her to do the same. She had no doubt that gentle person still existed. He just wasn't willing to show that side of himself to her anymore.

"Why are you shaking your head?" Crystal asked.

"What?" Andrea pulled her attention back to the present. She wanted to get to know her daughter and instead of being in the moment, she had allowed her mind to drift away to thoughts of Cole. "I was somewhere else for a moment. Sorry."

"No need to apologize. Anyway, we need to get to the table."

Andrea paid for her supplies, then joined the others. Most of the participants were senior citizens, and it didn't take long for Andrea to realize that though they were working on projects, they were there to gossip as much as they were to learn how to purl. They were a friendly bunch who eagerly welcomed Andrea into the fold.

Apparently, the librarian, who wasn't present, had recently gotten engaged and the women were discussing the surprise wedding shower they wanted to throw her. That was, if she ever set a date, something that she hadn't done just yet. But that wasn't slowing them down.

"Which would you prefer, Andrea?" the woman who had introduced herself as Rose asked. Since she was the one who had taught Crystal how to knit, Andrea had been especially interested in getting to know her. She seemed to have a mischievous streak and she adored Crystal, which made her okay in Andrea's book.

"What are my choices again?" She and Crystal had been having a side conversation, and Andrea had only been listening to the others with one ear.

"Would you want to have a sedate luncheon like Linea wants, or would you rather a more fun event with male strippers like I want?"

"Uh. I don't know." How did she get in the middle of this? And how did she get out without offending either woman? "Why are you asking me? I've never met her."

"Because you're about her age."

"I suppose there's a place for each of them. But the main thing is what would the bride like?"

The women looked at each other, and then as one, burst into laughter.

"We're just kidding you," Rose said. "We know that Veronica wouldn't want a boring old luncheon."

"So you think she wants strippers?" Andrea choked out. She looked at the women, not sure if they were still kidding her.

"Are you saying you wouldn't?" Linea asked.

"Honestly, I've always been a bit of a good girl. I think I would lean toward a luncheon with the traditional games."

"Then we'll go with that," Rose said.

"And if I'd said I'd prefer a stripper?" Andrea asked.

"We would have put that in the back of our minds for when you got engaged."

"Oh, I'm not seeing anyone. And remember, I'm just in town visiting. I'll be leaving at the end of summer."

"Famous last words." Rose smiled and looked between Crystal and Andrea. Was she noticing that familial resemblance? "What brings you to our humble town?"

Andrea breathed out a sigh of relief and scolded herself for her paranoia. There was no reason to think any of these ladies would be suspicious. Crystal resembled Cole much more than she did Andrea. Even more so now that Andrea had changed her hairstyle. "Vacation. I live in Chicago. It seems like a nice change of pace. I've visited places all around the world—Paris, Rome, Nairobi, but they were all big cities. I wanted to get the feel of small-town America, but I wanted there to be lots of activities for vacationers. Aspen Creek has the best of both worlds."

The other women nodded and murmured. "In that case, you might need a tour guide."

"I was thinking the same thing. Maybe my dad could show you around," Crystal said.

"That sounds like a plan," Rose said, as if that was that. "If ever a man needed a girlfriend, it's Cole Richards."

"Hold on," Andrea said, trying to stop the train before it could get too far down the tracks. Did Cole know that the matchmakers included more than his daughter? From the interest on the faces of the other women, the crew was made up of at least five others. "I'm already dating someone."

"You said it's casual," Crystal pointed out.

"Yes, because I'm not looking for a relationship right now. And if I was, I would never start one with someone in a place I'm just visiting. Long-distance relationships aren't for me. They eventually lead to heartache. I don't know about you, but I do my best to avoid pain at all costs."

And look where that had gotten her. Alone. Trying to get to know the child she'd walked away from while hiding her identity. You couldn't get any more painful than that.

When the class ended, the women gathered their belongings, but didn't leave. Instead, they stood around Andrea. Rose was apparently the designated spokesperson. "Andrea, it was good to meet you. Be sure to come back."

"I will. I enjoyed meeting all of you." These women reminded her of her late grandmother. They were mischievous and playful. Most importantly, they were very supportive of Crystal. They, like her grandmother had she lived, would never turn away a teenager who'd needed them.

"And don't automatically say no to long-distance romance. It can work out."

"I'll keep that in mind," Andrea said.

Rose nodded, and the older women left.

"I'm going to meet my dad for lunch. You're welcome to join us if you would like," Crystal said, when she and Andrea were alone. "I ordered our meal from the diner. I'm going to pick it up."

"Thanks for the offer, but I'm going to decline." She didn't think she could handle being around Cole twice in one day. "I will walk with you to the diner, though."

"Okay. Wait until I sign out."

Crystal let Rebecca know that she was leaving for the day. "What did you think about class?"

"It was fun. It didn't look to me that most of the people needed to learn."

"Only one or two are less experienced. But Rebecca is hoping that more people will come once they see how much fun it is."

They walked down the street to the diner where Crystal picked up her order. "Are you sure you don't want to join us?"

"I'm positive. Thanks for the invitation."

"I guess I'll see you around," Crystal said.

The urge to hug Crystal was strong, but Andrea resisted it. Instead, she smiled and nodded as she watched her daughter walk away. It had taken nearly sixteen years, but she was getting to know her child.

Life couldn't get better than that.

Chapter Seven

"Is there something you want to tell me, boss?" Gary asked, coming into the break room a few minutes after Andrea walked out. Though she was no longer there, her enticing perfume still lingered in the air, taunting him.

"Something like what?" Cole asked, stalling for time, even though Gary was too sharp to be fooled for a minute. He needed to pull himself together, but he still couldn't believe that Andrea had sought him out.

More surprising was the fact that he hadn't tossed her out on her ear. And most astonishing of all was the fact that he'd agreed to let her hang around Crystal. But then, Andrea had always possessed the ability to get him to do what she wanted. Too bad he hadn't been able to do the same with her. Then maybe they could have raised Crystal together.

"Oh, like who that woman was." Gary fixed him with a hard stare. "Your conversation might have started out at a low level, but you raised your voice a couple of times. It might take me a bit longer to get where I'm going and I might need glasses to read, but I have terrific hearing."

Cole's heart stopped, and then began to race. "You heard?"

"That she's Crystal's mother? Yes."

"Did Danny?"

"No. Don't panic. He was already gone by that time. And he was so busy looking at the catalog that he didn't see her when she walked in. I put the Closed sign on the door, so nobody else would walk in while she was here."

Cole's heart slowed down although it was still beating faster than normally. "That's good. Thanks."

Gary shrugged, staying silent even though clearly there was more he wanted to say. He generally spoke his mind freely, so the fact that he was hesitant to speak wasn't a good sign.

"What?" Cole asked cautiously.

"Why is she here? You've lived in Aspen Creek for years and have not mentioned her once. To be honest, most people in town believe that Crystal's mother died in childbirth or soon after."

"Really?" Cole froze in shock. Why would people think that? "I hadn't heard that gossip."

"The subject of gossip is always the last to know. That's kind of how the whole thing works. You know, people talk about you behind your back, and then stop talking when you come around."

"I know how gossip works. I just never knew people were talking about Crystal's mother."

"Well, they haven't in years."

"Why didn't anyone ask me?"

"If I had to guess, it would be because there was no right time. When you arrived in Aspen Creek you were alone with a baby. It was obvious to all of us that you didn't have a family to turn to. You needed our help, not a bunch of prying questions. You were in pain, and nobody wanted to add to it by bringing up a sensitive topic. We all figured you'd talk about it when you were healed enough to do so. But you never said a thing. And Crystal is such a charmer. What kind of mother would turn her back on such a sweet baby? I suppose it was natural for people to conclude that something tragic had occurred."

"Obviously, Andrea isn't dead."

"Obviously." Gary poured some coffee into a mug, took a swig, then leaned against the countertop. When Cole didn't speak, Gary prodded. "So, what is the true story?"

"This goes no further than here."

"I'm offended you think you have to say that to me."

"We're talking about Crystal's happiness here. That makes me cautious."

Gary nodded.

"We were eighteen when she gave birth to Crystal. She wasn't ready to be a mother, and her parents put a lot of pressure on her to put the baby up for adoption. My parents put pressure on me, too, but unlike Andrea, I wasn't going to let go of my little girl." Those two sentences didn't come close to capturing the pain and heartache Cole had felt—honestly often still felt—when he thought back to that time. Some things hurt too much for a man to get over. "She signed away her parental rights, and got to stay a part of her family. I kept Crystal—and got disowned for it."

"Why is she here now? I can't believe her being in town is a coincidence."

"She wants to get to know Crystal."

"What?" Gary's voice was nearly as loud as Cole's had been when he'd spoken with Andrea.

"You heard me."

"She has her nerve. Does she actually believe she can just barge into our Crystal's life like that? I hope you told her where she can go. Hell, I'll give her directions if she needs them."

Despite the seriousness of the conversation, Cole struggled to hold back a smile. It warmed his heart to see just how much Gary loved Crystal and the lengths he would go to in order to protect her. Once again Cole was reassured that he'd made the right decision when he'd chosen Aspen Creek as their hometown. The people here loved Crystal. They were her extended family. The ones who'd taken her to their hearts when the rest of her biological family turned away.

"Actually, she convinced me to let her get to know Crystal."

"Are you out of your mind? Why would you do that?"

"I've been asking myself that very question since she walked out the door." Cole looked up at the ceiling, then blew out a breath.

"Don't tell me that you're still sweet on that woman after all this time."

"What? No. Of course not. Definitely not. That's ridiculous."

Gary gave him a searching look. "That was a whole lot of words. The more you use, the less I think you actually meant what you said."

Cole placed his palms on the table, then looked dead into Gary's eyes. "Let me assure you then. I'm not still sweet on her. To be honest, it took all that I had inside me to be civil to her."

"You should have stopped at politeness. There was no need to give her access to Crystal."

"But I did. I can't take it back."

"The hell you can't. You just march over to wherever

she's staying and tell her to hit the road. I'll go with you if you think you might fall under her spell again."

"I'm not under her spell." He hoped. "But like it or not, she is Crystal's mother. And she just wants to spend some time with her. Then she'll go back home."

"You have Crystal to think about. How is she going to feel when this strange woman tells her, *surprise, I'm your mama. I didn't want you before, but I want to be in your life.*"

"Not so loud."

"The sign is still up."

"Even so. Crystal will be here any moment. And Andrea and I already agreed not to tell her who she is. The story is that she's on vacation. When she goes back home, then that will be the end of it."

"Humph."

"What does that mean?"

"You know things never go according to plan. I don't trust her."

"Still. It is what it is." Cole shoved his hands into his pants pockets. Gary had stirred up all of his doubts, and now he wondered if he'd been too hasty making his deal with Andrea. Still, it was too late to change things now.

The bell over the front door jangled. "Hey. Are you guys here?" Crystal called out, effectively putting an end to the conversation. Not that there was anything more to be said. "I have lunch."

"We're in the back," Cole replied.

"What are the two of you up to?" Crystal asked when she stepped into the break room. She set the bag on the table and gave them a searching look. "I was only joking, but you guys look guilty as sin. What *are* you up to?"

Cole was usually quick on his feet, but Andrea's unexpected visit had knocked him for a loop. He didn't expect to return to normal until she was out of town and their lives for good.

"You know better than ask questions this close to your birthday," Gary answered, much to Cole's relief. "Too many questions means no gift."

"If I could call back those words, I would. Especially since this is my sweet sixteen. Since I can't, I'll make sure no more questions come out of my mouth." Crystal mimed zipping her lips, and they all laughed.

"I suppose that will do. This time. What do we have to eat?" Gary asked. "I'm starved."

"Roast chicken, macaroni and cheese, and mixed vegetables. And when I called in the order, Mrs. Rose heard me. She asked me if some of the macaroni and cheese was for you and I said yes. So she told Rhonda to slide yours in the oven for a few more minutes so the cheese would get nice and brown just the way you like it. Mrs. Rose also told Rhonda to put in a second helping for your dinner tonight. She said it's her treat."

The expression on Gary's face was unreadable. Finally he spoke. "That was nice of her."

"I think Mrs. Rose likes you," Crystal teased, as she washed her hands and dried them on a paper towel.

Much as Cole disliked gossip, he knew that it couldn't be avoided altogether. He didn't give much credence to the tales that traveled around town, going from tongue to ear and back again. But when you heard the same story over and over, you started to believe it had to have some truth to it. And Cole had heard from many sources that Gary and Rose had once been sweet on each other. Nobody seemed to know what went wrong between them. Whatever the problem, they had remained good friends.

Given what he'd just heard about the gossip circulating about him and Crystal and how totally wrong it was, Cole was glad he'd paid the gossip no mind. It was no doubt just as inaccurate. After all, Gary and Rose were senior citizens. They'd had plenty of time to work out the problems in their relationship if indeed there had been one.

"Rose likes everyone," Gary said. Even so, a smile played on the edges of his lips. Obviously, he was touched by her thoughtful gesture.

"Yes, but does she know how everyone likes their macaroni and cheese?" Crystal asked, her eyes dancing with mischief.

Gary looked at Cole, his eyes beseeching his assistance. Cole pretended not to notice. Maybe now Gary would know how it felt when Crystal targeted him with her ceaseless matchmaking. Perhaps next time Gary wouldn't join in.

Sure. And pigs would fly.

Gary loved teasing him. Not only that, Cole was starting to suspect that Gary was a romantic at heart.

"You got me there," Gary said. "But doesn't everyone like their cheese toasty?"

"Nope," Crystal said, digging into hers. "But I suppose it takes all types."

Cole and Gary exchanged looks, and then laughed. As they ate, Cole was once more struck by the questions that Gary had raised. Was he right? Had Cole made a monumental mistake by allowing Andrea back into their lives? Would her presence disturb the safe, happy life he'd created for his daughter?

Those questions nagged at him long after Crystal had gone home and Gary left to meet up with friends for a game of cards. Or as he liked to refer to it, filling his wallet with suckers' spare cash.

Cole had never been one to waffle. Once he made a decision, he lived with it unless and until he discovered that he'd made a mistake. Then he made a U-turn and did his best to get going in the right direction again. Now he couldn't seem to settle his mind. One minute he thought it was right to let Andrea and Crystal get to know each other. The next he was asking himself if he had an ounce of common sense and wondering how he could have been so wrong.

He needed to stop brooding, but he second-guessed himself the rest of the day and all through dinner.

"I'm going over to Livvie's for a little while," Crystal said after they'd washed the dishes.

"Okay. Let me know when you're there."

She blew out an exasperated breath. "I'm only going a couple of blocks. And she's standing on the porch waiting for me."

"I can always walk over with you," he offered.

"I'll text."

"Thanks."

Two minutes later his phone pinged and he read Crystal's text. As if his hand had a will of its own, he scrolled the contacts until he found Andrea's number, which he'd added earlier. Before he could give it a second thought, he pressed the icon. As he listened to the phone ring, he wondered what had come over him. He didn't want to talk to Andrea. Or rather, he didn't *want* to want to talk to her.

Before he could hang up, her sultry *hello* came over the line. His mind was instantly filled with memories of talking to her on the phone for hours.

"It's me. Cole." He leaned back, covering his eyes with his free arm.

"Cole?" Andrea's voice was filled with surprise.

"Yes. Are you free to talk?"

"Sure. What's up?"

There would be no beating around the bush tonight. But then he had been pretty clear that they weren't friends, so there was no reason for her to expect him to make small talk. He may as well get right to the heart of the matter.

"I'm not sure about you spending time with Crystal." Andrea gasped but other than that she didn't make a sound. Cole waited a minute before he continued. "It seems like it's a disaster waiting to happen."

Still nothing. Just complete silence.

"Are you going to say something? If I wanted to talk to myself, I wouldn't have called you."

"What is it you expect me to say? Do you want me to beg for the opportunity to see the child I gave birth to?"

"A child you walked away from before." They'd already covered this ground, but apparently Cole wasn't ready—or able—to let it go.

"A child I carried inside my body for nine months. I felt her growing and moving inside me. I fell in love with her over and over every day. Do you think it was easy to let her go? My heart broke every time I thought about never seeing her again."

"See her *again*? You didn't even look at her once." To him, that showed how cold her heart had been toward his daughter. How indifferent she'd been toward that helpless baby.

"You think I don't know that?" Her voice was loud with indignation as if she were the injured party. Then she sighed and spoke softly. "I couldn't see her. Just like

I couldn't hold her. If I did, I would never have been able to let her go. *And I had to let her go.*"

"So you could get your precious education and continue the family legacy of being a doctor," he said bitterly.

"So I could keep my family and have the only future I was able to picture for myself. I don't expect you to understand my choice."

"I do understand. I just don't like it."

"So because of that, you've decided to punish me forever. I never thought you would be so cruel as to play with my feelings. Was this your plan all along? Let me get excited to spend time with Crystal, get my hopes up so you can dash them?"

"Wait a minute. How did I suddenly become the bad guy?"

"That's just it, Cole. Why does anybody have to be the bad guy? Why can't we accept that we each made what we thought was the best decision at the time?"

He sat with that for a moment. "I suppose you have a point. I just have so many conflicting feelings about this situation."

"Join the club."

"I haven't thought about you in years," he said, though even as the words came out, he realized that they weren't entirely true. Every once in a while when he wasn't holding on to his emotions as well as he should have, or when Crystal had a certain expression on her face, he thought about Andrea. But she didn't need to know that. "So don't think that I have been waiting for the opportunity to hurt you. I actually never thought I'd see you again."

"I understand why you want to keep me away from Crystal. I just wish I knew how to convince you that I have no intention of hurting her." She sighed. "I've lived sixteen years without her. I missed hearing her first word. I didn't get to see her take her first step. I missed so many of her milestones. I just wanted a few weeks with her, to be her friend. Then I'll leave, and everything will go back to how it was. Is that really too much to ask?"

Why was it so hard to say no to her? He should stick to his guns. That's what Gary would do. But Cole couldn't be that selfish. All this time, he supposed he had thought of her as the bad guy in the story—but she was right. Why did there have to be a bad guy at all? They were just kids back then, trying to figure things out. Trying to make good choices. He still didn't agree with the choice she'd made, but having a daughter who was nearly sixteen drove home to him just how young they'd been when Crystal was born. How much could he really blame the scared, conflicted teenager she used to be for making a mistake? He didn't want to hate her. And he didn't want to make her suffer unnecessarily.

"Okay."

"What does that mean?" Andrea's voice held cautious hope.

"That we can go back to the original plan."

"Thank you."

Cole knew that he should end the call—after all, he'd said everything he'd intended to say—but he couldn't make himself say goodbye. Now that he'd gotten over the shock of Andrea's presence in town, he was curious about her life. He wanted to know what she'd been up to. It would be easy to claim that his curiosity stemmed from the fact that Andrea would be in Crystal's life, at least temporarily, but that wasn't the entire truth.

"How have you been otherwise?"

"Are you asking me because you want to know or because I need to pass a background interview with you?"

"Because I really want to know."

"Okay." There was a pause, and he could picture her getting more comfortable in her chair. "College was intense."

"What did you major in?"

"Biology and biochemistry."

"Wow. I bet you graduated with honors."

"Yes. Summa cum laude. Number one in my graduating class."

"Why am I not surprised?"

"All I did was study and go to class."

"You didn't join a sorority? You always planned to join the one our mothers and grandmothers were in."

"That was before."

"Before Crystal?"

"Yeah. After…everything… I decided that I needed to focus solely on my future. I veered off track once and look what happened."

"You and I created the best thing that ever happened to me." He sighed. "But that's not how you looked at it."

"No. Not then. My family had high expectations of me. I felt like I had let them down once and I wasn't going to do it again. I wanted to make them proud of me again."

"Were they?"

"They seemed to be."

"That's the difference between you and me. I wanted my parents to be proud, but I wasn't going to walk away from my daughter in order to make that happen."

"I made a different choice. And you hate me for that."

He closed his eyes. "I don't hate you. At least not now. But I'm still struggling to understand. A part of me wants to make you live with the consequences of that choice forever, you know? That may be small of me, but that's the truth."

"And whenever that part of you raises its head, you want to make me suffer."

He didn't like the way that sounded...but he couldn't deny it either. "In a nutshell. But I'm going to work on getting over it. I don't want to be that kind of person."

He meant that. He didn't like feeling so torn up and conflicted over someone he used to love. He'd wanted to spend the rest of his life with her even before she'd gotten pregnant. He wondered if part of the reason he was so upset with her was that she'd walked away not just from Crystal but from him. She hadn't loved him as much as he'd loved her. That summer and early fall had been special for him, and he didn't regret a second of the time they'd spent together. Apparently, he was the only one.

"Anyway. How was medical school?"

"More of the same. There was a lot of hard work involved, but I loved it."

"You always did love a challenge."

"Yes. I already told you that I started a practice with two of my classmates after graduation. I've been working there ever since."

Andrea had answered every question, but her responses sounded a bit cut-and-dried. There was absolutely no emotion behind them. She had referred to their conversation as an interview. That was how her answers sounded to him. As if she was trying to convince him to hire her. But she didn't need to convince him of how driven she was. He knew it already. That was one of the qualities that had drawn him to her. That and her pretty face, sexy body and exciting personality.

"I can't believe you managed to sum up sixteen years of your life in under ten minutes. I'm impressed." Of course she had left out all personal things. What did she do in her spare time—besides knit? Was there a special man in her life? Did she want other children? Heck, for all he knew she could have another child.

He pushed the questions away. Andrea's life was not his business, beyond how it would impact Crystal. They weren't going to become friends again. Once the summer was over, she would be going back to her life and he and Crystal would remain here.

And that was the way he wanted it.

"What have you been up to? Apart from being a great dad to Crystal?" Andrea couldn't believe she'd asked that question, but she really wanted to know. They were having a good conversation and before things turned bad, as she had no doubt they would when Cole had some time alone with his thoughts, she wanted to learn as much as she could about his life over the past sixteen years.

"Being a dad is a full-time job. Especially when you're doing it alone. I had to earn a living and learn how to cook and keep house. Grocery shopping was really an adventure in the beginning. There wasn't room for much else."

"Ouch. Forget I asked."

"I didn't mean that as judgment. Honestly. It's just that being a parent takes a lot of time. First there were diapers and night feedings. Then there was teething and crawling. I don't think I slept for the first year or so. I was afraid of doing something wrong that would cause her harm."

Though it didn't sound pleasant, Andrea felt as if she'd missed out on something great.

"Luckily I found the people in the Aspen Creek area,"

Cole continued. "I worked at the Montgomery cattle ranch. They became the family support system that I needed. And Crystal just blossomed. She soaked up all of the love they lavished on her."

Andrea was glad to know that her daughter had been loved. That's what she'd wanted more than anything. Hearing that Crystal had enjoyed a happy childhood filled her with relief. It was as if her heart was released from a tight bind, and she could breathe freely for the first time since she'd known she was going to relinquish her parental rights to her Little One.

"Then she was crawling. There were horses all around and the Montgomerys had a dog. I think she crawled for so long because that was what she saw."

"Did you try to encourage her to walk?"

"Yes. We all did. Finally she realized that she could grab more things if she was upright. But she skipped the walking stage altogether and went straight to running. Speed was the name of the game."

"Did you live in town then?"

"No. I was a ranch hand for my first twelve years here. The job didn't pay a lot of money, but it came with a furnished cabin. Little did I know that it also came with a built-in family. Miles, Nathan and Isaac Montgomery became more than my employers' sons. They started as friends, and then became family. They're my brothers from another mother. And Crystal thinks of them as her uncles. Edward and Michelle Montgomery are like grandparents to her."

"Speaking of grandparents, are you in touch with your parents?"

"No. They made it clear that if I didn't do what they wanted, I was out of their lives completely—and so was

Crystal. They made their choice. Now they have to live with it."

"I think they regret it."

"Why do you think that?"

"Little things they've said here and there. Mind you, they are careful around me. Probably because they don't want to make me feel bad about the decision I made."

"Well, you found me. They could have done the same if they were interested. It's not as if I'm hiding. I lived in Chicago for nearly six months, scraping and doing without so I could care for my child on my own. Not once did anyone—and I mean my parents or grandparents or yours—reach out to me and offer a hand. They were willing to let me sink if that's what it took for me to bend to their will."

"Maybe they thought it would be for the best in the long run."

"What are you, their lawyer? They don't need you to advocate for them. I know they expected me to fail and come crawling back to them. I know they thought they were showing me tough love, forcing me to make what they thought was the right decision. But I succeeded in spite of them, and I don't need anything from them now. And I certainly don't want to hear anything about giving them a second chance."

"I wasn't trying to do that. You were talking about the family you made here, and I didn't want you to forget that you had a family in Chicago."

"They stopped being my family when they refused to help me. A real family stands by you and helps you when you need it. They love you even when they don't agree with the decisions you make for your life. Anything else is not acceptable."

"You're right. I'm sorry." Andrea sighed. "I just want so much for Crystal. The world. One of the reasons I agreed to give her up was so she could have a family."

"*I'm* her family."

"I know. And I'm not discounting that for a minute. But you and I grew up with loving families."

"Your definition of 'loving' leaves a lot to be desired."

"You know what I mean. When we were growing up, everyone was so supportive and caring."

"Until they weren't."

"Anyway, that's why I agreed to give Crystal up for adoption. I thought she'd be better off with a couple that was really ready for a baby—a couple with a whole support network behind them. Now, though, I see that you have given her everything that I could have wished for."

He was silent, as if absorbing her words. Maybe they'd shocked him.

"When did you move to town?"

Andrea couldn't see him, but she sensed the tension leaving his body. "Three years ago. The feedstore was for sale and Crystal wanted to move to town. She was getting older and wanted to be closer to her friends. She loves being closer to the action. Now it's easier to drive her around to her activities. And as I'm sure you've already noticed, everyone loves her."

"She is definitely a people person. I know she didn't get that from me."

"I don't know about that. You were very popular. And you were into a lot of activities."

"Yeah, but I was doing them more to make my college applications stand out than anything else. Looking back, I didn't enjoy things very much."

"You were certainly driven. Even so, I thought that you

had fun." His voice grew quieter. "Did you have even a little bit of fun?"

"Some. But that was never of primary importance. I was focused on my goals and determined not to let anything get in my way."

"And you succeeded."

Andrea couldn't determine whether he was being sarcastic or not, so she decided to assume the answer was *not*. It was better for a peaceful conversation.

"What does Crystal like to do?"

"For a while she was into basketball. She was pretty good. It helped that she's tall. She's really into dance. She's on a dance squad. They perform at a lot of the town activities."

"Like what?"

"High school football games. Town festivals and parades. The Aspen Creek summer carnival. Aspen Creek may be a resort town, but we have the same activities for residents as any other place."

Cole's and Crystal's lives sounded so different from the one Andrea lived in Chicago. She was completely focused on work. Not that she was still striving to get ahead. She'd already achieved the goals she'd set out for herself, and she was pleased with the size of her practice. It was just that she wanted to make her sacrifice worth it. Seeing the life that Cole had created for himself and Crystal made her wonder if she had prioritized the wrong things. Maybe things would have worked out if she had trusted Cole enough. But would she be as happy if she hadn't been able to become a doctor? If she was honest, she had to say no.

Andrea took a deep breath and crossed her fingers. "Is running a feedstore your new dream?"

He hesitated, and Andrea wondered if she had said the wrong thing. Maybe she'd touched a sore spot. "No. It's a new thing. Working on the ranch was great, and one day I hope to have a spread of my own. It won't be as huge as the Montgomery ranch, but I don't need something that big in order to be happy."

"Wow. I never would have believed you would move to a small town much less a ranch."

"You're not the only one who is stunned by the way my life turned out. But sometimes we plan and fate has something entirely different in mind. Something much better."

"So you're happy?"

"Yes. Very. Are you?"

Was she? "I have my moments."

And apparently that was as good as it was going to get.

Chapter Eight

"What are you doing tonight?" Crystal asked two days later as she finished knitting the sweater she was working on. The meeting was wrapping up, and the others were putting their needles and yarn into their bags and saying their goodbyes. This was always the worst part of the day for Andrea. She knew that she wouldn't be seeing Crystal again until the next session.

"I don't have plans. Why?"

"I wanted to invite you to dinner."

Andrea paused. Everything inside her wanted to say yes, but she didn't know how Cole would react. They hadn't talked since that one telephone conversation, and she hadn't seen him since. She didn't think he would appreciate her walking into the feedstore where anyone could see them together. On the other hand, she didn't want to reject Crystal and hurt her feelings.

"That sounds nice. What does your father think?"

"It's not a problem."

Andrea wasn't so sure about that. But then, he was the one who said she should keep her meetings with Crystal organic. It didn't get any more organic than this. "Okay then. I would love to have dinner with you. Can I bring anything?"

"No. Rhonda at the Aspen Creek Diner has been teaching me how to cook. It's really fun, and I'm getting good at it."

"Doesn't your dad cook for you?" Andrea's voice was sharper than she had intended. Of course at nearly sixteen Crystal was old enough to help with the cooking. Even so, the notion of Crystal needing to fend for herself was disturbing.

"Of course. He cooked all the time when I was little. Now we take turns. He makes the best waffles. They're always really fluffy and he puts whipped cream around the edges. We have them just about every Saturday. When I was little, I loved putting syrup in all the little squares."

"That sounds nice." It also sounded a lot like the waffles that Cole's mother used to make on the weekends. Cole might think that he had left all traces of his family behind, but clearly that wasn't the case. She suspected that despite all his protestations, he missed his family and he was keeping the connection alive in the only way that he would allow himself to. He'd brought at least one of the traditions with him and was sharing it with Crystal.

"It is. My dad is such a great guy," Crystal said, switching to what was clearly her favorite topic. "You can ask anyone in town, and they'll tell you the same thing. When our neighbor twisted her knee and was on crutches, dad drove her to the store and to the doctor whenever she needed. Some of our neighbors are senior citizens and Dad always shovels their snow and cleans off their cars in the winter. And he is really handsome. Aspen Creek has this bachelor auction every year. Well, they've had two. I've tried to get my dad to enter, but he wouldn't. I know he would have raised a lot of money for charity, but nothing I said could persuade him. The other men who entered are kind of cute, for guys in their thirties, but none of them look as good as my dad."

Andrea had to admit that Cole was still easy on the eyes. Andrea couldn't get the image of him at the feed-store the other day out of her mind. His plaid shirt had fit his muscular torso perfectly, emphasizing his powerful build. Every time he'd moved his arms, his biceps stretched the shirt fabric. Things might be tense between them, but her attention had been divided between their conversation and his physique. She'd been unable to keep her eyes from straying all over his handsome face and sexy body.

She'd always thought she preferred a man dressed in a suit and tie, but after seeing how good Cole looked in his casual shirt and faded jeans, she might have to reconsider that. Not that it mattered. She and Cole were not going to date. Their fling had been a onetime thing. She wasn't a teenager anymore. Thirty-four was old enough to know that physical attraction was not nearly enough to hold a relationship together. Even a shared past wasn't enough. Besides, there was too much stacked against them to make a romance work—even if they both wanted one, which they didn't.

But there was no way she could tell Crystal that without going into more detail that would make keeping her secret more difficult.

"Is this a friendly dinner or are you trying to set me up with your dad?"

Crystal laughed and gave what Andrea supposed was her innocent look. Andrea had no idea how Cole had been able to resist her all of these years. Andrea doubted she would ever have been able to tell her no.

"Just say yes. We're friends and you're new to town. I was raised to be kind. That's all I'm trying to do here."

"Okay. Then I'll be there."

"Great." Crystal gave Andrea her address. "See you at seven."

Andrea had brought lots of clothes with her, but as she did a quick mental inventory of her closet, nothing seemed right for tonight. Everything was either too casual or too dressy. Since she had time to kill and she knew the minutes would crawl by if she was alone at the cabin, she decided to do some stress shopping. Aspen Creek had plenty of high-end boutiques to choose from.

She strolled down the street, passing vacationers carrying shopping bags and families enjoying the warm summer day. She was still amazed by how easily she had begun to feel at home here. In addition to being a regular at the craft store, she had become a familiar face at the Sweet as Pie bakery and the Aspen Creek Diner. She'd visited the Main Space Art Gallery and had purchased two pieces of original art. One for the office and one for her condo.

She entered the Heavenly Garb boutique and looked around. Andrea didn't know what she was looking for exactly, but she knew she would recognize it the moment she laid eyes on it. The clothes were stylish and well-made, and Andrea was immediately drawn to a short orange print skirt. She'd always loved bold colors. Years ago, Cole had pointed out how good she looked in them. That had been all it took for her to wear them just about every day. Now, in order to look professional, her wardrobe mostly consisted of neutral dresses and skirts that she wore underneath her white doctor's coat, same as her mother did. And since she spent most of her time working, she didn't really bother to have a lot of options for clothes she wore just for fun. She might not wear this skirt again, but it would be worth it to feel extra pretty tonight.

There were two coordinating tops beside the skirts, and Andrea picked up one of each color in her size and headed to the dressing room. Once inside, she quickly changed out of her shorts and top and pulled on the skirt and blouse and turned to the mirror.

"I remember you," she said to her reflection. She liked the bright colors and wondered if she'd changed her style because of her mother's not so subtle comments about how a female doctor should dress. Was she still trying to regain her parents' approval—forgiveness even—after all these years?

How else had she changed herself?

Would she still be as driven as she was now if she wasn't trying to erase the disappointment she'd seen in their eyes when she'd told them she was pregnant, or would she have learned to relax a bit? Would she still strive to be number one in all things? That was hard to know because she had always wanted to be the best. But would that desire be as intense if she'd stepped away from their influence earlier?

She might not ever know the answer to those questions. And really, did it matter now? There was no changing the past. The only thing to do was live in the present and prepare for the future. And that started tonight with her dinner with her daughter and Cole.

"Something smells good," Cole said, stepping into the living room. He sifted through the mail, and then tossed it and his keys onto the coffee table. His phone had died earlier, and he plugged it into the charger. Maybe it was time to break down and get a new one.

"You always say that when it's my turn to cook," Crystal replied as she stepped into the room. She was wearing a green apron with a gold crown and the words *Cooking Queen* embroidered on the front.

"I'm just saying those cooking lessons with Rhonda are paying off." The women in this town had taken it upon themselves to be the mothers, grandmothers and aunties that Crystal was lacking. They always respected his role as father, but insisted that a woman's influence was important. Since he knew it actually did take a village to raise a child—and as long as Crystal was willing—he was happy for them to have a place in Crystal's life.

He sniffed. "What's that I smell?"

"Baked salmon, mixed vegetables and baked potatoes."

"No, that's not what I smell."

Crystal rolled her eyes. "I baked a chocolate cake."

"My favorite. I don't know what you want, but the answer is yes."

"You're so easy, Dad. You're lucky I'm not the kind of kid who would try to take advantage of you."

He slung his arm over her shoulder, pulled her close and kissed her cheek. "I always say I'm the luckiest dad in the world to have gotten such a great daughter."

He glanced at the table. It was set for three. "Are we having company?"

"Yep. I invited a friend. I didn't think you'd mind."

"I don't mind at all." She often invited friends for dinner on the nights she cooked.

She wrinkled her nose. "You made a delivery to a ranch, didn't you."

"If you can tell, I suppose I'm in need of a shower." He

had intended to take a quick one anyway, but confirmation was a good thing.

"You are such a smart dad. You must have been head of the class."

"Smart aleck."

Crystal grinned. "Dinner will be ready at seven."

"Then I had better hurry. I don't want you to start without me."

Cole raced up the stairs and headed to the shared bathroom, even though he knew there wasn't a need to rush. He didn't really think Crystal and her friend would start dinner without him. They would probably be too busy giggling and talking about the latest romance movie they'd seen or some boy they thought was cute. Cole wasn't sure how he felt about Crystal dating, but he knew the time was coming when a boy would show up on his porch, wanting to take Crystal to the movies. He'd been about her age when he'd started to think of Andrea as more than just a friend. It had just taken him a year or two to act on it. The notion that some other teenage boy might be thinking the same about his daughter was enough to turn his stomach.

He'd never tried to hide the fact that he'd been an unwed single father from Crystal. It had been clear that he was much younger than her friends' fathers. Once she had been able to add and subtract, she'd figured out that he was only eighteen years older than she was. Crystal was well aware of how hard he'd worked to make a good life for her. Of course she wasn't aware of all of the struggles—he'd done his best to protect her—but she was aware of the ways her life differed from those of her friends whose parents had built successful careers before they'd had children. Even so, Cole had made sure that she'd never lacked for anything. She'd had the dance and gymnastics classes, and gone on every school field trip.

The one thing he hadn't been able to give her was a mother. Oh, when he'd been in his midtwenties with a good job, the women had begun to come around. He'd quickly shut them down. He was focused on being the best father he could be and hadn't been interested in dividing his time or attention. But then, Crystal had gotten it into her head that it was up to her to find him a wife.

He'd tried to explain to her that he wasn't interested in a romantic relationship. More than once he'd told her that his heart wasn't in it. There was no good way to tell her that after getting his heart broken by her mother, he would never trust his heart with another woman again. He knew that Crystal had interpreted his words to mean that he hadn't gotten over her mother, and he'd let her. Whatever worked.

Unbidden, he thought about Andrea. They'd been each other's first lover. He had never felt the way he'd felt about Andrea for anyone before or since. She'd been his everything. It had taken years to be able to think about her without an ache in his chest. Talking about her had hurt, so he hadn't spoken of her to anyone for years. Being the empathetic person she was, Crystal stopped asking about her mother.

Now he wondered if he had been selfish. He'd told Crystal that her mother had loved her but that she couldn't be a part of her life. Perhaps that was how the rumor that she had died had begun.

Cole stepped out of the shower and quickly dried off. Maybe now was the time to talk to Crystal about her mother. After all, she was a teenager herself and could relate. Cole and Andrea could be a cautionary tale of what happened when you let your hormones get the better of your common sense. Or not. With Andrea in town, perhaps stirring up the past was the last thing he should do.

He dressed, and then started down the stairs. He'd heard the doorbell ring earlier, so he knew Crystal's friend was here.

"I'll be right back. I just need to check on the sauce," he heard Crystal say, catching a glimpse of her as she headed into the kitchen.

Cole stepped into the living room with the intention of greeting whichever teen had joined them. But instead of one of the usual crew, a woman dressed in a sexy outfit was sitting on his sofa. *Andrea*.

She looked up and he realized that he had spoken out loud. Thankfully Crystal was in the kitchen, banging pots and pans so she didn't hear his exclamation. He lowered his voice. "What are you doing here?"

The smile that had been on her face faded. She stood and he was temporarily distracted by the way her skirt skimmed her slender curves before stopping at the middle of her toned thighs. She was still so gorgeous and even now could take his breath away.

"Crystal invited me to dinner." Her brow wrinkled. "I left a message on your cell earlier. I said if you had a problem to let me know and I'd cancel. When I didn't hear back from you, I thought…" She flapped her arms, looking very uncomfortable.

He frowned. "My phone died. I've been putting off getting a new one. Besides, you could have stopped in the store."

"I thought we agreed that wasn't a good idea."

"You're right." He didn't know why he was being such a jerk right now. She hadn't done anything wrong. This was only dinner. Not a big deal. And it wasn't as if he and Andrea hadn't just eaten together at the park. Not only that, he knew Crystal was trying to get the two of them together. If not tonight, she'd find a way to push them together in some other time and place. She already sang Andrea's praises every chance she got. If he hadn't been preoccupied with his phone, he would have guessed that Andrea was Crystal's dinner guest.

"I can make up an excuse to leave," Andrea said reluctantly.

"Like what? An emergency call from your office?"

Andrea actually laughed, and Cole found himself joining in. "I don't suppose there are many emergencies on vacation."

"Where is that case of projectile vomiting when you need it?" Cole joked, putting a hand on Andrea's arm. Her skin was soft and warm, and he felt a jolt of electricity. Their eyes met, and he saw the surprise in hers.

"Okay, you guys, come to the table," Crystal said, as she entered the room. She had a platter in her hand and a satisfied grin on her face that grew wider as she looked between Andrea and Cole. Great. Now her matchmaking was bound to go into overdrive. Crystal set down the platter, and then stepped back into the kitchen.

"Sorry," Andrea murmured, although he had no idea why she was apologizing. He doubted she knew either.

"Let's just enjoy dinner. Later we can let her know that there is no spark." That last line was a bit of wishful thinking. He might not want to feel attracted to Andrea, but he was losing that fight. The part of him that had always found her sexy was still alive and kicking. "If we both tell her—separately of course—she'll have to believe it."

It was safe to say that claiming there was no attraction between them would be half right. He knew beyond a shadow of a doubt that Andrea was no longer attracted to him. It was clear by the way she went out of her way to keep from touching him. It was as if she found even the slightest contact repulsive.

"So, we just go along with it tonight," Andrea said, as if seeking clarification.

"Yes. Surely you can pretend for a couple of hours."

Andrea nodded slowly, and Cole knew she was reluctant to play this game. He also knew that she would agree to anything for the opportunity to spend more time with Crystal.

They walked into dining room, and Crystal shot Cole a meaningful glance. Sighing, he pulled out Andrea's chair for her. As she took her seat, she smiled at him and his pulse began to race. Why had his heart decided to respond to this woman and not another one? He would have been happier to remain numb.

"Thank you." Her voice was soft and contained a hint of surprise.

"I hope you like salmon," Crystal said, her expression momentarily concerned.

"I love all kinds of fish. Truthfully, I love all food. Especially when it's eaten in the company of friends."

Cole couldn't help but smile. Some things never changed. While she might sometimes get too distracted to remember to eat, once she sat down at the table, Andrea had always had a huge appetite. She'd never pretended that she couldn't eat a bite when they'd gone out to eat. She'd eaten nearly as much as he had. But she was always so busy, racing from one activity to another, that she'd needed a lot of fuel to keep going. He had a feeling her need to stay busy hadn't changed. He had no doubt that she joined the knitting group in order to get closer to Crystal. But Andrea had never felt comfortable if her hands weren't busy. She hated being idle.

"I made a lot, so help yourself."

"You mean this isn't all for me?" Andrea joked.

Cole barked out a laugh. How had he forgotten her wicked sense of humor? Andrea's personality was a complex and often contradictory mix of traits. She could be so serious and driven, but she had a great sense of humor and never minded laughing at herself. She'd been intensely competitive, but she'd always managed to be genuinely happy for the victor in those rare occasions when she hadn't come in first. Of course, a loss was often used as fuel for working harder to make sure that she came out on top the next time.

"That would be a no," Crystal said, laughing. "The cook always gets to eat, right, Dad?"

"Absolutely. That's the first rule of the kitchen."

"I may have heard that a time or two," Andrea replied, spooning a good size portion of vegetables onto her plate. "The second rule being the chef doesn't have to clean."

"Right. That's what we agreed to," Crystal said. "It sounds like you have that in common with us. I knew you would fit in around here."

Cole shook his head. Could Crystal be any more obvious? His gaze caught Andrea's, and he noticed that she had a small smile on her face.

"I hope that isn't a hint for me to wash dishes," Andrea joked.

"No," Crystal sputtered, clearly horrified. "That's not what I meant at all."

"I'm kidding. I wouldn't dream of getting in your father's way."

"Dad wouldn't mind the help," Crystal said. "Would you, Dad?"

Cole immediately envisioned being in the kitchen with Andrea, working together. He imagined brushing past her slender form as he put storage bowls filled with leftovers into the refrigerator and feeling the warmth from her body wrap around him. He was already close enough to her to inhale her tantalizing scent with each breath he took. Despite his intention to keep her at a distance, he felt his defenses lowering with each passing minute. Being with Andrea felt good. More than that, it felt right. The three of them having dinner together seemed natural. He might not want to admit it to himself, and he definitely would never say it to Andrea, but they were a family.

"I never turn down helping hands," he said, pleased that his voice didn't reveal his emotions. He was hopeful that once Andrea was out of his life that his desires would vanish right along with her.

When Crystal had been a toddler, he'd had to remind her to keep away from the stove because it was hot. She hadn't truly understood until she'd burned her fingertips. Cole had been burned by love sixteen years ago, and he'd more than learned his lesson.

They managed to keep conversation light as they ate despite the fact that Crystal was doing the hard sell. She went from pointing out how great Andrea looked with her new haircut—which was true—to mentioning how strong Cole was. All while managing to eat. It would have been amusing if it wasn't happening to him.

They had just finished eating dessert when Crystal's phone buzzed. Since dinner was over, the rule of no phone at the table no longer applied. Hopping up, Crystal grabbed her phone off the coffee table and after reading the text, her thumbs began to fly across the screen. Another text reply and she looked at Cole.

"Livvie is having an emergency. She needs me to come right now. Sorry to run out on you guys." Her grin was wide, and Cole suspected that she'd arranged the text message in advance.

Crystal walked back to the table and gave Andrea a quick hug. Andrea's eyes widened in surprise, and she blinked rapidly then closed her eyes. When Crystal pulled back, Andrea swiped at her eyes quickly, banishing any moisture before Crystal noticed. Cole saw, and his heart ached for Andrea and all that she had missed.

"What's the emergency?" Cole asked. He was skeptical, but it would be unfeeling of him not to ask.

"She wants me to help her choose her clothes for a date." Crystal grabbed her purse and before Cole could think of something to say, his daughter had flown from the room, the door shutting firmly behind her.

"Oh," Andrea murmured. It was clear that she was talking to herself, so he didn't feel the need to answer.

Though he and Andrea had managed to keep things light while Crystal was around, now that they were alone, he felt his lust for her building. He didn't know how he'd managed to stay under control with Andrea so close. Every time she laughed, something low in his stomach had stirred. It had taken every ounce of self-control not to reach out and caress her face or run his fingers through her hair. Every time she tilted her head to the side, he'd been drawn to her slender neck and the desire to place kisses there walloped him.

"I want to apologize again for showing up out of the blue."

"Do you mean tonight or when you arrived in town?"

"I meant tonight."

"No need. Crystal is a force of nature. Once she makes up her mind, it's darn near impossible to get her to change it. She was determined to get us together. One way or another she was going to make it happen."

"I wonder where she got that from," Andrea said, and then smirked.

"Surely you aren't talking about me?"

"Don't sound so surprised. Once you set your mind to something there is no going back."

"Funny. I was just about to say the same about you. If ever there was a more goal-oriented person in the world, I have yet to meet them."

Unexpectedly, her smile faded, and she seemed to sink in upon herself. "Do you think that is a bad thing?"

"Not at all. I always admired the way that you never let anything get in your way."

"Including my own baby."

"Yeah." He reached out and touched her hand. "But I wasn't thinking about that when I made that comment. It wasn't a backhanded slap."

"I know. You always preferred a frontal attack."

"I'm a fan of directness. Honesty is the best policy and all that. It leads to fewer misunderstandings." That was usually the case. He was hiding so many things now— from Crystal, from Andrea and even from himself.

"True."

A silence settled between them, but it wasn't entirely uncomfortable. Sexual tension lurked beneath the surface. At least on his part. Since he wasn't sure how long his self-control would last, and he knew better than to test the limits, he stood. "I guess we should say good night."

"I can help with the dishes," she offered, as she reached for her plate.

The idea of living out his earlier vision of working in the kitchen together made him shake his head. He couldn't trust himself to behave as he knew he should. Not when he couldn't stop himself from reacting to Andrea's nearness. He didn't want to tempt fate. "That's not necessary. I have it down to a science."

Andrea looked as if she might protest, and given his weakening self-control, if she'd pressed, then he might have agreed to let her, consequences be damned. She shook her head and stood. "Then I'll leave you to it. Thank you so much for your hospitality."

"You're welcome." He stepped back so Andrea could pass by. The space was tight, and she brushed against him as she headed for the living room. As quickly as that, his desire for her ignited. Completely unaware of her effect on him, she picked up her purse from the couch, draped the strap across her torso, then looked up at him. He would give his right arm to know what was going on behind those brown eyes.

He walked beside her to the door, opened it and let her out.

"Would you mind texting me to let me know when you get back to your cabin?" He couldn't believe he'd asked that. Her eyes widened. Clearly she was just as surprised by his comment as he was. "You know Crystal is going to ask me when she comes home. I want to be able to tell her that you got back safely."

Andrea gave him a long look. She'd always been able to see through him and know when he was lying. He mentally crossed his fingers that she'd grown rusty over time. "Sure."

Cole watched as Andrea descended the stairs and got into her luxury car. As she drove away, he felt unexpectedly sad to see her go. He knew he hadn't seen the last of her. He just wished he knew what part he wanted her to play in his life.

Chapter Nine

Andrea stared at the starry sky as she replayed the evening in her mind. As promised, she'd texted Cole the minute that she'd gotten back to the cabin. He'd replied with one word. *Thanks*. And that was that. She didn't know what she'd been expecting, but it had been more than that. After staring at her phone screen for fifteen minutes, she'd washed off her makeup, changed into a pair of shorts and a favorite T-shirt, then gone onto the front porch and dropped into a rocking chair, which had become her favorite place to sit. She'd texted Dana an update. Her friend had been on a date night with her husband and promised to call her back later.

Dinner had turned out so much better than she had anticipated. After she and Cole overcame their initial discomfort, the conversation flowed. They'd talked and laughed together so easily that it was almost as if the past sixteen years hadn't occurred. It was as if they were the friends they'd always been. Then out of nowhere, the sexual attraction that she'd been doing her best to ignore from the time that she'd arrived in town had hit her with full force. It started out so subtly that she hadn't noticed at first. Before she knew what was happening, she was paying close attention to the way his eyes crinkled at the sides when he smiled. Or just how good he smelled. Every time he laughed, a chill raced down her spine. The sound was so jovial and electric. And so sexy.

Andrea took a sip of wine and sighed. This wasn't the way to get her growing attraction under control. She was supposed to be keeping her distance, not recalling how good his touch felt. In fact, she'd done her best to keep from touching him.

She'd been attracted to him as a teenager, so it wasn't entirely surprising that she was attracted to the man he'd become. And now that he was all grown up, there was an ease to him—the way he talked and moved—that was purely masculine and very attractive.

She waved a hand in front of her face in an effort to cool down. There was no sense getting all stirred up when there was absolutely no possibility she and Cole could re-ignite their relationship. It was over and done. She wondered if they would have even continued to see each other if she hadn't gotten pregnant. Andrea hadn't had many boyfriends before Cole, and none of the relationships had lasted more than a few months before she'd ended things.

Cole had stuck by her side throughout the pregnancy, behaving as any good boyfriend would, swearing he was there for the long haul. She'd known that he meant well, but he wasn't the one who'd been sick for nearly four months, throwing up every morning and suffering bouts of nausea the rest of the day. He wasn't the one who was no longer able to participate in sports. Nor was he the one getting stared at while walking down the hallway be-tween classes. Most importantly, he wasn't the one used as a cautionary tale of what could happen if a girl went too far. That had been all her and her alone.

Instead of feeling comforted by him, she'd been angry

and resentful. A part of her knew that she was being unreasonable, so she'd kept her feelings to herself. It wasn't his fault that she was the one bearing the visible signs of what they had done together. That was simple biology. Nor was it his fault that she'd been ashamed of herself. She'd always prided herself on her single-minded focus. It had been disappointing to see the way that she'd let her physical desires derail her plans. That lapse in judgment haunted her. Looking back, she realized that was one of the reasons she'd let her parents persuade her to give up her baby for adoption. She couldn't erase what she'd done, but she'd wanted to make amends to her parents for embarrassing them. She'd wanted to prove she could still be the daughter they expected her to be.

Andrea sighed. She rarely allowed herself to think about the past. Now it was in her face, refusing to be ignored. Well, she could try to pretend it wasn't following her around. She just needed to stay busy. Since she was on vacation she decided to do some of the touristy things that the town was famous for. Tomorrow she was going to spend the day at a dude ranch. She'd signed up as a lark, but now she was glad to have something to occupy her mind so thoughts of Cole couldn't intrude.

The next day she woke up early as usual, anxious to get the day started. The guests would spend the day working the ranch, starting with a hardy breakfast so after drinking a quick cup of coffee, she headed for the dude ranch. According to Melanie, it was a new business that until recently had been a family run cattle ranch. The newness made it all the more appealing to Andrea. It wouldn't be sleek or phony. It would be authentic. The cabin Andrea was renting was only a few miles from the dude ranch, and as she drove the short distance, her excitement grew.

She saw a large wooden sign indicating that she'd reached the Triple W Dude Ranch so she turned onto the driveway and followed the road. A painted sign directed her to a patch of grass that had been converted into a makeshift parking lot. She pulled in between a luxury SUV and a battered pickup truck and got out of her car. The air was fresh and the sky was clear, a perfect start to what she hoped would be a great day.

About a dozen people were heading for a small building, so she joined them. She was nearing the entrance when she heard her name being called. She would recognize that voice for the rest of her life. *Cole.* Shivers raced down her spine as she turned to look at him. Dressed in a plaid shirt, loose fitting faded jeans, cowboy boots and a Stetson, he looked like the definition of a cowboy. He seemed perfectly at ease in these surroundings. If she didn't know he was Chicago born and bred, she would have taken him for a third generation cowboy.

"What are you doing here?" she asked.

"I was just about to ask you the same thing." He gave her a small smile and something inside her stirred. Andrea wasn't sure how to define the feelings she'd had for Cole as a teenager, so she couldn't claim that he was reawakening her emotions. But there was something about him that made her heart beat faster.

"I'm on vacation, remember?" she answered. "And from what I understand, the Triple W Dude Ranch is a popular destination for those of us who want to get a taste of cowboy life."

"Is that right?"

"Yes."

"You want to experience cowboy life?"

"Why is that so hard for you to believe?"

"Let's just say it doesn't fit the image I have of you."

"You're probably thinking about the old me. I'm the new and improved Andrea Taylor."

He folded his arms across his chest and rocked back on his heels. "I see. Well, I look forward to getting to know this version."

She placed a hand on her hip and tilted her head. "Do you have any suggestions of places I should visit or things I should do?"

She hadn't really expected him to answer in the affirmative, so she was pleased when he nodded. "There are several things you should do. Places you should visit. I'll get a list together and text it to you."

"Really?"

"Yes." He paused. "Given how close you are with my... *with Crystal*, I think we should put the past behind us and try to become friends again. At least for the rest of your visit."

He seemed as surprised as she was by his words, so she paused a moment to give him a chance to take them back.

"Oh wow. I hadn't expected you to say that." She inhaled. "I would like that very much."

"Good. Should we shake on it?" He held out his hand. The visible calluses on his palm were proof that even though he was a business owner, he still did physical labor.

"Definitely," Andrea said, slipping her hand into his. Electricity raced through her, reaching all the way to her toes. After a moment, she reluctantly pulled her hand away. "You never answered my question. What are you doing here?"

"I have a hay delivery. Malcolm, who co-owns the ranch with his parents, is a good friend of mine. Whenever there are dude ranchers here, I bring the hay to save him a trip to town."

"Oh my."

"What does that mean?"

She shrugged. "I'm beginning to get a picture of what we're going to be doing."

"You aren't planning on backing out, are you?"

"Not a chance."

"In that case, you'd better go eat. You're going to need a filling meal."

Andrea hesitated. "Will I see you later?"

His smile made her stomach all topsy-turvy. "Count on it."

Cole watched as Andrea disappeared into the newly constructed dining hall, not looking away until the double doors closed behind her. He almost would believe that he'd thought her up as Gary liked to say. She had been on his mind from the minute he'd seen her in town. Surprisingly, he wasn't annoyed to see her today. At dinner, he'd discovered that she was just as clever and amusing as she'd been as a teenager. She'd always been a great storyteller, and he'd been entertained as she'd regaled Crystal with tales of life as a pediatrician. When he'd let himself, he'd actually enjoyed her company.

"Who was that you were talking to?" Malcolm asked, coming to stand beside Cole.

There were so many ways that he could answer that, but the one thing he couldn't say was the truth. Cole hated that. He didn't like lying to his friend. But he couldn't exactly go blabbing that Andrea was Crystal's mother. That would only open a can of worms that he preferred to keep closed.

"She's one of your ranch hands for the day."

Malcolm shook his head and grinned. "I figured that out on my own."

There was an unspoken question lingering in the air, but Cole knew Malcolm wouldn't press him. "She's in town on vacation. She met Crystal in the craft store, and they've become friends."

"I get it now. She's the latest woman that Crystal has set you up with."

"Yes."

Malcolm laughed. "Well, I have to admit that she has good taste. But Crystal must be getting desperate if she's expanded the dating pool to include outsiders."

"She is determined to say the least." Cole paused, and then changed the subject. "Speaking of women, how are things with you and Veronica? Will I be getting an invitation in the mail anytime soon?"

"Are you not so subtly asking me when I'm getting married?"

"What can I say? I want to get the latest gossip before Gary for a change."

"I can't help you there. We're taking things slowly. Just the way we both like it. But that hasn't stopped the senior crew from talking. Word is they're planning a bridal shower. Veronica and I are holding the line, though. Eventually we'll convince them that we plan to stick to our schedule."

"I wish I could convince my daughter that I like being single."

"Do you, though?"

Malcolm's question caught Cole by surprise. For a second, he wasn't sure that he'd heard him correctly. When Malcolm only stared at him, a skeptical expression on his face, Cole realized that Malcolm actually doubted him. "Of course. What makes you ask something like that? Don't tell me that now that you're part of a couple you're turning into a matchmaker. Please don't try to snatch my bachelor card."

"Look, I get it. Something happened with Crystal's mother that made you reluctant to give love another chance. Trust me, I understand how that could happen. But when you find the right woman—and I'm not saying that Crystal's latest candidate is the one—life can be good."

"I'll keep that in mind," Cole said, though he intended to forget this conversation the moment he walked away. "I'll let you go make your welcoming speech and lay out the plans for the day. I need to get to work."

Though Cole intended to dismiss Malcolm's words, they remained with him. Would he be happier if he had a woman in his life? Who knew? If that woman was Andrea? The woman who'd walked away from him once before? He didn't want to think about that now. Especially since she was only in town for the summer.

Cole drove his pickup loaded with hay over to a flatbed truck. Ordinarily he would hang out for a while, shooting the breeze with the ranch hands while they unloaded the hay, but the knowledge that Andrea was inside having breakfast had his feet walking toward the chow hall. When he stepped inside, he looked around until he spotted Andrea. She was sitting at a table with two couples, a plate of pancakes, sausage, eggs and a mug of coffee in front of her.

He filled a cup with coffee for himself from one of the urns, and then walked over to her table. Andrea's back was to him, but the way she suddenly went still, her fork suspended between her plate and her mouth, let him know that she was aware of his approach.

"Do you mind if I join you?" Cole asked, standing behind the vacant chair beside Andrea.

"Please do," a man at the head of the table said. "I'm Derrick and this is my wife, Shelly." He gestured to a woman wearing obviously new western wear before pointing to a couple at the other end of the table. "That's Cliff and his wife, Ruth."

Cole nodded to a well-dressed couple who returned the silent greeting.

"Are you a first-timer like the rest of us?" Cliff asked.

Cole shook his head. "No. I own the feedstore in town. I just dropped off a load of hay that some of you lucky guests will be putting out for the cattle."

"I hope I'm one," Shelly said. "If it's not too hard."

"It won't be," Cole assured her. "I actually was a ranch hand for over a decade. Not on this ranch, but on a nearby one."

"What's it like?" Derrick asked.

"It's hard work, but lots of fun."

"I think I'll stick with the group going white water rafting," Ruth said, checking her perfectly manicured nails.

"Not me," Andrea said. "I'm going to get the true ranching experience."

"We're here for the week, but this is more of my husband's dream vacation than mine," Ruth said. "I'll have to ease into the real ranch experience you're talking about."

The others laughed and Cole glanced at Andrea. Before today, he would have put Andrea in the same category as Ruth. She'd always been such a girlie girl. Her wardrobe had been fashionable, and she'd never had a hair out of place. Everything about her had been impeccable. Yet here she was, about to embark on a cattle drive. Oh, her jeans and top were stylish, and even without a hint of makeup, she was still gorgeous. But seeing her this way made it seem as if she was stepping out of her world and into his.

"To each his own," Cole said. "After all, a vacation is to be enjoyed."

Andrea smiled up at him, and for a moment the two of them could have been alone in the room. Her eyes were clear and filled with pleasure. Happiness practically radiated from her pores. Derrick stood and spoke, his words breaking the spell. "I'm going to get another pancake. It sounds as if we are going to need a lot of fuel to get the job done."

Cole took a swallow of his coffee and looked at Andrea. "I didn't know you knew how to ride a horse."

Andrea winced. "I wouldn't exactly say I know how. But I've been on horseback and didn't fall off so..."

"The horses are well trained so you'll be fine."

"I'll take you at your word."

Her confidence in him boosted his ego. He tried to suppress the feeling, but the pleasure remained. "I need to get going. I hope you all have a great time." He looked around the table, encompassing everyone as he spoke, but his gaze lingered on Andrea.

Andrea touched his hand. "It was good to see you again."

"You really are going to have a great time."

Cole had taken care of his business and there was no reason for him to remain, so he was surprised to find himself whipping out his phone and calling Gary.

"Hey. I think I might stick around and go for a ride. That is, if you can handle everything alone for a few hours."

"Of course I can handle the store," Gary said, his voice slightly affronted although it was tinged with amusement. "I did it for years without you."

"I know that. I just want to make sure you didn't have plans. I was just trying to be courteous." That was only partially true. Part of him hoped that Gary wouldn't be available so he would have no choice but to return to the store. He should be keeping his distance from Andrea. Instead, he was looking for opportunities to spend more time with her. He hated to admit even to himself, *especially to himself*, that he liked being around Andrea. She was the only woman who'd been able to reach inside him and touch his heart. It was scary to know that she still could.

"I know you miss being on the ranch, even though I understand your reason for moving to town and I agree with it. So enjoy yourself today. I'll stay here until you're back."

Cole didn't dare ask the older man if he was sure. Gary never said anything he didn't mean. "Thanks. I appreciate it."

After ending the call, Cole sought out Malcolm. "Do you have a horse I can ride? I thought I might stick around for a while."

Malcolm laughed. "I knew you were going to ask me that. I already had one saddled for you."

"You're psychic. Who knew you could see the future?"

"I don't need to see the future. I could see the way you were looking at that woman. I've known you for years, and you've never had that expression on your face before."

"You're imagining things."

"No, I'm not. But you're entitled to live in denial for as long as you like. I hung out there for a bit myself. But take it from me, the real world is better." Malcolm clapped Cole on the shoulder before he walked away.

Cole joined the group assembling for the cattle drive. When Andrea spotted him walking in her direction, she smiled.

"I thought you were leaving. Did you forget something?"

"No. It's been a while since I've been on a cattle drive, so I decided to join this one. Do you mind?" Cole actually held his breath while he waited for her response.

Andrea smiled. "Actually I would love it. The people I met at breakfast are nice, but they've spent the past couple of days together. They've kind of bonded. Besides, I think I'll have more fun with you."

Chapter Ten

Andrea couldn't believe Cole actually wanted to spend time with her. Nor could she believe that she'd been as open with him as she had. They were still being cautious, tiptoeing around their feelings for each other. But they'd gone past politeness toward friendliness. Who knew what feelings would develop if they spent even more time together? Could they find their way back to some of the connection they used to share?

She knew that the chances of forming a true friendship with him again might be slim. Friendship, like any other relationship, required attention to flourish. She and Cole hadn't spoken to each other for nearly sixteen years. They had parted in anger. No friendship could survive that.

But it didn't stop her from hoping.

They walked together to the corral, where the horses had been saddled. When they found the mare that had been assigned to Andrea, Cole took the reins from the ranch hand who walked away and patted the horse's neck. The animal was bigger than Andrea expected, and trepidation filled her as she stared up at it. While she stood there, another hand wearing black jeans and the tan shirt with the ranch logo on it brought over a magnificent horse for Cole. He smiled and rubbed the horse's nose. It was much larger than the one she'd been assigned, but the size didn't appear to bother him. But then, he'd worked on a ranch for over a decade. Naturally he would be comfortable.

Andrea swallowed her concern, hoping Cole hadn't noticed her hesitation. She didn't know why it was so important for her to impress him, but it was.

"Do you need help mounting?" Cole asked.

She nodded and decided to come clean. "I might have oversold my riding experience."

He grinned. "It definitely isn't your first time doing something like that."

Laughter burst from her lips. "I can't believe you remember that time."

"You say that as if there was only one occasion. I can think of a dozen off the top of my head."

"You're exaggerating."

He raised an eyebrow and stared at her. Several inches taller than she was, he was quite an imposing figure. "You've always been a bit more confident in your ability than you should have been."

"True. But I always believed that if I tried hard enough, I would be able to anything. After all, if one person can do it, then every person should be able to do it."

"You've always said that, but I don't think that's true. Anyway, let's get you on your horse. Everybody else is already sitting in the saddle. We don't want to be the holdup." He beckoned her closer. As she walked over, she noticed that his eyes focused on her hips, and she added a bit more swing to them than was absolutely necessary.

"What should I do?"

"Stand on the left side, and then put your left foot into the stirrup. Then swing your right leg over the saddle."

"Piece of cake," Andrea said. And it would have been

easy if not for the fact that Cole was standing so close to her that they were all but touching. Her hands ached to reach out and caress his chest. She took a breath, hoping to steady herself. Instead, she got a lungful of his heady scent. She felt her body temperature rise and hoped she didn't start sweating.

She followed his instructions, and in a few seconds she was astride the horse. It felt a bit odd to be this high. The mare took two steps, and a gasp escaped Andrea's lips before she could hold it back.

"I take it that it's all coming back to you now," Cole said, as he swung gracefully into the saddle. Her experience on horseback wasn't the only thing coming back to her. The insatiable desire she'd felt for him that summer was back with a vengeance. It was burning even hotter the second time around.

"Like riding a bike," she joked. The horse moved again, and she tightened her grip on the reins. "A bike with four legs instead of two wheels, and a mind of its own."

"You'll get used to it in no time. I have faith in you."

His words made her feel all tingly all over. Oh no. She had to knock it off now. She was not going to lose her head over Cole again. There was no way they could make a relationship between them work. Just looking at him astride the horse or walking around the ranch proved that. He was in his element here. She, on the other hand, was a fish out of water. Sure she liked the town and the people she'd met, but she could never slow down enough to fit in for long. There was no doubt in her mind that she would be itching for more activity than Aspen Creek could provide before the summer ended.

And even if she found she wanted to stick around permanently, Cole hadn't done anything to make her believe he wanted her to stay any longer than she'd planned. Quite the opposite. He fully expected her to go back to Chicago when her vacation was over. At that time things would go back to the way they had been for sixteen years. They wouldn't see or speak to each other. The thought was painful, and she shoved it aside. She was going to enjoy today and the time they had together.

Malcolm, the partner in the dude ranch who had introduced himself to her earlier, called everyone to attention, then made a short speech, explaining the day's itinerary. They would be riding for about forty-five minutes to an hour before they reached the cattle's current grazing site. Then the group would help to move the cattle to their new site. Some people would be stationed at the front of the herd while others rode in the back. Halfway through they would switch so everyone could have the full experience.

There were twelve guests going on the ride—not including Cole—and they were split into groups of six. When everyone was in place, they took off across the ranch. They started slowly so they could get used to their mounts, increasing speed gradually. After about fifteen minutes, they were going at a steady clip. Andrea and Cole were riding side by side and though she was focused on staying in the saddle, she felt him glancing over at her from time to time. Each time she felt his eyes on her, she turned to look at him only to find that he was looking straight ahead. His lips curved up at the corners, a dead giveaway that he knew she was onto him.

"It's so beautiful," Andrea said. "You must love living here."

"I do."

"How did you decide to move to Colorado? If that's not too nosy."

Cole chuckled, and the sound did funny things to her stomach. "It's not a state secret. I moved here after I saw the job listing to work on the ranch I told you that. Living in Chicago was expensive. It was hard to find a job with only a high school diploma, much less one that paid enough for me to support Crystal."

"But a ranch in the middle of nowhere? That's a huge change from the city life we grew up in."

He shrugged. "I have to admit there was a bit of culture shock for a while. I went from a busy city to a place where three people in the same place is considered a crowd. There wasn't a lot to do for entertainment. Today, there are clubs and restaurants where the locals hang out, apart from the touristy places, but very little of that existed when I moved here. There was no nightlife to speak of. But then, as a single father, I wasn't going out a lot anyway. I only planned to stay long enough to save some money and get my feet under me. But time flew by, and the next thing I knew I had put down roots."

He glanced at her and she nodded.

"Coming here turned out to be the best thing for Crystal and me. Like I told you before, the family that employed me practically adopted us. Even though I work in town, we're still close. And it turned out that I love ranch life. It's as if I found my true destiny here." He gave a self-conscious chuckle. "I hope that doesn't sound too… out there."

"It doesn't." He'd mentioned being a single father so easily. She didn't hear any bitterness in his voice at what she knew had to have been a hard time for him. It was as if any struggles that he'd endured as a solo parent were of no significance.

Andrea lifted her face to the sky, letting the sun warm

her skin. She knew it was the exact same sun that illuminated the sky back home, but somehow it seemed brighter. The sky seemed bluer. Of course, she knew that part of that was due to the man beside her. Everything seemed more vibrant when Cole was around. She felt more herself when he was around. He made everything...*more*... just by his very presence.

"There does seem to be a lot to love."

"And now I live in town. It may not have the variety and amount of entertainment options that Chicago has, but there are still places to hang out and have a good time."

"The stylist who cut my hair mentioned some places I might like."

"She probably gave you recommendations for tourist traps. The locals very rarely go to those. But if you play your cards right, I'll tell you some of the best places to go." He gave her a wicked grin that made her shiver. Was he flirting with her?

Andrea tilted her head and gave her sexiest smile. "What cards might those be?"

Cole's grin grew more devilish, and he looked much too sexy for her good. Before he could answer her, the sound of cattle lowing filled the air, and she realized that they had completed the first half of the drive. Oh, if only they'd had a few more minutes to finish their conversation.

Two ranch hands swung open a wide gate and began to drive the cattle out of the fenced area. Cole and Andrea were among those stationed in the back, so she had to wait until the last of the cattle were out before her horse began to walk again. The cattle were huge, and she wondered if they stampeded often and what she should do if they decided to make a break for it today.

"What's that worried look on your face?" Cole asked.

"I'm not worried," she said. And that was true. She felt safe with Cole beside her. She knew he wouldn't let any harm come to her. "It's just louder than I thought it would be."

"I suppose you didn't expect all the mooing. Add in the sound of the hooves hitting the ground, the cowboys shouting, and the barking dogs and there's a lot of noise. I guess I'm used to it."

"I know. But the funny thing is the noise hasn't changed the way the atmosphere feels. It still feels really peaceful." Andrea shook her head. "That didn't make a lick of sense. Forget I said it."

"Actually it makes plenty of sense. The thing is, peace isn't limited to silence, although that is often a part of it. Peace also has to do with being in nature. The wide-open spaces are so relaxing. The animals in their natural surroundings provide a sense of comfort. And of course, the mountains in the distance don't hurt."

"The setting is definitely a plus."

"But one thing I've learned over the past years is that peace doesn't only come from your surroundings. Peace is internal. You have to be at peace with yourself and the decisions that you've made in life. Then you can be in the middle of Soldier Field with the Bears destroying the Packers and the crowd going wild and still feel peaceful inside. You know?"

"Are you really that fully at peace with the decisions that you've made?" Andrea asked, then wanted to kick herself. Things were going so well. Why would she bring up something so personal? Especially when she didn't want to answer that question herself.

"I am. But you know, I've never been one to second-guess myself. It serves no purpose. Once I make a decision, I live with it. But I'm not stupidly stubborn either. I'm willing to change directions if necessary."

"You always were so confident like that."

He seemed surprised by her compliment. To be honest, she was surprised that she'd actually spoken the words out loud. She was glad things were no longer tense between them, but she didn't want to fall into her old pattern of sharing her innermost feelings with him.

"Thanks. And get that worried look off your face. I'm not going to turn your question back on you. Whether you're at peace with your decisions can be your own secret."

"How did you know what I was thinking?"

"Some things never change. Your feelings are written all over your face."

She didn't tell him that she was a great poker player, winning significantly more hands than she lost. He was the only one who'd always known how to read her thoughts; the one who'd known how she felt simply by looking at her. To others, she was a mystery. And that was just the way she liked it. It would be terrible if everyone could see inside her by simply glancing at her.

While they'd been talking, Cole had split his attention between her and the cattle. Now he steered his horse toward the outside of the herd, nudging a couple of cows that had begun to wander down another path. Andrea couldn't tear her eyes away. Cole was so impressive, sitting tall and straight on the back of the majestic animal as the two of them worked in tandem to get the straying cattle back with the herd. It occurred to her then that although this was a vacation excursion for her, a time away from her real life, this was a part of Cole's real life. Or rather it had been his life and his profession before he'd bought the feedstore and moved to town.

He looked so happy—as if everything was right in his world. She knew he'd moved away from the ranch and into Aspen Creek for Crystal's happiness, and she couldn't be prouder of his choice. Though the range was beautiful and serene, she had the feeling it could be awfully solitary. There probably wasn't a lot for a teenager to do. Andrea learned quite quickly that Crystal was a people person. She was happiest when she was interacting with others. People tended to gravitate to her. It was as if they saw her inner light and wanted to experience the warmth that radiated from her sweet spirit.

Andrea knew she hadn't contributed to Crystal's nurturing, but she had contributed 50 percent of her nature. That gave her a reason to be proud of just how wonderful Crystal was.

"He looks so natural on a horse," one of the other riders said, coming up beside Andrea. The admiration in the other woman's voice was unmistakable.

"I know," Andrea agreed.

"I wonder if he has a wife or girlfriend. If not, I wouldn't mind spending some quality time alone with him." The woman laughed as if she had been joking, but Andrea didn't find it funny. Her stomach churned with jealousy. She didn't want to think about Cole with another woman. But even as the thought popped into her head, she tried to push it away. It would be ridiculous to be jealous. She had no claim to Cole. They weren't involved. He was free to date or have a meaningless fling with anyone of his choosing.

It was hard, but she forced the green monster away and pasted on a smile. Then doing her best to keep her voice light, she looked at the other woman. "You can always ask him."

The other woman gave her a searching look. "I would if I thought I had a chance. His interest definitely lies somewhere else."

"What does that mean?" Andrea asked, tamping down the ridiculous hope that sprouted at the other woman's words.

"I think you know. He hasn't taken his eyes off you all day. I know, because I'm a cop. I'm a trained observer."

"And what else have you observed?" Andrea asked, even though she wasn't sure she wanted to hear the answer. She didn't want to get her hopes up.

"That you're into him even though you don't want to be. Maybe it's because you're the practical type. You know that this is vacation, and you don't want to start anything you think will be difficult to maintain. The logical part of me agrees with that decision one hundred percent."

"And the part of you that isn't logical?"

"That part of me says you should go for it. You're interested and so is he. Live in the moment and let the future take care of itself. To paraphrase an overused saying, what happens in Colorado stays in Colorado."

"I don't know about that." Living in the moment had resulted in an unexpected pregnancy that had changed the trajectory of their lives. Worse, it had ruined their friendship. Now that she and Cole had buried the hatchet, she didn't want to risk destroying their tenuous peace.

"I do. Look at him. He may be focused on getting the cows back on the path, but he is acutely attuned to every move that you make. You guys have a connection."

Andrea glanced over at Cole and her heart began to thud. He had gotten the cattle back in line with the rest of the herd and was riding over to her. Immediately her eyes were drawn to his broad shoulders and muscular chest. The strength beneath the blue plaid shirt was undeniable. Unbidden, she wondered how great it would feel to be held in his strong arms again and feel sheltered by him one more time. She shut down the thought before it could take hold. She wasn't going to start longing for the impossible. That would only lead to disappointment.

"Catch you later," the woman said, turning her horse and going back to her place on the other side of the line.

"I see you made a friend," Cole said, coming up beside her.

Andrea was tempted to tell him that the woman was more interested in him than in her, but she wasn't certain she could keep the petty jealousy out of her voice. "I think she just wanted to get a better view of you working with the cattle. That was pretty impressive, by the way."

"It's nothing I haven't done lots of times. It wasn't hard. You could have done it."

Andrea chuckled. "I don't think so. It may be old hat to you, but I'm doing all I can to stay on this horse. I'm not sure I could nudge two cows back in line."

"Whatever happened to 'if one person can do it then every person should be able to do it'?"

"I may have to rethink that."

Cole chuckled. "Who knew it only took a herd of cattle and a horse to get you to change your philosophy? That is a definite first. I'm going to mark this day on my calendar to remember this momentous occasion."

Andrea laughed, and a feeling of contentment swept over her. She would be lying to herself if she claimed that she'd been madly in love with Cole as a teenager. She hadn't been. She liked him and thought he was a good friend. And she'd definitely loved his body. But it was lust and not love that had gotten the best of her. Truthfully, she wasn't certain that she had ever been in love with anyone, including the men with whom she'd had long relationships. Now, though, she was feeling emotions that she hadn't felt before for anyone. The strength of her feelings was staggering. It was too soon to be sure, but she had a feeling that she was falling in love with Cole. For real this time.

She shoved the disturbing idea aside. The notion of falling in love—really and truly in love—didn't frighten her, per se. In fact, she longed to feel what the poets and songwriters had written about since the dawn of time. But the thought of falling in love with Cole—someone who she knew still resented her for walking out on him and their daughter? Someone who would never return her feelings? That would be a recipe for disaster.

Thankfully one of the ranch hands approached them then. They were halfway to the new grazing area, and it was time for them to move up to the front of the herd. Just when she'd gotten comfortable where she was.

"Don't be nervous," Cole said, his voice gentle.

"I'm not nervous exactly. Maybe cautious," she said. She knew he was talking about the ride and not her worries about her growing feelings for him, so she stuck to that topic. "Those animals are huge. What if they decide to stampede just as I pass by?"

"That's not going to happen. For the most part they stay in line, following the ones in front of them."

"But those other two broke off. What if they decide to do that again?"

"They aren't going to try to go through a horse, if that's what you mean. The dogs are helping them to stay in line.

And if one or two should decide to take the scenic route, I'll get them back on track."

Andrea nodded slowly.

"Who would have thought that the very bold and confident Andrea Taylor would be afraid of a few hundred head of cattle?"

Andrea flashed him a grin. She didn't like the idea of backing away from a challenge as he well knew. "Well, when you put it like that... Lead the way."

Cole grinned, then steered his horse around the outside of the cattle. She did the same, staying close to his side. The cows didn't seem to be paying the least bit of attention to them, which was a comfort. When they reached the front, Cole led his horse over to Malcolm who was driving the cattle from the front. He tipped his hat and grinned as he looked at Cole. A look passed between the two men that Andrea couldn't decipher. It was a look of two friends who knew how to communicate without words.

Once she and Cole had been that close. They'd had entire conversations with only a single word. A touch. It suddenly hit her just how much she missed that. Even so, she was glad that Cole had found other close friends. It was a relief to know he'd found a new family to stand beside him.

Several weeks after she'd given birth, Andrea had gone to Cole's parents and asked them to support Cole. At the time, Cole and Crystal had been staying in the basement of one of their friends' parents. Cole's parents had refused, saying that this was for the best—that Cole would learn his lesson soon and that they'd welcome him then. She'd had her doubts, but since she'd already disappointed them along with her own parents, she'd backed down.

Looking back with the benefit of hindsight, she wondered what would have happened if they had helped Cole. She doubted they would be estranged today. The older couple had missed so much by not knowing their wonderful grandchild. As far as she knew, they had never made an attempt to find Cole. Did they even know how good a man he was? How successful? And was there a way to bridge the divide that separated them?

She didn't think so. After all, she'd mentioned seeing and interacting with them, and yet Cole hadn't asked a single question about them. He hadn't seemed the least bit curious about their lives. But then, as he'd said, they could have reached out if they were interested in restoring the relationship.

Andrea's horse stepped to the side and she squealed.

"Are you okay?" Cole asked, concern in his dark eyes.

She nodded. That's what she got for letting her thoughts wander instead of focusing on the here and now.

"Are you enjoying yourself?" Malcolm asked.

Andrea nodded and looked at him. His eyes were practically hidden by the brim of his hat, but she could see the smile curving his lips. He was a handsome man, but her heart didn't speed up when she looked at him as it did whenever she and Cole were near each other.

"Yes. This is an adventure."

"And one you don't intend to repeat anytime in the near future," he guessed.

"I can see myself riding a horse again someday." *But not anytime soon.*

He laughed. "You're diplomatic, I'll give you that."

"I try."

Malcolm tipped his hat, and then rode over to talk to another guest, leaving Andrea and Cole alone again. There were so many things that she wanted to say to him, but at the same time she felt that she'd said too much. So she turned her attention back to the cattle drive, determined to enjoy every moment of this. When she went back to Chicago, she would bring with her this wonderful memory to pull out on those nights when she missed the life she could have had.

Chapter Eleven

"**Y**ou're awfully cheerful," Crystal said that night at dinner. After the cattle drive, Cole had made his excuses and hurried away before his emotions got the better of him. Being around Andrea brought back good memories that he hadn't wanted to revisit ever again. The walls he'd built around his heart had begun to crumble, and he'd started wishing for the impossible.

"I'm always cheerful," Cole countered.

"That's not true, but I'll allow it," Crystal said, digging into her spaghetti and meatballs. After eating a bit, she continued. "My dance recital is this Sunday."

"I know. I'm looking forward to seeing you onstage." Crystal had started taking jazz dance when she was nine. She'd joined the class because all of her friends were taking lessons. Although a couple of her friends had lost interest, most of them had stuck with it. "I'll be sitting front and center."

"I don't want you to have to sit alone."

"I won't be. Gary and the Montgomery family are coming. Heck, most of Aspen Creek will be sitting with me. You're quite popular, you know."

"I know. But I invited one more person."

"Who's that?" he asked, playing it cool. He had a

sneaking suspicion she meant Andrea. That wasn't a problem for him. Surprisingly, he minded Crystal and Andrea's friendship less and less these days.

"Andrea." She set down her fork and looked him in the eye, talking fast so he couldn't interrupt. "I know she's only here on vacation, but we want to make her feel welcome. Like she's part of the community."

Cole knew Crystal had an ulterior motive. She was bound and determined to throw him and Andrea together whenever she could. He had spent the entire afternoon trying to get the image of Andrea out of his mind. Although he managed for a second here or there, he was never truly successful. The sound of her sweet laughter echoed through his ears even as customers spoke to him about their purchases. Her beautiful face, alight with happiness, flashed in his vision even as he read vendor emails. And her scent? It was so soft and sweet as it had been sixteen years ago. The perfume might be different, but her personal scent remained the same. The things that had made him fall in love with her years ago were having the same effect now.

Despite knowing that Andrea wasn't good for his mental state, not to mention his heart, he couldn't deny his daughter this opportunity. More than that, he wouldn't stand in the way of Andrea getting to see their daughter perform with her dance troupe. Since he'd agreed to let Andrea spend time with Crystal, it would be cruel to exclude her from a major event.

Crystal was only a year and a half younger than Andrea had been when she became pregnant. Cole was coming to understand just how afraid she must have been back then. Now as he watched Crystal plan her future, he had a clearer understanding of how horrified Andrea must have been when she realized the dreams that she had worked so hard to achieve were in jeopardy of not coming true.

Andrea had always wanted to be a pediatrician. She'd been focused on that goal and had done everything to make herself the best candidate for the top colleges and universities. Every club she'd joined, every job she'd volunteered for had been part of her master plan. When faced with the reality of it all being for nothing, it was no wonder that she'd chosen the path that seemed safer. Though he had never regretted his decision to raise his little girl, he was coming to believe that the decision that had been right for him had been right for *him*. That didn't make it the right decision for Andrea. He supposed understanding was the first step toward acceptance.

As a parent, he wanted the best for his child. Though he knew his parents had felt the same way on some level, he wasn't ready or able to forgive them. Try as he might, he couldn't understand the way they'd treated him and Crystal. He would never force his daughter to do something that would break her soul as they'd tried to do to him.

"I suppose that would be all right."

"Great."

"But, I don't want you to get your hopes up. A romance won't be brewing between the two of us. I hope that puts an end to your matchmaking, once and for all, because there's no spark there. No chemistry." He hoped his words sounded more believable to her than they did to him.

Crystal stared at him. Then she picked up her fork and started to eat again. In that moment she looked so much like Andrea that his heart nearly stopped.

"I don't know if you're lying to me or just plain deluded because there were enough sparks between you and Andrea at dinner to start a forest fire."

"You're just imagining things." Had his feelings been that obvious to Crystal? Had Andrea noticed?

"Sure, Dad."

He took a bite of garlic bread. When that didn't calm his suddenly jumpy nerves, he took a long swallow of water. "Like I said, don't be upset if she can't come. She might have something else to do." He hoped.

"I'm not worried about that."

"Why not?"

Crystal grinned. "Because she likes you, too."

Cole rolled his eyes. When he realized what he'd done, he shook his head. He couldn't believe he was acting like a teenager. But then, he was starting to feel like a lovestruck teenager again, looking for opportunities to be around Andrea. When they were together, he felt giddy and goofy. Look at the way he'd shown off today when they were herding cattle.

He might feel like a kid, but he was an adult. Even though he couldn't control his emotions, he could control his behavior. So whenever thoughts of Andrea popped into his mind, he was going to shove them away and think about something else. *Anything else.*

He reminded himself of that as he walked into the auditorium Sunday afternoon. As he greeted his friends and their wives or girlfriends, he suddenly felt lonely. For the first time in forever, he wished he was half of a couple. It was something he'd never thought he'd feel.

Until Andrea popped up in town.

He reminded himself of his vow to push all thoughts of her out of his mind. Somehow, that was easier said than done. He looked at his ticket, and then hurried to his assigned seat. The show was starting in about fifteen minutes, and people were beginning to filter in.

When he reached his row, the seat next to him was already occupied. Andrea. He should have known Crystal would have given them adjoining seats. She never left anything to chance.

Andrea smiled at him. His stomach stirred, and he accepted the fact that his body would always react to hers. It made no sense to try to fight it. "Hi. I hope you don't mind that I came," she said. "When Crystal invited me, I just couldn't say no."

Cole couldn't miss the hopeful expression on Andrea's face. There was so much yearning there that even the most hardened person would find it impossible to reject her at this time. "I don't mind. Besides, she already told me that she invited you."

"Ah. So you're forewarned this time." Her eyes sparkled in amusement.

"I wouldn't say warned. Given her belief that we're soulmates, I would be surprised if she didn't invite you."

"She thinks we're soulmates?" Andrea's voice squeaked. Cole didn't know if she was shocked or appalled.

"You have to understand that Crystal absolutely loves romance. She's seen every rom-com known to woman. Some of them ten times or more. She calls them her 'break in case of emergency' movies."

"So you're telling me she lives on a steady diet of meet-cutes and happy endings."

He heaved a heavy sigh. "That about sums it up."

"So what do you want me to do to change her mind about us?"

"Did you tell her that there was no spark between us?"

She shook her head slowly. "I didn't get a chance yet. But I will, if that's what you want."

"It might not make a difference."

"Why not?"

"I already told her I didn't feel a thing for you."

"And?"

"She didn't believe me." Probably because he'd been lying, but he wasn't going to tell that to Andrea. Or anyone.

Andrea only nodded. When she only sat there lost in thought, Cole wondered if he was supposed to say something else. He didn't think telling her that Crystal was incredibly astute was the way to go.

"So…we could…" Andrea's voice died off. Then she looked at him, her eyes wide. For a moment he was so distracted by the beauty of her face that he lost track of the conversation. Then she shrugged, and his eyes were drawn to her slender shoulders. "I got nothing."

He laughed and after a moment, she joined in. Her laughter was a merry sound that reached inside and touched his heart. He shook his head. "Who would have thought one teenaged girl could get the better of two adults?"

"You got me. I don't think I was this…single-minded."

"You're kidding, right? Andrea, you are the most focused person I've ever met. That was one of the things I admired most about you. One of the things I still admire about you."

The words were out of his mouth before he knew it. Then he realized that he didn't want to call them back. He wanted her to know how he truly felt.

"But I thought…" She swallowed. "I thought you resented me for sticking to my plan to become a doctor instead of marrying you and raising Crystal with you."

"I did before you came here. But now, with hindsight,

I understand that we each did what was right for us. And for Crystal."

Andrea blinked rapidly, and he knew she was moved by his words. His face burned with shame when he recalled the angry words he'd said to her when he'd first seen her again. But they'd put the past behind them, and they were well on their way to becoming real friends again.

"Would it be okay if I took a few pictures of Crystal?" Andrea asked.

He decided to take the change of subject in stride. "Sure. I always take a lot. And I know Crystal won't mind. She's a bit of a ham. She absolutely loves seeing pictures of her performance."

Andrea laughed. "A bit of vanity? Oh, thank goodness. From everything I've seen or heard, I was beginning to think she was too perfect to be real."

"Trust me, she's far from perfect. But you didn't hear that from me." He grinned and nudged her shoulder. "She loves the spotlight. Just like you did."

"I didn't love the spotlight as much as you think. But the roles did look good on my college applications."

"Crystal enjoys performing although I think she is beginning to think of her college applications now, too. Fortunately, she only does things she likes."

"I liked some of my activities."

"That's good. I would hate to think that you only did them for the prestige or how it would look. And speaking of looks. Crystal's starting to look like you."

"Do you think anyone has noticed?"

"No. People see what they expect to see. They know she's my daughter, so they pay more attention to our shared resemblances and dismiss everything else."

"That's a relief. I wouldn't want people to speculate."

"Neither would I."

The lights flickered, dimmed and eventually went out, signaling the beginning of the show. The last stragglers hustled to their seats, and the announcer welcomed everyone to the Mile High Dance Recital. Andrea leaned close, and her familiar scent wrapped around him. His attraction was growing stronger with each passing day. There was no use in trying to fight it. There were some things that just didn't change, and his desire for Andrea appeared to be one of them.

Given the secret they were keeping from Crystal, and the fact that Andrea would be leaving at the end of summer, that was a problem.

Andrea watched as her daughter moved gracefully across the stage, dancing a solo. Though she had intended to take photos and held her phone in her hands, she was too mesmerized by the performance to do anything other than stare in awe. Crystal was positively radiant. She lit up the stage, holding the audience spellbound with every jump and turn. Andrea knew she was completely biased, but she didn't care. It was a simple fact—her daughter was magnificent. Andrea's heart was so full that she didn't think she could hold her feelings inside much longer.

She felt something soft press into her hand and looked down. Cole had placed a tissue between her fingers. She gave him a perplexed look.

"You're crying."

"I am?" Andrea touched her cheek. It was wet. *She was crying.*

Taking the tissue, Andrea flashed him a grateful smile, then dabbed at the moisture on her cheeks. Try as she might, she couldn't stop the tears from falling from her eyes. Andrea wiped her face, and then swiped the tissue beneath her nose. She felt a strong arm wrap around her shoulders and looked into Cole's face. It was dim in the auditorium, but she could make out the concern in his eyes. Unable to resist, Andrea leaned closer to him. She inhaled and got a lungful of his masculine scent. His musky cologne wasn't familiar but his own personal scent underlying it was. It reminded her of home and happier times.

The weight of his arm was as comforting as the heat that warmed her body. Watching her daughter perform joyously on stage with Cole beside her was the best moment of Andrea's life, and she wished it could last forever. She focused on every small detail, from the blue and silver sparkles on Crystal's costume that caught the light with each pirouette, to the blue ribbon that held her ponytail in place. She would remember the bright smile on her daughter's face for the rest of her life.

And Cole. The tender way he held her would be indelibly etched on her soul. The gentle way he absently caressed her shoulder, silently letting her know that she wasn't alone, moved her beyond words.

Andrea relaxed against him, snuggling into his powerful chest. She might regret her behavior later, but right now she allowed herself to lean on him. She hadn't expected to feel so many emotions, and she couldn't contain them on her own.

"Are you okay?" Cole whispered, his voice soft. His lips brushed against her ear and a shiver raced down her spine.

"This is just so much." The whispered words didn't come anywhere near to explaining what she felt. But when Cole nodded, she knew the right words weren't necessary. He was the one person in the world who'd always understood her.

"I know. Just enjoy it."

She managed a watery smile. "I am."

They turned their attention back to the performance. It was a complete paradox, but time flew and slowed down at the same time. All the while, Andrea was completely focused on the performance even as she was totally aware of Cole's nearness. She knew each time he inhaled or exhaled. She was so attuned to him that she knew every time he blinked.

By the time the dancers performed the grand finale, Andrea was totally drained. And she'd never been fuller. When the entire cast and crew took a bow, the audience rose and gave them a standing ovation. Andrea wasn't sure her legs would hold her, but somehow she managed to stand. Cole's arm dropped from her shoulders to her waist to support her, and she basked in the peaceful feeling. For the time being, all was right in her world.

The curtain came down, and then the houselights came up. Andrea looked into Cole's eyes, unsure what she should do next. He took a step away from her, breaking the contact. Though she understood why he wanted to keep physical distance between them—it would be hard to convince Crystal there was absolutely no attraction between them with his arm around Andrea's waist—she missed his touch.

"We should probably sit down while we wait. It'll take Crystal a while to get back into her street clothes. And of course all of the kids will want to take pictures together and autograph each other's programs."

Andrea smiled and joy warmed her heart. She might not know what the rest of the evening would hold, but at least Cole wasn't trying to rush her out the door. She sat back down and turned to Cole. "I remember those days. Now that was part of the performance that I actually did enjoy. Just hanging around the rest of the cast and crew was so much fun."

"I remember seeing the backstage pictures from your performances in the yearbook."

"Ah, the yearbook. All of those memories. And signatures." At least for the first three years. After she'd become pregnant so many things changed. There were no more extracurricular activities for her. For her senior year, school became limited to her classes. "Do you still have any of yours?"

He nodded. "Surprisingly yes. All four. I can't believe that of all the things that I piled into my bags when I left, I included those. I'm not at all sure why. I couldn't tell you the last time I looked at them. They're somewhere in my closet gathering dust."

"That's good to hear."

"Why?"

"Because I can't bear the idea of you turning your back entirely on your past. I like knowing that you have something to remind you that everything wasn't bad back then. Tangible proof that there was a lot of good in your life."

The corners of his mouth turned down, a clear sign that he was giving serious thought to her words. "I suppose you might be right. It's not as if I forgot. I know there was good in my life back then. I just think that at some point the pain of the bad outweighed the memory of the good. But you don't have to worry about Crystal. I haven't let the memories of the past bleed into the present."

"I know. There is no way that she could be as sweet and open as she is if you were bitter."

Cole seemed pleased by her comment. In that moment, it felt as if they had truly put the past behind them. That was going to make the rest of her visit that much more pleasant. She didn't think they were going to play happy family, but the tension could finally release.

"Speaking of Crystal." Cole pointed down the aisle. Crystal was running over to them, her fabric bag dangling over her back.

"I was hoping you were still here," Crystal said, smiling at Andrea.

"I couldn't leave without telling you how great your performance was."

"I was nervous at first, but once I relaxed I had a lot of fun."

"I took a lot of pictures of you," Cole said. Then he nudged Andrea's shoulder playfully. "Andrea's phone never left her lap."

"She was in the moment," Crystal said, looking between Cole and Andrea. "And you can text her copies. That is if you want them."

"Of course I want them." Andrea held out her program. "And I would love your autograph, too. That is, if you have time for humble fans like me."

Crystal laughed and tossed her head into the air playfully. "I suppose. But be sure to hold on to this. My autograph is going to be valuable in the future."

Cole's and Andrea's gaze met and she saw the expression on his face. She'd once made that same comment when she was in high school. Andrea had also tossed her head in the same manner. Looking at Crystal wasn't exactly like staring into the past. She had too many of Cole's mannerisms to be Andrea's perfect replica, but it was close. And it made Andrea's heart ache for all that she had missed. She wished that she had been able to live the life she'd had as well as live the life that she'd missed. Of course that was impossible. She'd had to choose, and she had.

"I'll cherish this forever," Andrea said, taking the program after Crystal scrawled her signature beneath her photograph. She injected a bit of humor into her tone to mask the fact that she meant every word. This simple program was more precious to her than everything she owned. This was now her greatest treasure, tangible proof that she had shared this moment with her beloved child.

Crystal smiled and turned her attention to Cole. She took his program, and then signed her name for him, too.

"I'll add this to my collection of valuables."

"I think it is beginning to border on clutter at this point," Crystal said with a laugh.

"Nonsense. When you make it big, those programs and art projects will fund my retirement."

"I doubt anyone will be interested in my silver-and-gold spray-painted macaroni art other than you."

"You never know. Not that I will ever sell them. They hold too much sentimental value."

The banter between father and daughter continued, and Andrea felt a crack grow in her heart. With each laugh and shared inside joke, the crack widened until it was a gaping chasm. By sheer will, she tried to force it closed. This was what she'd wanted for her child. Crystal had grown up in a loving home. The wealth that Andrea's and Cole's parents had felt was so essential hadn't been necessary. Crystal hadn't missed out on a single thing.

"You should see the boxes Dad has of my schoolwork," Crystal said, pulling Andrea back into the conversation.

"I think he kept every test that I ever took from the time I was in kindergarten."

"Only the ones where you got a hundred."

"Like I said, *every* test I ever took."

"I didn't miss that humble brag," Cole said. "Although I'm not sure there was anything humble about it."

"Anyhow," Crystal said, laughter dancing in her eyes. She looked so much like Cole that Andrea was pulled into a happy past that had been filled with laughter and fun. "I think it's time to let some of that stuff go."

"Never. You'll understand when you become a parent," Cole said.

"That's your favorite line." Crystal turned to Andrea. "No matter what we're talking about, Dad always pulls out the parent card. Especially when he wants me to do what he wants. It's his ace in the hole as Gary likes to say. Don't ever disagree with my Dad, Andrea. You can't win. According to him, being a parent makes you the automatic winner of every argument. Since you don't have children, you won't stand a chance."

The hole that had begun to close in Andrea's heart immediately burst wide-open at Crystal's innocent remark. Crystal had no idea that Andrea was her mother; the one who'd sheltered her inside her body for forty weeks and endured an intense labor while giving birth to her. She was simply making a joke to someone she believed was childless. And wasn't that the case? She might have given birth to Crystal, but she'd long since given up the right to claim her as a daughter.

Crystal might not have known the impact of her words, but Cole's gasp let Andrea know that he was aware of her pain. He seemed to be searching for words when one of the other dancers approached them. "We're going out for pizza now. Are you still coming?"

Crystal gave Cole a hopeful look. "It's the cast party. Everyone is going."

He nodded, pulled out his wallet and handed over several bills. "Have fun."

Crystal kissed his cheek. "Thanks. I'll text you when I'm ready for you to pick me up. See you later, Andrea. Thanks for coming."

Andrea could only nod, still stinging from Crystal's words.

"I'm sorry," Cole said when they were alone.

Now that Crystal was no longer around, Andrea let down her protective shield. She didn't need to pretend in front of Cole. He knew that her heart was broken.

"I need to get out of here." She was at her emotional end. Grabbing her purse, she turned to leave.

"Andrea, wait. Let's talk about this. Crystal didn't mean to hurt you." He reached out to touch her shoulder, and she flinched. She was already on edge. If he touched her, she would break down completely. And if she started to cry, she wasn't sure she would be able to stop.

Cole's hand froze, and then dropped to his side. Then he took a large step back, allowing her to pass. She avoided his eyes, afraid of what she would see there. Summoning her strength, she strode from the auditorium, picking up speed as she went. She was practically running by the time she reached her car.

How had a day that started so happily turned into such a painful disaster?

Chapter Twelve

"How are things going?"

Andrea heaved out a sigh of relief as her best friend's voice came over the phone. She hadn't quite managed to keep the tears at bay while she drove back to the rental cabin. Lacking the strength to go inside, she'd barely managed to drop into the rocking chair before her legs gave out. Truthfully, she didn't know what she was crying over. Crystal hadn't said anything that Andrea hadn't said herself numerous times over the past sixteen years. If anyone asked, she'd always said that she didn't have children. For all intents and purposes, that was true. Somehow, the statement hit differently when it was coming from the little girl that she'd given birth to.

"It's been better," Andrea said. She and Dana had gone to high school together although they hadn't been friends at the time. When Andrea and her friends formed their practice, they hired Dana as a nurse. In no time, the two had become close friends. Since Dana had known her back when, Andrea hadn't needed to edit her life story. Dana had been sympathetic, and she'd made it clear that she would never tell anyone about the child Andrea had given up.

"What happened? Do I need to come out there? I can be on the first plane."

"No. Thanks. I don't think Cole would appreciate having a class reunion."

Dana laughed. "I don't know. He always liked me."

"True. But then he liked everyone." Cole had been a friend to everyone. He'd been the rare kid who'd fit in every crowd, from the jocks to the geeks and everyone in between.

"I thought you guys were becoming friends again. You said Cole was okay with you coming to the dance recital today."

"He was. And the performance was so good. Crystal is very talented. I was so proud of her."

"So what went wrong?"

Andrea hesitated. It was still so painful to talk about. But holding it in wouldn't help.

"After the show, Crystal and Cole were joking around. It is always so great to see the two of them together. They have the best relationship." Andrea knew she was beating around the bush, so she took a deep breath and got to the point. "Crystal said that I should never argue with Cole because he thinks that being a parent means he automatically wins every argument. Then she said that since I don't have kids, I'd lose."

"Oh, Andrea. You have to know that she didn't mean anything bad by it."

"I know. And I know that I'm being ridiculous, but it still hurt. Maybe getting involved with her was a mistake. Perhaps I should have left well enough alone. I know she's happy and has a great life." She sighed. "It might be a good idea for me to back off. The whole reason I took this trip was to make sure that she's happy. Now that I know she is, maybe I should just come home."

"What? You can't be seriously thinking about running away simply because your feelings are hurt."

Andrea swiped at a stray tear that leaked from her eye. "It's more than that. I don't belong here. Cole and Crystal have made such good lives for themselves. She is practically an adult. She doesn't need a mother now."

"I don't believe that and neither do you. I may be an adult and a mother, but that doesn't stop me from needing my own mother."

"But you and your mother have spent a lifetime building a strong relationship together. Crystal and I have only known each other for a few weeks. And she doesn't think of me as her mother." Just saying the words hurt. But this situation was the inevitable result of the choice she'd made years ago.

"Maybe not. But she sees you as a friend. And every teenaged girl could use a woman's influence."

"Crystal has plenty of them. Every woman in this town has stepped up to fill the gap that I left in her life. She has plenty of aunties and grandmas. If there is a more loved person in this world, I have yet to meet them."

"So what are you saying? That there isn't place for you?"

Was that what she was saying? Was that why her feelings were so hurt? She'd thought she was coming here to see if her daughter needed her only to find that not only had she survived without her mom around, she had also thrived. Andrea hadn't been necessary. "Maybe. I don't know."

"I do. You and Crystal are building a relationship. Is it the one you would have had if you'd been a part of her life for the past sixteen years? Of course not. But you can't change that. The past is gone and no amount of regret will bring it back. But you can still build something beautiful. Don't forget, Crystal cares about you enough to invite you to watch her perform. Are you really thinking about backing away because she inadvertently said something that hurt you?"

Andrea looked at the mountains in the distance, somehow comforted by their solid presence. "I hadn't thought about it that way."

"Of course not. Because you're all in your feelings. You're too emotional to think straight."

Andrea sighed. She was being ridiculous. "You're right. I guess I was being a bit sensitive."

"You're entitled. How was Cole tonight?"

Very charming and way too sexy. "He's still the same. It was almost like the old days when we were friends. I was worried that he would want to keep me from coming today, but he's too good a man to hold a grudge for long."

"It sounds as if you admire that about him."

"I do."

"Could something be developing between the two of you? You know, a second chance romance?" Dana's voice was alive with hope.

"No."

"Don't answer without thinking."

"I didn't. I've given this plenty of thought. Is Cole handsome? Sexy? A good man? Yes. He's all those things and more. But we have so much history. A lot of it is good, but a lot of it is really bad. And a real relationship with him? I don't even know what that would look like. It wasn't what we had before. I was just infatuated with him back then and let things get out of hand."

"That doesn't mean you can't fall in love with him now. But if you don't think you can love him, I think you're right not to start something."

Andrea leaned back in the rocking chair and closed her eyes. "I'm just so confused. I am starting to wonder if things could work between us. But I'm not sure if my feelings are really because of him or because I'm thinking of how good it would be to be part of the family that he and Crystal have created. If I don't trust my feelings, I certainly can't expect him to."

"Let's pretend that the two of you didn't have a past."

"I can't play make-believe. That is the best way to end up hurt. We have a past and it isn't going anywhere."

"So let's start where you are. You and Cole have been getting along."

"Lately, sure. We've had a few decent conversations. We agreed to be friends for the summer. But I don't think he'll shed any tears when I drive out of town."

"You don't know how you feel, so you shouldn't assume you know what he's feeling."

"Fair enough."

"Now, back to what I was saying. Is it possible that you might fall in love with Cole?"

"I hope not," Andrea said emphatically.

"Why?"

"For so many reasons. First, I don't think he could ever fall in love with me. And even if he could, getting together would mean having to deal with the fact that we're lying to Crystal. That's huge. If I was going to be a permanent part of her and Cole's lives, we'd have to tell her the truth. Can you see that working out? Because I can't. At least not for me. She has a great relationship with Cole, so she could forgive him. But she and I don't have an established past. She might not be able to get over the deception. Not to mention the whole issue of me walking away when she was a baby."

"I hear you making a lot of excuses, but I don't hear you denying that you could fall in love with Cole."

Andrea sighed. "I'm scared."

"Don't let fear hold you back."

"I can't help it. The truth is, I don't know if I can fall in love with anyone. I've been involved with men yet something keeps me from giving my heart."

"Before Rodney and I got married, I dated a few nice guys, too. But I didn't feel for them what I feel for Rodney because we weren't meant to be together. Maybe it's the same with you."

"Maybe. But there's no guarantee that Cole is the one that I'm supposed to be with. Remember, I told you that I wasn't in love with him in high school."

"That's not surprising. You still had a lot of growing up to do at that point. You're not the same person you were then. That's why high school romance often isn't the real thing."

"Maybe not, but the people actually believed that they were in love. I knew I didn't love Cole back then. He was such a great guy that I just thought that I *should* be in love with him."

"When are you going to stop beating yourself up about that? Maybe the time was wrong. But if you don't think you can ever love him, you're right not to lead him on."

Though she knew Dana couldn't see her, Andrea nodded. But a quiet voice inside her whispered the truth that she was too afraid to face. A part of her knew that she absolutely could love him. But if she did fall in love with him, her heart would be shattered when she had to leave.

* * *

Cole stared at his phone. He'd been home for hours and was now waiting for Crystal to text him to pick her up from the pizza place. But he wasn't staring at his phone because he wanted to receive a text. He was debating whether or not to reach out to Andrea. Everything inside him was telling him to leave her alone, but he couldn't stop thinking about the way she'd looked before she'd run from the auditorium. The pain in her eyes had been palpable, and it had broken his heart. In that moment he realized that he had fully put the past behind them. He cared about Andrea, and her happiness mattered to him.

"Forget it," he said. Debating with himself was giving him a headache. He was normally decisive. His strong feelings for Andrea were making him question his every move when it came to her. But going back and forth was ridiculous when he knew he was eventually going to call her. If it was a mistake, then he would live with the consequences.

He hit the icon by Andrea's number, dropped into his chair and listened as the phone rang. It wasn't very late, so he guessed she was still awake. Besides, she'd never been able to sleep when she'd been upset. Maybe if they talked, he could help her feel better. Then she would be able to get some rest.

"Cole?"

"Yes."

"Is everything all right?"

"I was calling to ask you the same thing."

"Really? Why?" The genuine surprise in her voice stung. Was it really so inconceivable to her that he truly cared about her?

"Why? Because you were upset earlier. Let's not pretend that you weren't."

"I was. But I realize now that I shouldn't have been. I totally overreacted."

Cole knew Andrea well enough to notice how carefully she was speaking. She was trying to hide her feelings from him. "You had every right to be hurt."

"Well, I'm over it now."

"So you weren't over there brooding? You weren't thinking that you'd made a mistake coming here to meet your daughter?"

Andrea's sigh came over the phone. "What would make you say something like that?"

"People don't change. Not really. You've always needed things in your world to be straight before you can go to bed."

"Maybe you don't know me as well as you think you do. For all you know, I could already be in bed."

The image of Andrea dressed in a silky nightgown that caressed her slender curves flashed in his mind, temporarily distracting him from the conversation. He knew he shouldn't even think of her in that way, but some things were inevitable.

"As long as you're fine," he said. "I'll let you get back to what you were doing."

He paused, but when Andrea didn't say anything, he accepted defeat. He said good-night and ended the call. He didn't know what he'd been hoping would happen, but he knew that wasn't it. Maybe it was time to accept that he really didn't know her as well as he thought he did. Though they had agreed to bury the hatchet and try to be friends while she was in town, that didn't mean they would ever be close friends again. And it certainly didn't mean that there was a possibility of them having any type of romantic relationship. Every once in a while when he was alone, Cole fantasized about starting over with Andrea. When she'd cuddled close to him tonight, he'd begun to think his fantasy might become reality. Maybe it was time for him to accept the fact that their chance at being a couple had come and gone years ago.

He reminded himself of that fact all night and the next day when he was back in the store working.

"Well, look who's back in the ranching game," he heard Gary say and looked up. "It's Sheriff Morrow."

The sheriff laughed. "I never got out of the ranching game."

"Good to see you, Hank," Cole said, coming from around the counter. Hank and Cole had become good friends over the years. Though Hank was the sheriff, he still lived on the horse ranch that had been in his family for generations.

"So how are things going with the superstar?" Gary asked.

Hank sighed. "I forgot that nothing happens in this town that you don't know about. Perhaps I should deputize you. It would make my investigations go a lot more smoothly. Heck, I would be ahead of the criminals."

Cole laughed. "Wait a minute. I thought we were friends. Yet here you are trying to steal my best employee."

"Sorry," Hank said, grinning. "I lost my head there for a minute."

"I notice you didn't answer Gary's question about Shayna. Is she doing well? How is she adjusting to small-town life?" Cole asked.

"Oh, that's right. Sometimes I forget you didn't grow

up here. Shayna is actually from Aspen Creek. She grew up on a small ranch near mine. She started singing while we were in high school. Once she became a superstar, she and her family moved to California."

"So, why is she here?" Gary asked, undeterred. He was determined to get the information he wanted.

"Just a visit," Hank said. He picked up a catalog and began paging through it.

"I suppose that's enough to satisfy the rest of the gang," Gary said with a laugh. "You can't get in the card games if you aren't able to ante up."

"Glad I was able to help you lose your money," Hank said, then laughed.

"Who said anything about losing?" Gary said, before walking out the door.

Cole shook his head, and then glanced over at Hank. "What can I get for you today?"

"Nothing. I'm just making the rounds, checking on businesses today. How are things going with you?"

Cole shrugged. The only major thing going on in his life was the situation with Andrea—but that wasn't something he was willing to talk about. Not when no one but Gary knew the truth. "First, tell me about you and Shayna. Did you know her in high school?"

Hank nodded. "We were friends of a sort. Living together is a different kind of thing altogether."

"Crystal is all into celebrity gossip, so I'm surprised that she didn't know that Shayna was in town."

"We were trying to keep her presence under wraps. Obviously since Gary knows we're not doing a good job of that."

"Crystal did say that she read that Shayna has a stalker.

I don't give much credence to the tabloids, but do I need to be on the lookout for strangers?"

"Aspen Creek is a vacation destination. It's filled with strangers twelve months out of the year. It's nigh impossible to determine who is here for a good time and who is up to no good."

"True. But I want to help if I can."

"I've got it covered." Hank tossed the catalog onto the counter, then stared out the window for a moment before turning to look back at Cole. "Now, back to you. How are you? Really?"

Cole blew out a breath. "Do you ever wonder what life would have been like if you'd made a different decision in the past?"

"More times than I can count. But then I remember that there is no going back. The only way to go is forward."

"I know. But I can't seem to do that. I'm stuck inside my head."

"Does this have anything to do with the woman you were sitting with at the dance recital?"

"You weren't there. How do you even know about that?"

"Gary isn't the only one with a network of spies," Hank said with a smirk. "One of the deputies' daughters was part of the crew. She worked the lighting. He went to the performance. I worked his shift for him and got a full report afterward. So, is this introspection about her?"

"Yes." He paused. Was he really going to tell Hank about Andrea? He was sharp and it would be easy for him to put the pieces together. "You aren't the only one with a high school friend in town. Crystal doesn't know it, but Andrea and I knew each other in high school."

"And now she's in town. What are the odds of that?"

Hank was silent for a moment, and Cole wondered if he had already put two and two together. "You moved here when Crystal was a baby. The whole town always wondered about her mother."

"I'm trusting you here."

"I know that. I hope our years of friendship would be enough for you to know that nothing you tell me will go any further."

Cole ran a hand over his jaw. "I don't know what to do."

"Are old feelings coming back up?"

"On my part, yes. It's confusing, though. I've carried a lot of resentment toward her for so long that even being friends again was unthinkable."

"But now that you've been around her?"

"I'm not sure how I feel. Not that it matters. We can't go back. Our time has passed."

"That's not necessarily true. You just have to decide what you want. And then hope she wants the same thing."

"You know what I want? I want my life to go back the way it was before Andrea came waltzing into my life again. I hate deceiving Crystal, but I can't tell her the truth. How could I tell her that the mother who walked away from her when she was born is her new friend? Oh, and now she wants to be a part of her life, but only for the summer. When her vacation is over, she plans on going back home and leaving Crystal behind. Again. Having a friend leave will be hard enough on her. Having her mother leave? Again? I can't hurt my little girl that way."

"Andrea could change her mind. It's been known to happen."

"She won't. Even if she did, how would I explain not letting Crystal know from the beginning that Andrea was her mother?"

"That does put you in a tough place."

"The toughest. And the longer I wait, the worse it becomes. But I want to respect Andrea's wishes. Our parents ignored what we wanted. They pushed Andrea until she eventually gave in and signed away her parental rights. They were so sure that they knew what was right that they refused to listen to us at all. I don't want to do the same thing to her. I can't."

"And Crystal?"

"What she doesn't know can't hurt her. Or us."

"Well, this is a twisted knot of a problem. Here's hoping it works out for you," Hank said before walking out the door.

"You and me both," Cole muttered to himself. "You and me both."

Chapter Thirteen

"My birthday is tomorrow," Crystal said. She and Andrea had finished their sweaters and were adding them to the donation box.

"I heard something about that once or twice," Andrea said with a grin, striving to keep her voice normal. Every year, the day was one of great pain as well as joy for her. This year she hoped the joy outweighed the pain.

"You know what that means." Crystal had been quite vocal about the fact that she couldn't wait to get her driver's license.

"I need to stay off the sidewalks?" Andrea joked.

Crystal groaned. "Your dad jokes are just as bad as my dad's. Besides, I've had my permit for a year and Dad has ridden with me a lot, and I haven't run over a single mailbox. But anyway, that wasn't what I was going to say."

"Okay. So then what's on your mind?"

"I was hoping that you would join me and Dad for dinner."

Andrea's heart nearly jumped out of her chest. Over the years she'd fantasized about being a family with Cole and their daughter. She'd often imagined the three of them celebrating Crystal's birthday together. Now she was getting that opportunity.

"Are you sure? I don't want to intrude on a family tradition." Though she longed to be there, a part of her knew that she had no right.

"My dad and I always spend our birthdays together. But when it's your birthday, you get to choose what you want to do and who you want to include."

"And do you always include other people?"

"Not usually at dinner. But there is nothing that says I can't. I generally have a party with my friends."

"If you're sure it's okay with your father, I would love to have dinner and help you celebrate your birthday."

"Good. Then I'll see you tomorrow at seven."

Andrea waved goodbye and headed for the shops. For sixteen years she'd haunted the stores, looking for the perfect gift for her child. She hadn't bought anything, other than the card she tucked away each year, but she'd scoured the shelves, imagining what the perfect present would be. Would her two-year-old daughter like the baby doll in the pink dress or would she prefer the one in overalls? Was her eight-year-old into Barbies or did she prefer puzzles? Was she artistic? Would she like the paint set? Was she a reader? The unanswered questions had plagued Andrea for years. These past weeks she'd been able to fill in some of the blanks. Andrea would never know the little girl that Crystal had been, but she had the opportunity to get to know the young woman that her daughter had become. Over the past few weeks, the holes in her heart had begun to fill in and she was finally beginning to feel whole.

This year she would finally be able to give her child a birthday gift. She had gotten to know Crystal and knew her interests. But the most obvious idea—giving her daughter crafting supplies—didn't appeal to her. As she walked down the streets of Aspen Creek, she bypassed the boutiques and the boho clothing store and headed for the jewelry store.

When she'd been growing up, she'd always received jewelry from her parents for her birthday. At first it was a pair of gold hoop earrings. Later it was a set of diamond studs. On her sixteenth birthday, as was tradition, Andrea's parents gave her a diamond bracelet, similar to one her mother had been given when she'd turned sixteen. Crystal wouldn't know the significance of the gift, but Andrea would.

Andrea went inside the store and glanced around. Though all the boutiques in Aspen Creek were upscale, this jewelry store was on another level. It would fit right in on Chicago's Magnificent Mile. She took a step and sank into the plush blue carpet that coordinated well with the rich silver window treatments and blue-and-silver-patterned wallpaper.

"Welcome to Saucier and Cornelius Fine Jewels. I'm Francois. How may I be of service?" The man's voice was low and cultured. He was dressed in an immaculate gray suit that had clearly been tailored to fit, a pristine white shirt and black cowboy boots. That last touch threw her for a second, but then she reminded herself that she was in ranch country after all.

"I'm looking for a diamond bracelet for a teenager." She didn't want to be too specific about the age just in case he knew Cole and Crystal. Andrea didn't think that all small-town people knew each other, but she knew people. They were the same all over. No doubt the people in this town gossiped as much as the doctors and nurses back home.

"Wonderful. We have a wide selection in a variety of price ranges."

Andrea wanted to say that money was no object, but

that wasn't true. She couldn't spend thousands of dollars no matter how badly she wanted to. Crystal would be confused and maybe even a little worried if someone she'd only known for a few weeks spent too much money on her.

She followed the salesperson to a glass counter. Diamond bracelets gleamed against the black velvet lined trays. Andrea studied the bracelets for a few minutes before she looked back at Francois. "These are exquisite. I don't know how I can choose."

"That's where I come in. First, we eliminate by price. There's no sense falling in love with something that is out of your budget. Then we'll sort by cut of diamond. And then type of bracelets. Bangles, cuffs, tennis. By the time you walk out of here, you'll wonder why you ever thought you could have chosen another one."

Andrea smiled. "That sounds like a plan I can get behind."

Francois asked Andrea a series of questions, nodding and rubbing his chin as he contemplated each of her answers. There wasn't even a hint of stubble. She would have expected him to take notes in order to keep the information straight, but he seemed content to rely on his memory. After she had finished replying to his inquiries, he opened the case and pulled out a bracelet and let it dangle in his hand. The single strand of square cut diamonds was so beautiful.

"May I?" Andrea asked.

"Be my guest."

Andrea took the delicate piece into her hands, and then draped it over her wrist. Although she hadn't made a conscious decision, this bracelet was very similar to the one she'd been gifted on her sixteenth birthday. "This is the one I want."

"Do you want me to wrap the box?"

"I'll do it." This was the very first, and possibly only present Andrea would be giving her daughter, and she was determined to enjoy every little detail.

"Very good." He wrote up the bill and handed it to Andrea. She ran her credit card through the reader, and then took the bag.

Andrea practically floated down the street on air, the bag secured in her hand. She stopped at a store and purchased two different kinds of wrapping paper, plus tape and a bow. She lingered over the cards, looking for just the right picture and the perfect words before choosing one. As she drove to the cabin, she imagined Crystal's reaction. Once she was inside, she pulled the bracelet out of the box and stared at it. Words could not describe how beautiful the bracelet was. She couldn't wait until Crystal saw it.

She returned the bracelet to the box, and then studied the wrapping paper. After a minute, she decided that the paper decorated with pink balloons was much too immature for a sixteen-year-old, so she decided to go with the silver-and-gold-striped paper.

Andrea took her time centering the box and measuring the paper. She had always been meticulous when it came to making her gifts look good. Even so, she checked and double-checked before she cut. Her hands trembled and she dropped them into her lap. Unexpected tears filled her eyes, and she brushed them away. She needed to get a grip on herself. If she was this emotional right now, how was she going to act tomorrow when she gave the bracelet to Crystal?

After taking a deep breath, Andrea set to work wrapping the box. When she was done, she tied ribbon around it and added a bow to one corner. Then she placed the box on the middle of the coffee table where she could see it from almost any place in the cabin.

Only a few more hours and she would be celebrating her daughter's birthday with her.

Cole picked up the wrapped package, and then headed for the dining room. From the time Crystal had been a baby, Cole had done everything in his power to make her birthday special every year. He'd made it an event. She'd had every type of birthday party over the years. She'd had horseback riding parties, swim parties, and sleepovers that included lots of giggling girls. Last year she'd included the senior citizens group in her bowling party. That had become a little raucous when the older group challenged the teenagers to a competition—and won. Though the type of party Crystal wanted had changed from year to year, one tradition remained unchanged. Cole and Crystal had dinner together on her birthday.

For the past few years, they'd had dinner at one of the many fancy restaurants in town. He'd planned the same this year, but a couple of days ago she'd told him she wanted to order in and have dinner at home. Since it was her day, it was her choice.

He stepped into the dining room. She'd gone all out with the decorations. There were flowers on just about every surface in the living and dining rooms.

"You look so nice," Crystal said as she joined him. Even though they were staying home, she'd insisted that they dress up.

"So do you."

"This is a new dress," Crystal said, turning in a slow circle, holding the full skirt as she showed off the pink floral dress. "Mrs. Rose helped me pick it out. She says it makes me look like a proper young lady."

Cole felt a twinge in his chest, but he managed to nod anyway. His little girl was growing up so fast. Before long she would be going away to college. Where had the time gone?

When she'd been a little girl, she'd loved shopping for clothes with him. It had been a fun outing, and he'd always made a day of it. But when she'd turned thirteen, she told him that she wanted to go school shopping with her best friend and her mother. Though he'd felt a bit rejected, there had also been a sense of relief. He and Crystal had started to bump heads, disagreeing on what was appropriate for a girl her age. That wasn't a problem when Crystal went shopping with Olivia and her mother. The girls often bought matching clothes and wore them on the same day, calling each other twin.

"You most certainly do. Do you want to open your gift now or after dinner?"

Before Crystal could reply, the doorbell rang. She dashed away and opened the door.

"I hope I'm not too early."

Andrea. What was she doing here today of all days? He was still asking himself the question when the answer came to him. She would never have shown up if she hadn't been invited. Obviously, Crystal had wanted to include Andrea in her birthday celebration. He knew Crystal liked Andrea, but he also knew this dinner invitation was more of her matchmaking. Otherwise, she would have simply included Andrea in her big, blowout party that she was having in a couple of days.

Though he was past his anger and wanted the best for

Andrea, he didn't think playing happy family in this way was a good idea. It was only asking for trouble.

Cole inhaled deeply, and then slowly exhaled. This was Crystal's birthday, and he didn't want to spoil it.

"Come on in," Crystal said. "Dad, look who's here. It's Andrea. I invited her to my birthday dinner."

The dinner that had always been just the two of them. Father and daughter.

Andrea glanced at Cole. Her expression was a mixture of emotions. She looked uneasy as if she didn't want to intrude. He also picked up on the hope and joy in her eyes. This was the first time she would celebrate her child's birthday with her. Surely he was big enough to allow her to do so.

"Hello, Andrea."

"When Crystal invited me to share her birthday dinner, I couldn't say no."

Crystal was staring at them, a pleased expression on her face.

"This is for you," Andrea said, holding out a wrapped box to Crystal. "I hope you like it."

"I like all presents. Dad always says a gift is whatever someone wants to give you. He says you should be grateful that the person even thought of you."

"That's a nice way to look at life." Andrea glanced at Cole, and then back at Crystal. "Of course, if you don't like it, let me know and you can choose something else. My feelings won't be hurt."

"Dad and I usually open our gifts before dinner. I think it makes the food taste better and he's just too impatient to wait."

"Hey," Cole said, pretending to be indignant. Now that

his shock had worn off, he was actually okay with Andrea's presence.

"Let's go into the dining room," Crystal said. She led the way and Andrea and Cole followed. As Andrea passed Cole, he got a whiff of her perfume. This one was slightly fruity, awakening a hunger inside him. She was wearing a royal blue dress that clung to her body, hugging her perky breasts and emphasizing her tiny waist and sexy hips. Although she was petite, her legs were long and shapely.

Desire began to burn its way through him, and he forced his eyes away. His daughter's birthday dinner was not the place to give his lust free rein. But he was starting to accept the fact that he wanted to explore those feelings. And he got the sense that Andrea did, too.

"Sit down so I can open my presents," Crystal said.

"I thought you said that your father was the impatient one," Andrea joked. "That sounded pretty impatient to me."

"I'm glad that you pointed that out so I didn't have to," Cole said.

"I guess that I might have inherited that trait from my dad. But anyway, let's get started."

"If you insist," Cole said. He pulled out Andrea's chair, and then sat beside her.

"I'm going to open yours first, Dad."

"I hope you like it."

Crystal had never been one to rip through the wrapping paper. Even as a little girl, she had taken the tape off strip by strip as if trying to prolong the moment. By the time she had removed the paper, all in one piece, his nerves were on edge.

When the box sat on the wrapping paper, Crystal's

mouth dropped open. "This is jewelry from Saucier and Cornelius. I recognize the box."

"So it is. Go ahead and open it."

Crystal's hands were shaking as she lifted the top of the box. Then she gasped. "Diamond earrings. I love them."

"I'm glad. I thought you should have them now that you're a proper young lady," he said, deliberately quoting Rose.

"Thank you, thank you, thank you." She gave him a big hug.

"You're welcome," he said, hugging her back.

"I'm going to put them on." She jumped up, then looking at Andrea, she sat back down. "After I open Andrea's gift."

"You can put on your earrings first," Andrea said. "I don't mind waiting."

"No. That's rude. I can wait. Besides, I can't wait to see what you got me."

"If you open this present as slowly as you opened the one from your father, it'll be tomorrow until you get it opened."

Crystal laughed, then once more slowly unwrapped the box. Cole and Andrea shared an exasperated look and she smiled.

"Christmas morning must last forever," Andrea said.

"You have no idea."

"I like the anticipation," Crystal said. She slipped off the last piece of tape, and then removed the paper. "Oh. Another box from Saucier and Cornelius."

Cole's pulse sped up at the sight. He knew Andrea had received a diamond bracelet on her sixteenth birthday. It was a tradition in her family. Was there a diamond bracelet in the box?

"Oh my goodness!" Crystal exclaimed. "A diamond bracelet. This is too much. I don't know if I can keep it."

"Of course you can keep it," Andrea said. "I got it especially for you."

"Can I, Dad?" Crystal's voice was hopeful.

There was no way he could say no without raising Crystal's suspicions. Though he and Andrea knew the tradition behind the gift, Crystal did not. Besides, wasn't he the one who said a gift was what someone wanted to give you? He nodded. "Yes."

"Thanks." Crystal's glee was unmistakable. "You know, the bracelet and earrings match."

Cole had noticed that, too. He'd seen the bracelet when he'd gone shopping two months ago and had considered buying it along with the earrings. Knowing the tradition in Andrea's family, he'd left the bracelet behind, choosing to start his own tradition. But he'd thought the bracelet was perfect for Crystal and planned to get it for her for Christmas.

Crystal put on the earrings and bracelet, and then stared into the mirror. Her smile was wide. "I want to show Livvie my gifts."

"Now? Before dinner?"

"I'll only be a minute. Please, Dad."

Cole nodded. Crystal was too excited to eat anyway.

"I'll be right back," she promised.

In a flash, Crystal had run out the door, leaving Andrea and Cole alone. Andrea looked at him. "I think she likes her gifts."

Cole only stared at her. "Of all of the gifts you could have gotten her, you had to give her a diamond bracelet?"

"You know why, Cole. Because my parents gave me a diamond bracelet for my sixteenth birthday. The same as my grandparents gave my mother. It's a family tradition. Crystal's my daughter. So why wouldn't I give her a diamond bracelet for her sixteenth birthday?"

"What?"

Andrea and Cole turned at once. Crystal was standing there, her eyes wide with shock. Her mouth worked but nothing came out.

"Crystal," Cole said, trying to find the right words—or any words—to say. He drew a blank

"She's my *mother*." Crystal's voice rang with hurt and anger. Worse, betrayal. Tears rained unchecked down her face. "And you knew it? Of course you knew it. Why didn't you tell me? Why did you lie to me?"

Before he could reply, Crystal turned to Andrea. "You pretended to be my friend."

"I—" Andrea tried to speak, but Crystal cut her off.

"All this time I thought that my mother was dead. Dad told me that she couldn't be with us, and I couldn't think of anything else that would keep a mother away from her daughter. But that wasn't it at all, was it? You weren't with us because you chose not to be. I don't want you in my life. You didn't want me when I was born. Well, I don't want you now." She unclasped the bracelet from her wrist and tossed it to Andrea. "Here. I don't want it. I don't want anything from you."

"Crystal, please. Let's talk. I can explain," Andrea beseeched, her hands outstretched.

"Never. I never want to talk to you again. I hate you," Crystal said. Wiping tears, she turned to look at Cole. "I can't believe you did this. I don't want to talk to you either."

Crystal turned and ran from the house, slamming the door behind her.

Silence reigned in the room. Neither Cole nor Andrea moved, frozen in shock. In under ten minutes, the celebratory mood had become almost funereal.

Cole had no idea what to say to Andrea. He was furious with her for not being more careful with her words when they knew Crystal would be back soon, but he was just as angry with himself. *Angrier* with himself. He was the one Crystal had trusted, and he'd betrayed that trust.

"I didn't know she was back," Andrea said, her voice small. She sounded so miserable. Any other time Cole would have been sympathetic, but the look of pain on his daughter's face was etched on his mind. From the moment the nurse had put his baby in his arms, he'd sworn that he'd always, always put her first.

"Yeah." Angry words came to his mouth, but he swallowed them. He'd been so involved in the conversation that he hadn't known Crystal was back either. Truthfully, he hadn't expected her to come back so quickly.

"I didn't mean for any of this to happen. I would never intentionally hurt her. I hope you know that."

"Andrea, it isn't the best time for me to talk to you." His head was spinning as he tried to figure out how to salvage the situation. He sucked in a breath. He wouldn't be able to concentrate on that if he had to try to carry on a conversation. "I'm barely holding it together. I need to focus on Crystal right now. I think it would be best if you left."

Andrea's eyes grew wider and her tears began to fall even faster. "But I want to talk to her. I can't leave things the way they are between us. I want to try to explain."

"I don't think she's in the frame of mind to listen to explanations tonight. Please, just go."

Andrea flinched, but without saying another word, she set the bracelet on the table, picked up her purse, stalked across the room and out of the front door. He hated the pain he'd seen etched on her face. But he couldn't concern himself with Andrea's feelings now. Not when his baby girl was so upset. And who could blame her? She'd been betrayed by the one person she should have been able to trust. Him.

Cole paced the room, the emptiness oppressive. The silence weighed heavily on his shoulders. He walked into the dining room. The flattened wrapping paper mocked him, reminding him of the happiness that had filled the room only minutes ago. The aroma from the food that he'd ordered for dinner floated in the air, and he went into the kitchen. His appetite was long gone. Besides he couldn't eat Crystal's birthday meal without her, so he packed up the food and put it into the refrigerator.

That done, he went back into the living room and dropped onto the couch. He replayed the conversation in his mind. Crystal had heard Andrea clearly state that she was her mother, something they'd kept from her. Would Crystal ever get past his deception? Why hadn't he told her the truth before? He'd had plenty of opportunities. His reasons for secrecy seemed so ridiculous now.

He jumped up and began pacing the small house. He should have gone after her. He checked the time. Thirty minutes had passed with no word from Crystal. Though he knew that she was probably all right, he couldn't stop worrying. He called Crystal's cell phone. It rang twice, and then went to her voicemail. As usual, he could hear the smile in her voice as she announced that she was busy and invited the caller to leave a message, promising to return the call when she was less busy.

Cole didn't know what to say, so he hung up without leaving a message. Asking Crystal to call him would be futile. She didn't want to talk to him. She was too hurt and needed time to come to grips with what she'd learned. But sitting here with nothing but his regrets to keep him company was stressing him out. What if she couldn't forgive him? He knew better than most that betrayal and disappointment could wreck a relationship. He and his parents were a perfect example of that. But surely Crystal wouldn't shut him out of her life forever simply because of one mistake. Especially when he'd had her best interest at heart and had only been trying to protect her.

His cell rang and he answered immediately. "Crystal?"

"No. It's Lynn." Olivia's mother. "I just want you to know that Crystal is over here. She's upset and doesn't want to talk, but I didn't want you to worry about her. I let her know that she could spend the night, but only if I called and let you know where she was."

He sighed with relief. "Thanks for letting me know. I appreciate it."

"I don't know what went wrong, but rest assured that Crystal loves you. She's talking to Livvie now."

Cole thanked Lynn again, and then ended the call. Though he had suspected Crystal would go to her best friend, his heart was finally able to beat normally now that he knew for sure that his daughter was in good hands. A moment later, guilt filled him. He wasn't the only person who was worrying about Crystal. Andrea was just as upset as he had been. Maybe even more.

Cole looked at his phone. He could call her, but somehow that didn't seem good enough. He needed to see her in person so he could assure himself that she was all right. Since Crystal wouldn't be returning tonight, there was no reason for him to stay in the house.

He grabbed his keys, jumped into his truck and headed

down the highway. He didn't question why it was so urgent that he see Andrea tonight. He just knew that it was. His feelings for her were growing stronger every day. And he was tired of fighting them.

At the same time, given what had just happened with Crystal, he knew that now wasn't the time to act on his feelings. It wasn't even the time to discuss them. But even though Crystal came first, Andrea's feelings also mattered.

When he reached the cabin, he parked behind her car and jogged up the stairs. Suddenly his heart began to pound, and he took a deep, steadying breath. He knocked on the door, and then waited. When Andrea didn't open it, he knocked again. After another few seconds, the door swung open and Andrea stood there. He took one look at her, and his heart dropped to his feet. Never in his life had he seen Andrea looking worse. She'd changed out of her pretty dress and was now wearing a T-shirt and shorts. There was nothing wrong with the clothing, per se. It's just that the colors clashed in a way her clothes never did, and he suspected that she'd just put on the first thing she laid her hands on. Her face was tearstained, leaving streaks in her previously flawless makeup. Her eyes were red as if she'd been crying nonstop from the time she'd left his house.

Remorse filled him. He shouldn't have sent her away like that when she was so upset. What if she'd gotten into an accident on the drive to the cabin? He'd never have forgiven himself.

"What do you want?" she asked, one hand on the doorframe, looking ready to slam the door in his face if she didn't like his answer.

"To talk. Can I come in?"

She looked at him for a moment, and then walked away as if she didn't have the energy to reply. Since she'd left the door open, he took that as assent and stepped inside.

The place was in chaos. There were cleaning supplies on the table, which she'd pushed under the windows. The vacuum cleaner was in the middle of the area rug. It was still running, so he turned it off. Her open suitcases were on the couch, her clothing tossed inside in a haphazard manner.

"Going somewhere?" he asked unnecessarily.

"Back home where I belong. I just need to get packed and get this place cleaned." She picked up a can of furniture polish, shook it, and then sprayed a lot of it the table. A lemony cloud filled the air and they both coughed.

"Could we talk about that first?"

She rubbed a rag against the table as if the furniture had offended her somehow. "What's to talk about? You never wanted me here. You even told me to leave the first day you saw me. I should have listened."

"Andrea."

She shook the can again and sprayed a table leg. Thankfully she used less this time. She began to scrub again. Clearly she wasn't going to look at him while they talked. He couldn't blame her. She'd never wanted anyone to see her when she was upset. Even back when they'd been close, she'd always retreated to cry alone. But this wasn't about them. It was about Crystal. They needed to plan on how to go forward. In order to do that, they needed to clear the air. Literally and figuratively.

She reached for the bottle again and he grabbed her hand. "Can we go outside and talk? Or at least open the windows to let in some fresh air."

Andrea dropped the rag onto the floor, then as if realizing that he was holding one of her hands, she pulled away from him and stood up. "Fine. Let's go outside."

Cole stepped back as she brushed in front of him. The warmth from her body reached out to taunt him with the knowledge that after this disastrous night, the odds of him ever touching her again were nearly zero. He followed her out the door and onto the front porch. She leaned against the porch rail, crossed her arms over her chest and stared off into the distance. There were two rocking chairs, so he sat in one. He knew better than to suggest she sit by him. She'd deliberately chosen to stand.

"Why did you come here?" she asked.

"I was worried about you."

"About me?" She turned to face him, her expression empty. "I'm fine. You should be worried about Crystal."

"Crystal's safe—Olivia's mom called me and said that she'll be spending the night there."

Some tension eased from Andrea's shoulders, and he was glad that he'd been able to lay one of her fears to rest.

"That's...that's good," she managed to say, her voice wobbly. She turned away from him again.

"You can talk to me, you know," he said. "We agreed to be friends."

"Until I leave. Well, I'm leaving now, so this is the end of our friendship—such as it was."

"Leaving would be a mistake."

"Not my first. Yet somehow I've managed to overcome them and move on with my life."

"Have you? That's not the way it looks from where I'm sitting."

"I thought I was doing the right thing for all of us by relinquishing my rights. And I still do."

She didn't sound very confident, but Cole didn't bother

pointing that out. He was here to get things back on track, not add fuel to the fire. But he couldn't let that last bit go. "Then why did you show up out of the blue? If you're so happy with what you chose to do, if you think it was right to leave us, why did you just blow up Crystal's life?"

As soon as the words were out, he regretted them. He knew that Andrea had never wanted to hurt Crystal. He shouldn't have been so blunt.

As if her legs could no longer support her, she slid down the rail and sank onto the floor. Her eyes filled with tears as she stared at him. "That was never my intention. And I told you why I came so there's no reason to repeat myself. But…the more time I spent with Crystal, the more I began to love her."

"Crystal has that effect on people."

"I know."

"Anyway, we're getting off track. You were talking about leaving."

"I'm not just talking about leaving. I *am* leaving. As you pointed out, I blew up her life by coming here. So I'll go back to Chicago, and she can pretend like she never met me." Her voice broke and she tossed her head. Clearly she didn't want him to see her cry again.

"You don't know Crystal very well if you think that."

Andrea gasped, and he realized he'd said the wrong thing. Again. Before he could clarify his statement, Andrea gave him a sad smile. "We've already established that."

"That came out wrong. What I am saying is that going back to Chicago is the wrong thing to do."

"I just don't want to cause any more harm."

"I know you're trying to do what's right for Crystal, but I'm telling you that hurting her is exactly what will happen if you leave without making things right. You can't put toothpaste back into the tube." He met her eyes. Hers were filled with sorrow and remorse. "We're where we are and now we have to deal with it. Crystal is hurt and angry for the moment, but when those feelings pass— and they will pass—she's going to have questions. You are the only one who has those answers. Stay for her. Stay for yourself."

"Are you sure I won't make things worse just by being around? Because I don't want to do that."

"Staying is the best way to fix things."

"If I could go back in time I wouldn't have made the trip."

"It's too late for regrets. Coulda, woulda, shoulda, doesn't change anything. The only thing we can do is move on. Together."

Andrea's chest rose and fell as she took a deep breath, and then slowly blew it out. Even though they were having a serious conversation, he couldn't stop his gaze from following the up-and-down movement of her chest. Lucky for him, Andrea was looking at her hands and not at him. "If you think I should stay, then I will. For Crystal."

"For Crystal."

He reached out a hand to help her stand. When she was on her feet, he could have let her go—maybe even *should* have let her go. Instead, he pulled her soft body close to him and wrapped her in his arms. Andrea raised her head and Cole looked into her face. Seeing the yearning in her eyes, he lowered his head and kissed her tentatively. When she responded, he deepened the kiss, giving his desire free rein.

There was a lot to work through, but for the time being, he was going to enjoy this moment.

Chapter Fourteen

Andrea sighed and opened her mouth, giving in to the longing that she'd denied for far too long. As her tongue tangled with Cole's, flames of desire began to lick inside her until her body was a raging inferno. She pressed her body more tightly against his, needing to get even closer to him. Gradually she became aware that Cole was pulling away and she tightened her hold on his neck, reluctant to break the connection. She felt Cole's smile on her lips and the gentle rumble of laughter in his chest.

"I don't want to end things," he said, his lips still touching hers, "but we already have one mess on our hands. We don't need to make another one."

Cole's words were like a bucket of ice water dousing her desire so thoroughly that not even a smoldering ember remained.

"You're right." She managed to keep her voice calm. Cool. "We need to focus on Crystal."

After all, she was the one who mattered most. Crystal was the reason Andrea was in Aspen Creek. She'd come here to see her child, not to start a romance with Cole. Any attraction she felt for him was simply…simply… Well, it was something she couldn't prioritize right now. No matter how badly she wanted to.

"Well, I suppose you should leave now," she said, even though she didn't want to be alone just yet. But she didn't want him to feel as if he had to look out for her. She'd been crumbling before, but she was mostly better now.

"It's nice out here," he said. He spread his feet, put his hands on his hips and stared into the distance. There was something about his stance that was at ease and powerful. Something that she found nearly irresistible.

She nodded. Since she really didn't want him to leave, she replied, "It's a big change from the city, but I like it."

"It reminds me of the years I worked as a ranch hand. I loved it."

Andrea was hungry for any information she could get about those years she'd missed. Especially now. "How did Crystal like it?"

"She loved it. Particularly when she was little. She rode horses just about every day. She and some of the other kids spent a lot of time swimming at the watering hole. Life was good then. Mr. and Mrs. Montgomery still refer to her as their first grandchild."

Andrea smiled. "I'm glad to know she was loved. It sounds as if you both were very happy."

He lifted one shoulder in a way that was much too sexy for her peace of mind. "I liked the work, but I also like owning my own business."

He'd given up a life he loved to make their daughter happy. She might not have been in love with him all those years ago, but she'd been right about the type of man he was. He was the best father any girl could ever ask for. "You mentioned buying your own ranch someday."

"Yes. When the time is right."

"When will that be?"

"Who can see into the future?" He paused, and she had

the feeling that he was deep in thought. She hoped that if she was patient enough, he would expound on that answer, and a few moments later, she was proven right. "I suppose when Crystal graduates from college. She was happy living on the ranch, but she is thrilled to be in town. Ranch life can be a bit isolating. If I bought a ranch, it would be a small one. I wouldn't need a ranch hand so I would be the only one around. Crystal needs more than me in her life."

She could use a mother. The words hung in the air, but Andrea wasn't going to say them out loud. "It sounds as if you are doing all the right things. No surprise there. You always made the right decisions."

"Oh, I don't know about that. I've made plenty of mistakes in my life. I just learned to forgive myself and do my best to move on."

"Do you think you could find a way to forgive me?" The words were out before she could call them back. Then she realized she didn't want to retract them. She wanted the past to be over for real. These pretend apologies and fake forgiveness were too hard on her soul.

"I already have. After everything that went on with Crystal tonight, I realized just how easy it was to make one decision that could change everything. You do the best you can in the moment. That's what you did back then."

"Do you think Crystal will eventually see it that way?"

"You've met her. She has a sweet nature. A loving heart."

"I know."

"But honesty is very important to her. We lied to her, so she's not happy with either one of us right now."

"But you have a close relationship with her. That will make it easier for her to forgive you. But me? You heard what she said to me. And she's right. I walked away from her. Then I pretended to be a stranger so I could insinuate myself into her life as a friend. I didn't tell her that I was her mother."

"I kept the truth from her, too."

"Again, it's not the same thing."

"How about this?" Cole said, covering her hand with his. Though she was upset, she still felt the tingling in her fingers. "I'll do my best to convince her to listen to you. And believe me, she likes you so it won't be that hard."

Andrea nodded. She wanted to believe him, but she couldn't let herself hope.

After sitting in companionable silence for a while, Cole stood. "I suppose I should get going. Like I said, Crystal is spending the night with her best friend, but I should be there just in case she decides to come home."

"Do you think she'll come back tonight?"

"Honestly? No. But I expect she'll be back in the morning."

"When you hear from her…"

"I'll call."

"Thanks."

She expected Cole to walk down the stairs, but instead, he stopped in front of her. As they looked into each other's eyes, her pulse began to race. His dark brown eyes looked nearly black as they stared into hers as if trying to read her soul. She couldn't move to save her life. Ever so slowly he reached out and caressed her cheek. Her skin tingled and she leaned her face into his palm. "Everything will work out, Andrea. You just have to believe that."

She swallowed. She could believe anything when they were together. When she replied, her voice came out in a hoarse whisper. "I'll try."

"That's all I ask."

After a moment, Cole lowered his hand and walked away. Immediately she missed the contact and wanted to call him back and say... What exactly would she say? Kiss me again? Hold me in your arms for a little while longer? Make love to me like you did all those years ago?

No. She couldn't say any of those things. Kissing him had already shifted things between them on a basic level. They didn't need another layer of emotions to shovel through now.

So why did her heart ache as she watched the taillights of his truck grow smaller and eventually disappear into the night?

I can't believe I kissed Andrea. It had been so good that he hadn't wanted to stop. He'd actually wanted to pick her up and carry her into the bedroom and make love to her for the rest of the night. Thankfully, he'd managed to stay in control, stopping before his desire got the best of him.

Things were complicated enough right now. But adding complications wasn't the real reason that he'd stopped. What was one more issue given what they were already facing? No, the real reason was that he remembered how emotional Andrea had been when he'd arrived. She'd been distraught when she'd opened the door, holding on by a thread. She'd been a mess of feelings and in no way able to make a wise decision. She would have done anything to escape the pain she was in. What would be easier than losing herself in his arms for a while? No matter how badly he wanted to make love to her again, he didn't want it to be something she might later regret.

There was a lot for the three of them to work out. And he knew it wouldn't be easy. It would take a lot of time and effort. He just hoped Crystal would be open to hearing them out. Though he had told Andrea that he was confident Crystal would forgive them, he wasn't as certain as he'd pretended to be. Crystal was honest and expected honesty from everyone in return. He'd never seen her this angry. This hurt. He knew his betrayal stung more than Andrea's. But he also knew that when push came to shove, Crystal would forgive him more easily than she would forgive Andrea.

He needed to find a way to make her see Andrea's point of view. Getting mother and daughter together was suddenly the most important thing in his life. They needed each other.

That thought stuck with him all night. When morning arrived, he still hadn't thought of a solution. Perhaps inspiration would strike with a cup of coffee.

He didn't know when Crystal intended to come back, but he needed to be home when she did. So he called Gary and explained the situation to him.

"I knew that woman was up to no good," Gary said, his voice rising with anger. "You should have run her out of town the minute you saw her."

"She didn't set out to hurt Crystal. And Andrea's hurting pretty bad, too." He thought about what Andrea had said to him not long after she'd first come to town, then added, "There aren't any bad guys here, Gary. Just people doing their best."

"Their best? Our Crystal is hurting. And it's all because of that woman. You can't possibly be taking her side."

"There are no sides. She only wanted to see Crystal. Things just snowballed after that. It's not any more her fault than it is mine."

"Fix this, Cole. I mean it. I don't care what you have to do. Just make it right." Gary's voice shook with emotion.

"What do you think I'm trying to do?"

Gary's sigh came over the phone. "Sorry. I know you are doing your best. I just love that little girl like she was my own. When she hurts, I hurt."

"I know. So do I. But we'll get through this."

"I hope so," Gary said, and then hung up.

Cole was still holding the phone when he heard the key in the lock and the front door opened.

Crystal stepped into the living room, and then stopped. "I thought you would be at the store by now."

"No, you didn't," Cole said. "You knew I would be here so we could set things right between us."

"I was *hoping* you would be gone." Her voice was belligerent, something that was rare for her.

"Were you?" Cole asked, keeping his voice even. She might want to turn this into a fight, but he wasn't going to let that happen. Still, even though he knew she had a right to be angry, her words were like knives shoved into his heart. "Because I was waiting for you to come home so we could talk."

Crystal folded her arms across her chest and glared at him. "You lied to me."

"I didn't tell you the truth about Andrea when you introduced us. That's true. If I could do it again, I would change that."

"That's not what I mean."

"Then what?"

"You didn't tell me she was still alive. I thought she was dead."

"You said that last night." He dropped onto the couch,

hoping she would sit beside him. "What did I do to give you that impression?"

"Are you kidding me? Look around. There isn't one picture of her anywhere in the house. If there had been, I would have recognized her. And you never talked about her. You never said one single word—not even her name. When I used to ask, you would say that she loved me but that she couldn't be with me. What was I supposed to think?" A tear trickled from the corner of her eye. "But she wasn't dead. She just didn't want me."

Immediately Cole jumped to his feet and closed the distance between them. He pulled her into his embrace. Initially she struggled against him, then she put her head against his chest. Tears drenched his shirt, and her shoulders shook as she sobbed. "Why didn't she want me?"

"Oh, Crystal. It's not that simple."

"*You* wanted me," she said, as if he hadn't spoken. "You stayed to be my dad even though you were only eighteen. She's this big shot doctor. She's rich. Now that I'm grown and she doesn't have to make sacrifices for me, she wants to be in my life. I wanted a mom so bad when I was little. But I'm not little anymore. I don't need her now. I hate her, and I never want to see her again."

"No, you don't hate her. You could never hate anyone. It goes against everything inside you."

"I'll make an exception in her case." She spotted the diamond bracelet on the table where Andrea had put it. "I don't want that bracelet anymore. Can you give it back to her? I don't even want to look at her face."

"Before you decide you don't want to keep her gift, can I show you something?"

"Whatever."

Something Crystal had said had given him a burst of

inspiration. He gave her shoulder a squeeze. "I'll be right back."

He raced into his room and dug through an old box of mementos. He rummaged around until he found his senior year yearbook, then jogged down the stairs. Crystal was sitting on the couch, her arms folded over her chest.

"What do you have?" Crystal asked. He wondered if she knew her voice betrayed a bit of interest.

"My yearbook. I never showed it to you."

"Why are you showing it to me now?"

"Because I want you to see something."

"That you were goofy looking? I already know that. I have the picture of you holding me when I was a baby on my bedside table." One of the nurses had snapped that picture when Crystal had been a few hours old.

He shook his head at her, amused in spite of himself. They might not be on the best terms now, but she never missed a chance to roast him. "No. I want you to see someone else."

It took a moment for it to dawn on Crystal that he was talking about Andrea, and when it did, she pushed the book away and stood. "I'm not interested."

He took her hand and gently pulled her back beside him. "I just want you to look."

"You're on her side." The accusation was filled with hurt.

"I'm on your side. Always. But maybe you and Andrea are on the same side here."

"I'll never be on her side."

Though her tone was definite, Cole was relieved to note that she didn't stand up again. He opened the yearbook to Andrea's page, and then handed the book to Crystal.

Her picture was one of two on the page, her list of accomplishments long. "This is her."

Huffing out a sigh, Crystal looked at the page. Then she froze. After a long, tense moment, she glanced at Cole. "How old is she here?"

"Seventeen. We took yearbook pictures in early September of senior year. This picture was taken about a month before you were conceived."

"She was only about a year older than I am now."

"I know."

Crystal's finger went from Andrea's face to the list of activities Andrea had participated in. "She did a lot of things. She was voted most likely to succeed."

"Yes."

"I guess having a child would have ruined that for her."

"At eighteen? Most likely. Even carrying you to term was a challenge for her. Everyone could see she was pregnant. There was plenty of whispering about her behind her back. I think a lot of people expected her to drop out, give up. But that wasn't Andrea."

Crystal didn't say anything, but Cole knew she was taking it all in. She flipped the pages until she found Cole. She grinned. "Your list of accomplishments isn't nearly as long as Andrea's."

"Nobody's was. She was the most driven person I've ever met. When she set a goal, she didn't stop working until she accomplished it."

"I suppose keeping me would have gotten in her way." Crystal looked at him. "It says here that you wanted to be a doctor. That didn't happen. Was it because of me?"

He shook his head. "It was because of *me*."

She smiled and leaned her head against his shoulder. Then she pulled away and looked at him, her eyes sad.

"Andrea didn't feel the same way. Being a doctor was more important than being a mom."

"It wasn't just being a doctor that she chose. There was a lot more wrapped up in it. Our parents were furious with us. They tried to push both of us into giving you up for adoption. They said that if we didn't, we were on our own. Not just no money, but no support, no babysitting, no contact of any kind—we'd be totally cut off. Andrea idolized her parents. The idea of being disowned…it was too hard for her to take."

"Wait. I have grandparents."

"You did sixteen years ago. Andrea mentioned them not that long ago, and she talked about them in the present tense, so I guess they're still alive. But I'm not sure whether anyone would let me know if they were dead." His heart must be growing soft because suddenly the thought of his parents no longer being alive brought him pain.

"Wow. They didn't want you to keep me. Didn't they like Andrea?"

"They loved her. And her parents loved me. Or at least they did until I got their seventeen-year-old daughter pregnant. Our parents were best friends. But they had dreams for us. Just like I have dreams for you."

"They didn't want you to throw your life away."

"I never looked at raising you as throwing my life away. Being your father is the best thing I've ever done. There is no greater joy to me."

"So Andrea agreed to give me away so she could go to school and make her parents happy?"

He turned and looked deep into his daughter's eyes. It was important that he get this right. "Don't think it was easy for her to give you away. She stressed and cried over the decision for months. In the end, she thought that she was doing what was best for you. She loved you and didn't think she would make a good mother at eighteen."

"Sure."

"Do you think you would be ready to be a mother in a couple of years? You're going to be a junior this year. Andrea was pregnant our senior year."

"No. I don't think I would be. But I wouldn't just walk away from my child."

"You wouldn't be in the same situation. Because no matter what, I'd be in your corner one hundred percent. I would make sure that you could still follow your dreams. Andrea didn't have that support."

"But you managed."

"It was rough for a while. Thankfully I found Aspen Creek. So many people opened their hearts to us. But it didn't have to be that way. We got lucky. It could have gone wrong so many times."

"Do you think Andrea regrets deciding not to be my mother?"

"I don't know. But I know that she wanted to get to know you."

"How do you know that?"

"She found you."

Crystal turned back to Andrea's photo in the yearbook. "She was only a little older than I am." She seemed to be talking to herself more than him, so Cole didn't reply. "I guess I can understand why she did what she did. I don't think I could take care of a baby by myself. It would be hard even with your help, Dad. I want to go to college and join a sorority. I want to go to ball games and dances."

"You can do all of those things."

"But I couldn't if I had a baby to take care of."

"It would be harder, that's for sure."

"So I guess I can understand why she didn't think she could be a mom back then." Her eyes filled with tears. "And I'm so happy that you decided to be my dad. You didn't get to do any of those things after I was born."

"I didn't miss them. But I would have missed you."

"But I don't forgive her for coming around and not telling me who she was. She shouldn't have lied to me. And I'm kind of mad at you for pretending not to know her. You should have told me who she was."

"And what would you have done?"

"Well, I wouldn't have tried to get you to date her. That's for sure." She shook her head. "That was such a stupid idea. Especially since you dated before and it didn't work out."

"What we had in the past didn't last, but I don't regret a second of it. We made you together." He pulled her closer and she leaned her head against his chest. "What else would you have done differently?"

"I would have told her to stay away from me."

"Maybe at first. But later, when you had time to think about it, would you have asked her why she was here?"

"I wouldn't care," Crystal insisted, but he heard a slight waver in her voice. It was enough to make him press.

"Really?"

"I know what you're trying to do. You're trying to make me talk to her now."

"Yes," he admitted. "But not because I want to control how you feel or what you think. But because I want you to have a chance to ask questions. Because I want Andrea to have a chance to explain to you why she came here. The two of you might not get a second chance to talk if you don't take this one."

"You mean she'll get an attitude? Her way or the highway, like with your parents?"

"No, that's not it. I mean you're both hurting now. People tend to run away from situations that hurt them. Just like you did last night. You don't owe her anything. Nor do you owe me a thing. But maybe you owe yourself a chance to talk to her. A chance to listen to what she has to say."

"I don't know."

"You could take the opportunity to give her the bracelet back."

"You aren't going to do that for me?"

"No. She gave it to you. You're old enough to give it back to her if you don't want it."

Crystal jumped to her feet. "Fine. Let's go. I want to get this over with."

Cole had hoped to calm her down a bit before the meeting, but now that she was all riled up again, that didn't seem likely. This might be as good as it would get. He stood and shot off a quick text to Andrea.

When they were inside his truck, Crystal turned to him. "I want you to know that nothing she says will change my mind."

"Then why are you going if you aren't going to give her a fair chance?"

"Because I love you and this is important to you. I just want to lower your expectations so you won't be disappointed when I don't give her a big hug and say all is forgiven."

He nodded, even as his stomach sank. This was going to be harder than he expected. He wondered if he'd given Andrea false hope. Crystal did have a soft heart, but now that she knew what it felt like to have it broken, she might not want to risk feeling that pain again. Well, it was too late to worry about it now. He'd put the wheels in motion and would have to ride it out and see how things ended up. Crystal might be angry, but he knew at some point she would have questions, and he didn't want her to miss the opportunity to get answers.

Normally their car rides were filled with laughter and conversation. Today, the only sound came from the radio, which was tuned to Crystal's favorite radio station. Though many of her most loved songs came over the air, she didn't sing along to the lyrics or bob her head to the beat. Instead, she sat stone still, facing the windshield. The tension in her body was unmistakable.

Cole knew he wouldn't be successful in drawing her into conversation, so he kept his attention focused on the road. When they finally reached the driveway to the cabin, he breathed a sigh of relief. One way or the other, this would be over soon.

Crystal jumped from the passenger seat and slammed her door. Loaded for bear as she was, Cole thought she might storm up the stairs, but she didn't. Instead, she walked around to his side of the truck and waited until he was standing beside her before she took a step. Clearly her anger had been masking her fear and trepidation. It couldn't be easy coming face-to-face with the person who had walked out of your life the day you were born. Knowing her mother was still alive had to hurt even more than believing she was dead.

Cole took Crystal's hand and gave it a comforting squeeze as they walked up the stairs together. Was it only last night that he'd been here, talking with Andrea? Kissing her? The contentment that had filled him then escaped him now.

The door swung open when they reached the top step.

Andrea stood there, her arms wrapped around her midsection as if she already expected the worst and was holding herself together. "I've been waiting for you. Come on in."

Crystal made a major production of ignoring Andrea as she swept into the house. Andrea's shoulders slumped, and Cole gave her an encouraging smile as he stepped inside behind Crystal.

"Thank you for coming," Andrea said. "Please, have a seat."

The room had been put back in order and the windows were open, letting in fresh air and blowing out the remnants of furniture polish scent that lingered.

Crystal sat down and folded her arms over her chest.

"I want to apologize for not telling you who I was when we first met," Andrea said, getting to the heart of the matter. Perhaps she knew that her time was limited and didn't want to waste a moment. "I actually hadn't planned to meet you at all. I just wanted to see you to be sure you were okay. I may have given up my maternal rights, but I never stopped loving you. I never stopped thinking about you. But I mostly managed to keep those thoughts limited to one day a year."

"One day? One *whole* day?" Crystal sneered. "I was only worth thinking about for one day? Why did you bother?"

"You were worth thinking about every minute of every day. But I couldn't function unless I put my thoughts of you aside and focused on what was going on in my life. But on your birthday…" Andrea's voice broke off.

"What about my birthday?"

"I can show you better than I can tell you." Andrea picked up a large scrapbook and offered it to Crystal who stared at it as if debating whether to take it. Finally she did.

"What is this?" she asked.

"It's letters I wrote to you on your birthday every year. Birthday cards I would have given you if I had been in your life. It was one day when I indulged my feelings and allowed my love and pain to escape from the box where I'd kept them."

Crystal opened the book, and then looked at the first page before turning it.

"You can take out the cards and letters and read them if you want," Andrea said.

Crystal removed the lined paper and read the letter. Replacing it, she took out the birthday card with the large number one on the front. When she finished reading it, she replaced it, then turned the page and repeated the process.

As she slowly flipped through the book, Cole tried to guess how she was feeling by looking at her face, but her emotionless expression gave nothing away. When she reached the end, she closed the book. "What are the pictures of toys?"

"Every year I donated a toy to a homeless shelter. I couldn't give you a gift, but I gave one in your honor."

Crystal didn't reply, but Cole could tell that she was moved by the gesture.

"Why is there a card for my sixteenth birthday? You knew you were going to have dinner with me and Dad."

"No, I didn't. I bought that card in Chicago. When I came to town, I thought I would be celebrating your birthday alone like I had every year."

"But when I invited you to dinner..."

"This card says for my daughter. Obviously, I couldn't give that to you."

"No. Because you wanted to keep lying to me."

Chapter Fifteen

Andrea's heart fell at those angrily spoken words. She should have known that it wouldn't be easy to get through to Crystal. But when she had begun to page through Andrea's memory book, taking care with each letter and card, hope had begun to spring up in Andrea's heart. But she couldn't be surprised by the anger that was coming off Crystal in waves. Her parents were supposed to protect her, not put their own feelings ahead of hers. When it came down to it, Andrea was no better than her own parents. "I suppose there's some truth in that."

Crystal's head swung around. She hadn't been expecting that. "So you admit that you were going to keep lying to me."

Andrea held Crystal's gaze, determined to let her daughter know that she was being completely honest. "Yes. My plan was never to become a permanent part of your life. I knew that would be unfair to you. I only intended to make sure that you were happy, and then go back home."

"Why?"

"I don't understand. Why what?"

"Why did you need to know that I was okay after all this time? I'm almost grown now."

"So many reasons." Andrea sighed. "You're almost the age I was when I started dating your father. I know how hormones can get the best of a teenager. And I suppose I was also beginning to question my life. It wasn't easy to let go of you sixteen years ago. It broke my heart. But once it was done, I was determined to make the sacrifice worth it. I threw myself into my classes like never before. When I got to college, I didn't go to parties or football and basketball games. To my mother's horror, I didn't pledge her sorority."

"Dad gave up his chance to go to college and become a doctor. You did both of those things. So just what did you sacrifice?"

"The chance to raise my little girl. The chance to be your mother."

Crystal's mouth opened as if she was going to speak. Then she snapped it closed. Andrea didn't want Crystal to censor herself. "Say whatever you want. I won't be upset."

"You could have been my mother a long time ago. But you didn't want to."

"I did want to. But I was afraid."

"And selfish."

"Crystal," Cole said softly.

"It's okay," Andrea assured him. She appreciated him coming to her defense, but she needed Crystal to say what she felt. "I didn't intend to be selfish, not that my intentions matter. The result is what's important. And the result here was that you didn't have a mother when you needed one."

"Correct." Crystal stared at her with eyes so cold Andrea nearly shivered. "Is there anything else? If not, I'm ready to go."

"No."

Crystal stood and walked toward the door.

"Wait. There is one thing."

"What is it?" Crystal didn't turn around, leaving Andea with no choice but to talk to her back.

"I love you. I've loved you from the second you were born, and I'll love you forever. You don't have to love me in return. That won't change my feelings."

"Good, because I don't love you."

The words were daggers, stabbing holes in Andrea's heart, making breathing painful. Crystal pulled the diamond bracelet from her pocket, turned around and held it out. Andrea couldn't make her arm move to take it, so Crystal dropped it on the table, then looked at Cole. "I said everything I want to say. Can we go now?"

Cole didn't look too happy, but Andrea didn't want him to pressure Crystal to stay longer.

"Thank you for coming," Andrea said, preventing Cole from interfering. "I appreciate you letting me explain."

Crystal looked surprised by Andrea's response. Perhaps she had been looking for a fight. But Andrea wasn't going to give Crystal additional ammunition.

"I'll be in the truck," Crystal said, then stalked from the room.

Andrea managed to hold on to her composure until she heard the front door close behind Crystal. Then her shoulders slumped under the weight of her heartbreak. "I know that I deserve her anger, but it hurts so much to know that she hates me."

"She doesn't hate you," Cole said, taking Andrea into his arms and giving her a comforting hug. Then he leaned down so he could meet her gaze. "Remember, she's a teenager. For all of her maturity, she still is only sixteen. That's why you said you were going to give her time."

"It seems so hopeless."

"It's not. You're just emotional right now. I don't want to make light of your feelings. And I certainly don't want to sound condescending."

"But?"

"But maybe you should do something that relaxes you. Knit. Or, I don't know. Take a warm bath and listen to music. Do something that brings you peace so you can take your mind off things."

"I know that's better than brooding." But somehow she didn't think she would do either of the things he suggested. That would take more energy than she had right now. Just talking took effort.

"In the meantime, I'll work on softening Crystal's heart."

"Don't pressure her," Andrea said quickly. "I want her to feel whatever she feels. If and when she comes around, it has to be her decision. Not because she wants to please you. That's the only way it will work."

Cole didn't look pleased with her comment. Nevertheless he nodded. The truck horn blew and he shook his head. "She's really pushing it."

"Be patient with her. She's hurt."

"So are you."

Andrea spread her arms wide. "I'm the adult here."

"That doesn't make your pain any less real."

Cole's tenderness and understanding was making her weak. It would be so much easier to handle this if he was the angry man he'd been when she arrived in town. She cleared the lump in her throat. "Thank you for talking to her and convincing her to give me a chance to explain."

"You're welcome." Before she realized what he intended, he put a finger beneath her chin and lifted it. Then he brushed a gentle kiss across her lips. Despite her inner turmoil, his kiss made her knees weak and she barely managed to keep from wobbling. "I'll talk to you later."

Andrea could only nod as Cole left. She missed the warmth of his arms, the safety and serenity she'd found in his embrace. She didn't move until she heard his truck engine start. Then she slumped onto the couch and burst into tears. Once she was all cried out, she grabbed a pen and paper and wrote a letter to her Little One.

The ride back to the house was quiet. Cole wanted to know what Crystal was thinking and feeling, but he resisted the urge to ask. She was dealing with a lot of conflicting emotions, and she deserved time to process them on her own, without his interference. Besides, he didn't trust himself not to try to convince her to give Andrea a second chance. That was exactly what Andrea had asked him not to do. He knew that she was right. Crystal had to work through her feelings on her own. He just didn't like knowing that both Crystal and Andrea were miserable.

He pulled in front of the house and turned to Crystal. "Are you working today?"

"No."

"Do you want to hang out at the feedstore like you used to?"

"No. I want to stay home."

He blew out a breath. Maybe time alone to think was what she needed. "I'll see you later then."

"Bye."

Crystal got out of the truck and Cole watched until she was safely inside the house before he drove off. Gary was waiting inside the store when Cole stepped inside. "Well? What happened?"

Cole looked around. It was just the two of them. "Crystal came home. We talked and she agreed to listen to what Andrea had to say, so I drove her to Andrea's cabin."

"And?"

"It didn't seem to do a bit of good. The rational part of me knows that Crystal has to work through her feelings. She won't even be able to consider forgiving Andrea until that happens. But there was a part of me that hoped Crystal and Andrea would reconcile today and everything would be perfect."

"That was...irrational." Gary paused. "But I can see how you would think that way. I suppose there's nothing wrong with hoping."

"I suppose there's nothing I can do but wait."

Gary harrumphed. "Are you here for the day?"

"Yes."

"Then I'm out of here." When Gary reached the door, he turned and looked back at Cole. "I know you're doing what you think is best for everyone."

"I'm trying."

"I just happen to think Crystal is the only one who matters." With that parting shot, Gary left.

Gary's obvious disappointment in Cole hurt more than it should have. But then, Gary was more than an employee. He was a friend. He'd often offered Cole fatherly advice—usually unsolicited, but always with the best of intentions.

Cole tried to work, but it was hard to focus. After a few hours, he called in an order at the diner even though he didn't have much of an appetite. It would be a lonely meal since it was just him today. After hanging the Closed for Lunch sign on the door, he walked to the diner. He was passing by the craft store when the door opened and someone called his name.

"Yes?" He turned to see Mrs. Rose standing there.

"Do you have a minute?"

Though it had been couched as a question, Cole knew that it was a command. He nodded and stepped inside. The senior ladies of the knitting group were assembled around a circular table. Their bags filled with yarn with knitting needles sticking out the top were leaning against the chairs.

"I don't want to interrupt your meeting," Cole said.

"We were finished. I saw you walking by and knew this would be the perfect time for us to talk," Rose said.

"Of course." He glanced around the room, trying to determine whether he was about to be yelled at or comforted. Their faces gave nothing away, so he supposed either was possible.

"I called Crystal when she didn't show up for work today." Rose gestured to the other women who nodded. "We all wanted to know how her birthday went."

"She told us what happened," Diana Lowery said, folding her arms across her chest. It was clear from her posture that she blamed Cole for Crystal's unhappiness.

"You shouldn't have lied to her," Rose added.

Not the first time that he had heard that. He loved the people of Aspen Creek and considered them to be extended family. He knew they adored Crystal. That was the only reason he didn't tell them to remove their noses from his business. He folded his arms over his chest, mirroring Diana. "I did what I thought was best."

"We know that. And in your situation, we might have done the same thing," Rose said gently.

"I wouldn't have," Diana said, sniffing. Though she was barely five feet tall, she managed to look down her nose at Cole, making him feel small.

Rose shot Diana a look, and then turned back to Cole. "But the thing is, what are you going to do now?"

"I'm doing the only thing I can. I'm giving her space."

"And Andrea?"

"All I can tell you is that she has apologized and is giving Crystal space also."

"That's good," Rose said.

"But what about you and Andrea?" Diana asked. "Are you going to convince her to stay in Aspen Creek?"

Cole blinked. All five of the women seemed to be awaiting his response. "Why?"

"Because it would be good for Crystal," Rose said, as if it were the most obvious thing in the world. "And for you, too. Andrea is a good woman."

"You're not upset with her?" Cole asked. He'd been ready to protect her from criticism, but now it seemed that wasn't necessary.

As one, the women shook their heads. Rose said, "That's a waste of time. At our age we don't have time to waste. We are as disappointed in her as we are in you for not being up-front about this from the start. But now that the truth is out there, you can all move forward."

"I don't know what Andrea is going to do. I think we should let her have some time alone to figure out her next move."

"Bah. That woman has had enough time on her own. She needs to know that there's someone on her side." Rose gave him a pointed look.

"You mean me?"

"Who else?" Rose asked.

"But I've already told her that I'm going to do everything in my power to get her and Crystal's relationship back on track. She asked me not to influence Crystal, and I'm respecting her wishes."

"And what about your relationship with Andrea?"

Cole laughed. He should have seen where this conversation was going. No doubt Crystal had talked about her matchmaking plans with them. "That's not something I want to discuss."

"Figures. You always were too shut off for your own good."

"What's that supposed to mean?"

"It means that it's okay to let people in," Diana said. "I know you look at us as a bunch of busybodies, and that may be true. But we're busybodies who care about you and Crystal. If you'd talked to us in the beginning, we could have helped you before everything blew up in your face."

The other women nodded and murmured in agreement.

"And even before then," Rose said. "You've lived in Aspen Creek for nearly sixteen years. You should know us well enough by now to know that we want the best for you and Crystal. You've built a wall around yourself. We never mentioned it before, because it didn't appear to be hurting anyone. But now we see that we were wrong. We should have asked more questions even if it meant overstepping.

"You know that we love Crystal. But I don't think you really believe that we love you, too. You're our family. You can count on us. We'll do our best not to let you down."

Rose's words hit Cole hard and he staggered back under the power of them. Had he doubted they loved him? Doubted that he could rely on them? He often referred to them as his found family. But considering the way his biological family had treated him, people who'd told him that they loved him for eighteen years, it wasn't totally illogical for him to keep a bit of distance, even if he'd been doing it subconsciously. Now it finally occurred to him that he really hadn't let them in. Although he knew he could depend on his Aspen Creek family for material help, he'd made sure not to need them emotionally. "I guess I didn't really believe that until now."

"We know. That's why we decided to come out and tell you."

"Thanks." Cole hugged each of the women, then stood there, unsure what to do next.

"Now go. And trust that everything is going to work out," Diana said.

"We'll make sure of that," Rose said confidently.

Cole left and went to the diner to pick up his lunch. Suddenly he was famished. Though the situation was unchanged, he was feeling better. He'd always known the people in Aspen Creek were in his corner. But maybe he'd kept them at a distance because he feared that if he let them down, they would turn their backs on him like his parents had. But his fears hadn't come to pass. They might not have agreed with the way he'd handled things with Andrea, but they were standing beside him.

Five days later, his optimism had begun to fade. The situation with Crystal didn't appear to be changing. She'd enjoyed her sixteenth birthday party with all of her friends, but the light inside her seemed dimmer. Initially he thought that giving her time on her own was a good idea, but he was starting to question if that had been the wrong thing to do. Crystal wasn't the type to keep things bottled up inside. She liked a sounding board to help her work through her problems. Often that had been him.

Deciding a change of tactics was needed, he went in search of Crystal. She was on the patio, reading a book.

"What are your plans for the day?" he asked, pulling out the chair across from her and sitting down.

"I don't have anything planned. Why?"

"I thought we might go for a hike."

Crystal sighed. He knew she liked stomping around in the mountains. "Just the two of us?"

"Of course. Unless you want to invite someone."

She shook her head. "I just wanted to be sure that you didn't."

"Which trail do you want to hike?"

"I don't know. Let's figure that out while we're driving."

Ten minutes later, they were in Cole's truck and headed for the trails. Crystal's mood seemed to improve the closer they got to the mountains. When they reached the head of the trail, she was in great spirits.

"We haven't done this in a long time," she said.

"I know. I figured we should get back to doing things together again like we used to."

She gave him an odd look. He expected her to say something, but instead she took a swallow from her water bottle and began to walk. After about fifteen minutes, she broke the silence. "I've been getting information from colleges."

"I know. I'm the one who generally gets the mail from the box."

"I'll be going away to school."

"I know."

"You'll be alone."

"Oh no, Crystal. Please don't try to set me up again. Surely you remember what happened last time." He'd started falling in love again. But that would be his secret.

She actually giggled. "I don't have anyone specific in

mind this time. But it can't get any worse than discovering the woman I wanted to set you up with was…"

It was as if she couldn't refer to Andrea as her mother. Given everything, he supposed that was understandable. "True."

"Can you tell me more about you and my… Andrea?"

That was a happy change, that she was finally asking questions. "Sure. What do you want to know?"

"What was it like when you guys were dating? What was she like?"

"We'd known each other for a long time. Practically from the time we were born. Our parents met in medical school and became best friends."

"So they're all doctors too?"

"Yes."

"It's weird to think that I have a family that I've never met. People I don't know a thing about."

"I imagine that it is." But the rest of her family hadn't been interested in knowing a thing about her. That's why he hadn't told her about them. He couldn't bear to tell his little girl that her very own grandparents hadn't cared about her. He'd held out hope for a long time that their attitude would change and that they would reach out to him. It had hurt when he realized that nothing would change. The last thing he wanted to do was transfer that foolish hope to his daughter.

"Back to Andrea and you."

Cole stepped over a fallen branch before answering. "We were friends at first. Well, not so much when we were little kids. I preferred to play with boys, and she preferred to play with girls. We just saw each other when our parents got us together. But once we got to high school, we became good friends. That's when we really started hanging out. Then one day, like a bolt of lightning hit me, I fell in love with her."

"Did she feel the same?"

"I don't know."

"What did she say when you told her how you felt?"

"I didn't tell her."

"Why not?"

He shrugged and grinned. "I was fifteen and goofy."

"She must have felt the same way at some point since I'm here."

"Yeah." He'd thought so back then. With benefit of hindsight, he now suspected it had been raging hormones on her part.

Crystal stopped. Then she turned to look over the vista. They weren't very high, but the view was still impressive. "So why haven't you ever dated again? Some of my friends' parents are divorced, and they date other people. Some of them have even remarried."

"I guess I never found the right time."

"Or the right woman."

Cole put his hands on Crystal's shoulders and turned her so that she was facing him. "What is it that you really want to know?"

"Before I knew who she was, I told Andrea that I thought the reason you didn't date was because you were still in love with my mother. Are you?"

"You also thought she was dead so…"

"Nice dodge, Dad. Besides, that part is really your fault." She inhaled. "Are you still in love with Andrea? Because it's all right with me if you are. And I won't mind if you want to date her. I don't have to see her. And in a couple of years, I'll be going to college, so I won't be around much anyway."

"You're my daughter, Crystal. You mean more to me than anything in the world. If I have to choose between you and anyone else in the world, you would win hands down."

"I'm still kind of mad at her."

"You have a right to your feelings."

"But it was kind of sad to see the cards and letters she wrote to me over the years. I could almost feel how lonely she was."

"She missed you."

"I missed her, too." Her voice was so soft Cole could barely hear it.

"I'm sorry." Sorry that he hadn't been able to give his little girl the one thing that she'd wanted most in the world.

"You didn't make her leave. She did that on her own." Though she'd said these words before, this time they were lacking the fire and anger that had been there previously. Before they had been an accusation. This time the words were meant to assure Cole that she didn't blame him for her mother's actions.

"But she came back for you."

Crystal nodded. There was a boulder nearby and she sat on it and took a long drink from her water bottle. Cole knew she was thinking, and he left her to do it without hovering. He'd gotten an inkling of her thoughts from the questions that she'd asked, but he didn't have the slightest idea how she would process the information or what conclusion she would reach.

Cole leaned against the tree and took a drink from his own water bottle. Crystal's questions dredged up a lot of memories that he'd tried to keep buried. He remembered how heady it had felt when he and Andrea had begun to date. How he'd begun to notice every little thing about her:

the way she combed her hair; the sound of her laughter; the feel of her soft skin whenever they'd touched. He'd lived for the minutes that he'd spent with her. Sixteen years later, he was starting to feel the same way. Though he tried to ignore his growing feelings, it was impossible. He was falling in love with her all over again. And his heart ached to be with her. But he'd been telling Crystal the truth. She mattered more to him than anyone in the world. If she couldn't forgive Andrea and didn't want her in his life, then that was the way it had to be. He'd lived without Andrea before. He would do it again.

"I'm getting hungry. Are you ready to go?" Crystal asked suddenly.

Cole nodded. He'd hoped this hike would last a little longer. Not only that, he'd hoped that Crystal would tell him what she'd concluded. Apparently, he wasn't going to get what he wanted.

Chapter Sixteen

Andrea stepped into the craft store and looked around. It had been over a week since she'd last been here. The space hadn't changed, but the trepidation she felt replaced the warmth and welcome she'd experienced in the past. Crystal had texted her yesterday afternoon and asked her to meet here this morning. Dread and hope had battled inside her, and she'd tossed and turned all night. She wandered over to a corner where two chairs were grouped. The store had just opened, and the clubs wouldn't be meeting for another couple of hours, so Andrea didn't have to worry about running into anyone she knew.

"You're here."

Turning, Andrea looked into Crystal's eyes. They gave nothing away.

"You asked me to come," she replied simply. She wiped her suddenly damp palms on her denim skirt and stood erect, forcing herself not to betray her nerves.

Crystal opened her mouth, and then clamped her lips closed. Andrea sighed. She didn't want Crystal to feel uncomfortable around her.

Crystal sat down so Andrea did the same. Neither spoke for several minutes.

Andrea sighed and pulled a sealed envelope from

her purse. This was going even worse than she'd feared. Clearly Crystal needed more time and space. But while she was here, there was one thing she needed to pass along. "If you've changed your mind about talking, I understand. I've been carrying this letter around for days. I just want you to know that I'm going to be leaving town soon."

"You're leaving?"

"Yes. I think it's for the best." She had been debating it for a while, and seeing how uncomfortable Crystal was around her this morning tipped the scales. Though Cole had urged her to be patient with Crystal while she worked through her feelings, Andrea thought it might be easier for Crystal to do that if she wasn't worried about running into Andrea.

"Best for whom?"

"You. Me. All of us." Andrea sighed. "I think it's time to get back to the original plan. I never intended to disrupt your life. I came to town to make sure you were okay. Clearly you're more than okay. You're phenomenal. You're even better than the dreams I dared to have of you."

"I thought your original plan was to stay until the end of summer. It's not over yet."

"That was before."

"Before your secret was out?" Crystal's voice was sharp. Accusing. So different from the sweet girl she was at heart. Andrea hated knowing she was responsible for the change.

"Yes. You seemed so much happier when I was just your friend. Now that you know that I'm your mother, you seem so…"

"Angry?" It was an admission.

"Yes. I know I deserve it. But it's your sadness that

bothers me most. Maybe when I'm gone things can go back to the way they were for you. More than anything, I want you to be happy."

"Dad always says there's no going back when you mess up. You just have to start over where you are and do the best to make things right."

Andrea smiled. "That sounds exactly like something Cole would say. He always was wise beyond his years."

"But you're not starting over. You're running away."

"I—I imagine it seems that way."

"That's because it *is* that way," Crystal said. She'd definitely learned how to tell it straight from Cole.

Andrea sighed. "I suppose your dad wouldn't approve."

"Nope." Crystal tilted her head, a shy smile on her lips. "What was he like when you dated him?"

Talk about a quick change of subject. Andrea decided to go with it. After all, she'd promised to answer all of her daughter's questions.

"He was the smartest, kindest, funniest guy I knew." He'd also been the most handsome with the sexiest body that had made Andrea lose all sense, but that wasn't the kind of information Crystal was looking for.

"That sounds like how he is now."

"That's not surprising. Our character generally doesn't change."

"Dad said that you were the most driven, goal-oriented person that he knew. Are you still like that?"

"I suppose so. One of the things that I planned to do while I was here was learn how to relax and slow down."

Crystal laughed. Andrea had been missing that sweet sound. It lifted her heart, and she felt lighter in that moment. "Your goal was to learn how to relax?"

"When you put it like that, it sounds strange."

"I don't want to hurt your feelings, but it *is* strange."

"Sadly, it's one goal I have yet to achieve."

"Dad said that you never let anything get in the way of you reaching your goals. So you can't quit now. You have to stay until you master relaxing."

"Oh, Crystal. I would love to stay." It would be wonderful to have more time with her child. And Cole. But Crystal hadn't said anything about wanting to spend time together. To be honest, Andrea wasn't sure why Crystal had wanted to meet.

"You haven't been back to the knitting group."

"Of course not."

"Why?"

"Because I know you don't want to see me. I've avoided coming to town because I don't want to accidentally run into you."

Crystal picked at the cuticle of her left thumb. "I thought you were staying away because you were upset with me because of the things I said. I thought you didn't want to be around me."

Andrea reached out and covered Crystal's hand with her own. "There is absolutely nothing you can do to make me not want to be around you. *Nothing.* I know that may be hard to believe because I left you in the past. But that wasn't because I didn't want you. I did want you. I left because I wanted better for you."

"Better than what?"

"Better than me. I had nothing to offer you."

"You had love," Crystal said simply. Growing up with Cole as a father, it was natural that she would think that way. To Cole, love was all that mattered.

Andrea nodded. "Yes. And that love made me walk away so you could have a better life."

Crystal was silent for a long while, mulling over everything. Though it was difficult, Andrea didn't say a word. Finally Crystal looked up. "I don't understand why you left. I don't think I ever will. But I read the letters you wrote to your Little One." She inhaled. "The letters you wrote to *me*. At first I didn't want to admit it, but now that I've had time to think, I can say that I know they were filled with love."

Andrea's eyes began to water, and she blinked quickly. A lump developed in her throat making it impossible to speak above a hoarse whisper. "Every ounce of love in my heart."

Crystal nodded, silently absorbing Andrea's words. After a moment, she spoke again. "You don't have to leave because of me."

"You don't have to say that. I know that you're dealing with a lot. I don't want to make it harder for you."

"You being gone won't stop me from thinking about things. And if you're here, I can ask you questions. Do you want to stay?"

"Yes. I do."

"Then stay." With that, Crystal got up and walked away.

Andrea sat for a few seconds, her heart filled with hope. Perhaps the situation wasn't lost. Maybe their relationship could be salvaged.

Her daughter wanted her to stay.

"I talked to Andrea today," Crystal said, as she and Cole sat in the living room that evening. Cole had been pleasantly surprised that Crystal hadn't gone to her room immediately after dinner as she had every night since she'd learned Andrea was her mother. Though it wasn't family night, they were watching a movie.

Hallelujah! "How did that go?" Even though Cole was jumping for joy on the inside, he managed to keep his voice calm. He and Andrea had talked every night since Crystal's birthday, and he always filled her in on how Crystal was doing. Their conversations weren't especially long, and they didn't talk about anything deep or earth-shattering, but he looked forward to them. Hearing Andrea's voice as he lay in bed was intimate, and it made him miss her. He'd wanted to meet in person so he could see for himself that she was doing okay, but she'd shut down that idea with a quickness. She hadn't wanted him to do anything that might make Crystal angry at him.

"It was good. She was going to leave town, but I convinced her to stay."

What? Andrea hadn't said a word to him about leaving. "You did? Why?"

"I don't know." She avoided his eyes, suddenly quite interested in a spot on the wall. "It seemed like the right thing to do."

"I hope you didn't feel pressured by me."

"Sort of." Cole felt a deep pang of guilt, but it eased slightly when she added, "You're the one who's always told me to do the right thing."

"And I meant that. But not at the cost of your own feelings. It's never the right thing to ignore how you feel just to make someone else feel better."

"I didn't. Actually, I think Andrea being in town is right for me. I'm not angry at her any longer."

He raised an eyebrow. "Is that right?"

"Yes. And once I wasn't angry, I was able to think

clearly." She picked up her knitting needles and began to work on her project.

"And…?" he prompted when she didn't say anything else.

"*And* I think we should invite her over for dinner. We kind of owe her one. *And* I think we should let her hang out with us again."

"That's a big change."

"Not really. I liked her before I was upset with her. Now that I'm not upset any more, I like her again."

"Are you sure?"

"I'm sure. Is it okay with you? I mean it can't be easy having your ex-girlfriend around."

"That was a long time ago. I actually haven't thought about her that way in years." That was true as far as it went. Before she'd come to town, he really had packed away all of his old attraction to her. But now his feelings had started to reappear. Not that it mattered. Andrea was only here for the summer, and that was rapidly coming to an end. He had no intention of setting himself up for yet another heartbreak.

"Still, it must have been really awkward having me matchmaking." She didn't sound especially sorry.

"It was no more awkward than your matchmaking in general. Perhaps you should give it a rest." That last bit was wishful thinking, and he knew it.

"Maybe. In the meantime I think you should call Andrea and invite her to dinner tomorrow. I'll cook."

"I'll do you one better. How about we go to the Aspen Creek Resort? They have a very nice restaurant." Crystal's change of heart called for a celebration.

"Oh, we're going to have a fine dining experience?"

"Too much?"

"No. I like it. So call Andrea and invite her." She stood and picked up her knitting project. "I'll give you some privacy."

Grinning, Cole picked up his phone. After making a dinner reservation, he called Andrea.

When she answered, he blurted out, "What's this I hear about you wanting to leave town?"

He hadn't intended to say anything about that, but he was hurt that she hadn't even discussed her decision with him.

"Crystal told you?" Andrea's voice was filled with surprise and a hint of guilt.

"Yes. I should have heard it from you."

Andrea's sigh came over the line. "It was a spur-of-the-moment thing."

"Even so. You might act on the spur of the moment, but only when it's something you've been on the fence about. So you must have been thinking about it. But you never mentioned it once."

"I thought you would try to talk me out of it. I'd been hurting. And lonely. And you can guess how guilty I've been feeling."

"You should have told me instead of keeping it to yourself. I would have done something to try to make it better."

"What could you have possibly done?"

He had no idea. But he would have done *something*.

"I thought my presence in town was causing her pain. That if I was gone, she would feel better. Happy."

Cole sighed. "She just needed time to work through her feelings."

"I know. And now I'm not leaving. At least not until the end of summer."

That reminder of the limit to their time together, though

painful, was necessary to keep him from letting his feelings for her grow. They might have regained their friendship, but they wouldn't be rekindling their romance—if there had ever been a romance to rekindle. "To celebrate, let's go to dinner tomorrow. And before you answer, you should know this was Crystal's idea."

"It was?"

"Yes. She offered to cook, but I think we can do better than that. I was able to get reservations at the Aspen Creek Resort. The restaurant has great ambience and even greater food."

"For the three of us?" He heard the cautious hope in her voice.

"Yes."

"Count me in."

"Great. We'll pick you up at six."

They talked for a few more minutes before ending the call.

The next evening, he pulled in front of the cabin and parked.

"Breathe, Dad." Crystal's voice held a hint of humor. It was amazing. Once she had gotten past her anger, she had become her usual cheery self. That meant she was once more on her matchmaking kick. He didn't have the heart to tell her that nothing would ever happen between him and Andrea.

He looked over at Crystal. She was wearing a blue dress, looking every bit the young lady she was becoming. Cole got out of the truck, put on his coal-black suit jacket, then headed up the stairs. Before he had a chance to knock, the door swung open.

And there she was. Andrea looked like a dream. She had on a purple satin and sequin dress that clung to her curves and stopped midthigh. His eyes went immediately to her shapely legs. She was at once incredibly sexy and elegant. Her whole look screamed date night. Seeing how good she looked made him glad that he'd put on his best suit and tie.

Andrea's smile was bright enough to blind him. His heart thumped against the wall of his chest as he moved closer to her, drawn like steel to a magnet. She held out her hand and he immediately clasped it, noting how perfectly it fit into his. Her skin was soft and warm, a reflection of her heart. Being near her felt so good. He would happily stand there all night.

The sound of someone clearing their throat broke the enchantment, and Cole and Andrea jumped apart as if they'd been caught doing something wrong. Andrea blinked and slid her hand free of his. She looked over his shoulder, a tentative smile on her face. "Crystal. It's good to see you."

"It's good to see you, too, Andrea. And I really like your dress," Crystal replied. "Purple is Dad's favorite color."

Andrea nodded. "I know. He's also the person who convinced me to wear bold colors back when we were kids. I had gotten away from them for a while, but I'm getting back to my old style. And might I add that you look quite nice, too. Blue is a good color on you."

The conversation was a bit stilted and awkward. Cole wished he could do something to get them closer together, but he knew he couldn't force a relationship to grow between them. It was humbling to know that he had no more power to unite them than he'd had to keep them apart.

After a moment something shifted. Andrea started down the stairs at the same time that Crystal started up.

In the blink of an eye, mother and daughter were in each other's arms. Cole's vision blurred and he blinked away the moisture. When they pulled apart, they were both smiling.

Andrea linked arms with Crystal and turned to Cole, holding out her hand. "We're ready to go. How about you?"

He took the hand she offered, giving it a gentle squeeze as they walked across the driveway. Once they were all inside the truck, he headed toward the resort. The Aspen Creek Resort was family owned, but it boasted every amenity the corporate resorts had. At this time of year, the mountains were covered with colorful wildflowers, and Andrea and Crystal oohed and aahed over them.

"Did Dad tell you that they hold weddings here?" Crystal asked.

"No, he didn't mention that."

"They do. If you come on the right day, you can catch a glimpse of the bridal party taking pictures."

"Is that right?" Andrea said.

"The food is good too," Cole said, doing his best to steer the conversation away from weddings and marriage. He knew that Andrea was going back to Chicago, and he didn't want Crystal getting her hopes up. It was understandable that she would fantasize about her parents getting together, but that wasn't going to happen. Andrea wasn't going to walk away from everything that she'd worked so hard to build in Chicago and start over in a small town in Colorado. They would just have to find a way to build a familial relationship that worked for all of them.

He pulled into the resort parking lot, and they got out of the truck and walked inside. Cole had never cared much about decor, but now he tried to see the venue from Andrea's eyes. She'd grown up in the lap of luxury and was used to visiting the most lavish five-star restaurants, at home and abroad. The marble floor glistened in the large foyer, and light from the enormous crystal chandeliers illuminated the space. Large urns filled with flowers were scattered along the walls. Though they were in the mountains of Colorado, this restaurant could hold its own in any major city in the world.

As they crossed the lobby to the restaurant entrance, Cole was filled with a sense of peace. This was the first time the three of them were going out together with no secrets between them. They knew they were family. Now they just had to figure out a way to navigate that new reality.

Chapter Seventeen

Andrea swallowed the last bite of chocolate cake. Dinner tasted every bit as delicious as Cole had promised. But the delicious beef dish she'd enjoyed couldn't compare to the pleasure she'd gotten from the conversation the three of them had.

They'd talked about everything during dinner, laughing and teasing each other. It was as if they'd been together for years. By the time dessert was served, Andrea had felt comfortable enough to ask about Crystal's childhood. That set off a chain of stories that alternated between the humorous and the sentimental. Some of the stories were accompanied by pictures.

"This is Crystal's sixth grade picture," Cole said, pulling a small photo from his wallet. Most people had pictures on their phones, and Cole had an abundance of those, but his wallet was also thick with pictures of Crystal.

"Please don't show her that one," Crystal said, covering her face with her hands. "It's so embarrassing."

"Well, now you know I have to see it," Andrea said with a laugh. "You were so cute in all of the other ones."

"That was before Dad let me choose my own clothes and comb my hair by myself."

"Ahem," Cole interrupted. "If I recall correctly, you insisted. Vehemently."

"I had more attitude than skill."

Andrea took the picture and looked at it. "You were adorable."

"You mean a*dork*able," Crystal said. "My face couldn't seem to make up its mind what to do."

"Actually, you look a lot like I did back then."

"Do you have a picture?" Crystal asked.

"Not one from school. And definitely not in my wallet. But I may have a picture of a picture on my phone." Last year, Andrea's mother had put together a collage as part of her and Andrea's father's fortieth wedding anniversary celebration. She'd emailed Andrea a few pictures from the collage. Andrea scrolled through her phone's photo gallery and pulled up a picture of herself at eleven years old. She held out the phone to Crystal. "This is me at my tap dance recital."

Crystal took the phone and studied the image. "You were so cute. It's funny how much you look like I did— with a neater hairstyle."

"I guess that means you're cute, too."

"When you put it like that…" Crystal chuckled and struck a pose.

"Let me see," Cole said, extending his hand for the phone. Crystal gave it to him.

"I know you took dance lessons," he said. "I just never knew you performed in recitals."

"That's because you never came."

Crystal took the phone back. "I love your little hat and cane. I can't believe you took dance lessons just like me."

"That's something we have in common." When she'd been a kid, Andrea had loved to dance. That's one of the activities she'd wanted Crystal to be able to enjoy. Cole had given Crystal everything Andrea had dreamed of for her. And more.

Crystal began to scroll through the phone, stopping occasionally to ask Andrea about a photo. It took a moment for her to realize that although there were pictures of Andrea with her family, Crystal never asked about any of them. But then, they were all strangers to her. That reality was heartbreaking, but there was nothing Andrea could do to change the situation. She didn't have the ability—or right—to get them all together.

When Andrea noticed Crystal yawn for a second time, she reluctantly spoke up. "I suppose we should get a move on."

Cole motioned for the waitress, who brought the bill.

"I had a really good time," Crystal said.

"So did I," Andrea said. "We should do this again."

"Yes." Crystal glanced at her hands and spoke tentatively. "It's almost like being a family."

Cole cleared his throat, and then took one of Andrea's hands and one of Crystal's. "We *are* a family. Nothing that happened in the past and nothing that will happen in the future can change that."

"Do you feel that way too, Andrea?" Crystal asked.

Andrea replied without hesitation. "Absolutely."

Crystal smiled. "Then it's official. We're a family."

"It's also official that we need to get going," Cole said, coming to his feet.

As they walked back to the truck, Andrea felt like she could float to the moonlit sky. Sixteen years ago, she hadn't believed it would be possible to be a family with Cole and their baby. It had still seemed impossible only days ago. Yet it was a reality now.

She was lost in thought and was surprised when Cole pulled in front of the cabin. Andrea glanced in the back seat. Crystal was either sound asleep or doing a good imitation.

Andrea grabbed the door handle.

"I'll get it," Cole said. "I have to walk you to the door."

Andrea smiled as she watched Cole circle the truck and open her door. Before she could get out, Cole grabbed her waist and lowered her to the ground. Her body brushed against him and desire bloomed inside her at the contact. She knew she should step away, but she was powerless to move. She sought his gaze, and the fire in his eyes sent all good sense flying into the atmosphere.

Ever so slowly, Cole lowered his head and she raised hers until their lips met. Andrea closed her eyes and pressed against Cole's hard body. The need inside her was strong and no matter how close she got, she wanted to be even closer. Moaning, she opened her mouth to him and his tongue swept inside and tangled with hers. She ran her hands over Cole's chest, feeling his steady heart-beat beneath her palms, then wrapped her arms around his neck. Andrea felt Cole's hands caressing her back and she sighed. Nothing had ever felt this good, and she wanted the feeling to last forever.

An owl hooting in the distance brought her back to awareness of her surroundings. She and Cole were mak-ing out while their daughter slept in the truck not a foot away from them. Her desire cooled, but it didn't go out entirely. She felt sure that nothing in the world would ever completely erase her desire for Cole. But given the reality of their situation, she was going to have to try.

"What happened?" Cole asked, leaning his forehead

against hers. Though he'd stopped caressing her, his hands were wrapped around her waist, holding her in place.

She gestured to the truck. "We're not alone."

He smiled. "I know. But she's asleep. And I don't think Crystal is the reason you pulled back so suddenly."

She could have told him the truth, but she didn't want to ruin this perfect moment with talk of its eventual end. "I felt myself getting carried away."

His smile became devilish. "I know that feeling."

Smiling, she shook her head. "Good night, Cole."

Andrea pressed another kiss upon his lips, then turned and started up the stairs. She'd taken two steps when she realized Cole was walking beside her. She gave him a questioning look. "I said I would walk you to your door and that's what I intend to do."

"Such a gentleman," she said, taking his arm.

When they reached the cabin door, he turned to face her. "One more kiss for the road?"

"You read my mind."

This kiss was just as fiery as the previous one, and when they pulled away, they were each breathless. Had they been alone, Andrea would have dragged him into her bedroom and had her way with him. That would be the perfect memory to take back with her to Chicago, warming her on cold nights. But since their daughter was sleeping in the back seat of Cole's truck, Andrea opened the door and stepped inside, closing it before she could give into temptation.

Cole rubbed a thumb over his bottom lip as he recalled how good it felt to kiss Andrea. They'd kissed since she'd been back in town, and that been good, too. But last night's kisses had been something special. Even though he knew that they had been purely made of longing and desire, with nothing else mixed in, it hadn't made the kisses any less satisfying. He had already accepted the fact that the end of summer would bring the end of their relationship. But there was still time before Andrea left. And he intended to make the most of it.

"You're in a good mood," Gary said, breaking into Cole's thoughts. "You haven't stopped smiling all day."

"We went out last night. The three of us. And it was good."

"And Crystal?"

"She's happy. I might have been against Crystal and Andrea meeting, but now that things have worked out, I'm glad to say that I was wrong."

"So what is going to happen next? Is she going to move here and be a real mother to Crystal? Are you going to get together?"

Cole shook his head. The questions hurt his heart because he knew Andrea didn't plan to stay in Aspen Creek. She'd worked hard to become a pediatrician, making incredible sacrifices to earn her license and build her practice. He wouldn't pressure her by asking her to uproot herself.

"She has a full life in Chicago. It wouldn't make sense for her to move here, especially when Crystal will be going away to school in a couple of years. But she and Crystal are going to keep in touch."

Gary paused. "So Crystal is good."

"Yep."

"And you?"

"What about me?"

"It's obvious that you're still in love with her. I didn't like her for hurting Crystal, but if that's all in the past, then she's okay with me. Go ahead and pursue her. You never know what can happen."

Cole knew exactly what could happen. Summer would end, Andrea would leave and he would be devastated. But that wouldn't stop him from enjoying the time they had. He just would keep his heart out of it.

He'd already called her and invited her to go ice-skating at the indoor rink this evening. Crystal was having dinner with Olivia and her family, and Cole intended to take advantage of his time alone with Andrea. It had been years since he'd been on the ice, but he was certain he could stay on his feet.

Andrea was sitting on a wooden bench in the lobby when he arrived. She stood up when she saw him. "There isn't anyone else here. I thought ice-skating would be more popular here. Isn't Aspen Creek home to a bunch of winter Olympians?"

"Yes. And if we were here in January, the ice would be crowded. In summer people tend to enjoy the outdoors."

She gave him a sly smile. "Are you saying we'll have the ice to ourselves?"

"If not, pretty close to it."

They rented ice skates from the pimply faced teenager playing games on his phone, and then sat on a bench beside the ice. Andrea toed off her shoes and pulled on her skates. While she laced them, she looked over at him. "It's been forever since I've been skating. I hope I still remember how. I'm going to take a spin while you get your skates on."

Andrea stepped onto the ice, and then took a cautious step. Then another. When she was sure she wasn't going to fall, she pushed off and began gliding across the ice. Cole watched, mesmerized by her slender figure as she gracefully circled the rink. The way she jumped and spun was so joyous that he could only stare in awe.

"Are you coming, or are you just going to sit there?" Andrea called as she sped by.

Cole shoved his feet into the skates, tied them, and then joined Andrea on the ice. When she noticed him behind her, Cole thought she would slow down so he could catch up. Instead, she dug her blades into the ice and began to go faster. Laughing, he sped up. His legs were longer and in a few strides he was beside her. She held out a hand and he grasped it. They skated around the rink hand in hand. The music playing over the speakers switched from a fast number to a ballad. Without stopping, Cole slid his arm around Andrea's waist and turned her so that they were facing each other. Cole hummed along to the song as they danced across the ice.

One song bled into the other and time flew. Before long, the music ended and a recorded voice came over the loudspeaker, announcing that the rink would be closing in ten minutes. They made one last turn around the ice, and then hurried to the bench where they swapped out their skates for their shoes.

After returning their skates to the rental booth, they went to the parking lot and leaned against Cole's truck. The sun had set and the sky was filled with bright stars. A gentle breeze blew Andrea's hair into her face, and she tucked it behind her ear.

"That was fun," Andrea said, looking up at him. The streetlight illuminated her face just enough for him to be mesmerized by her happy smile.

"How about an ice cream?"

"That would be perfect."

The ice cream parlor was only two blocks away, so they

decided to walk. When they reached their destination, Cole turned to Andrea. "What do you want?"

She studied the board. "Is that a soft serve machine? I'll take a swirl."

"They have handmade ice cream and you want soft serve?"

"I'm a simple girl."

"Said no one ever about you."

Laughing, Andrea punched him in his biceps. "Maybe not. But I haven't had a cone in so long."

"That does sound good," Cole admitted, and got one, too.

Once they had their cones, they began to walk down the street. The night was balmy, so there were others walking around. After a few minutes, Andrea sighed. "This is such a great little town. I'm going to miss it when I leave."

She said it so matter-of-factly that it took Cole's breath away. He knew a few kisses hadn't meant she was falling in love or that she'd consider staying. But he thought she would have a little bit of regret about leaving him behind. He'd been telling himself all the right things: there was a difference between love and lust; a little friendly kissing never hurt anyone. But he knew those platitudes didn't apply to him in this situation. Stupidly, he'd fallen in love with Andrea again. But that was his problem.

Angry at himself, he squeezed the cone and his ice cream spilled over the top and plopped on the ground. "Damn."

Andrea handed him a couple of paper napkins. He scooped up the mess and dropped it into a trash can. Inhaling, he forced himself to calm down. He'd known the score from the start. He could either pout and spoil tonight for Andrea or he could enjoy the time they had together.

Andrea swiped her tongue around her rapidly melting ice cream, her eyes dancing with amusement. "I would offer to share, but I haven't had soft serve in ages."

"Be that way." He looked at his empty cone, and then dropped it into the can beside his now discarded treat. "I suppose I'll just have to look on in sorrow. Longing for a taste."

"If you're trying to guilt me into sharing, it's not working."

"Can't blame me for trying." Cole laughed and held out his arm. When she took it, they continued down the street. "So when are you leaving?"

Andrea stumbled and tightened her hold on his biceps. He wanted to tell her that he would always be by her side to catch her when she needed him, but he bit his lip. Their time—if it had ever existed—was gone. He wasn't going to drop not too subtle hints that might come across as pressure.

"I'm going back the last week of August."

"So soon? I thought you would be here until Labor Day."

"I wish. This has been the best vacation of my life. And you know why. But I can't stay that long. I have a lot of school and sports physicals to do. You played sports. You know how it is."

He remembered. Not to mention that he'd had to go through the same thing with Crystal. He wasn't going to make Andrea feel bad. And he certainly didn't want her to know just how badly he would miss her. "Crystal is going to miss you. We'll throw a party when you leave."

She gave him a look he couldn't decipher. "I'm getting tired. I suppose the ice-skating and walking has worn me out."

"Really?"

She nodded. He could have walked for hours with her by his side, but then he recalled that because of the tension that had existed between her and Crystal, she hadn't slept well for days. No doubt, that had caught up with her. Despite the fact that he wasn't ready for the night to end, he walked her back to the parking lot.

When they reached their cars, she tapped her key fob, and the lock clicked. She opened the door and stepped behind it as if using it as a wall to keep them apart. There was no mistaking what that meant. She had no intention of kissing him again tonight. What in the world had made her irritated with him all of a sudden? He replayed the last few minutes, but nothing came to mind. Perhaps he was misreading the situation, but he didn't think so.

One way or the other he had to set things straight between them for their daughter's sake. Crystal deserved parents who got along. He smiled and infused his voice with warmth and gentleness, as if he hadn't noticed that Andrea was suddenly as cold as the ice in the rink where they'd passed the evening. "It was wonderful spending time with you. Let's do it again soon."

"I'll call," she said. Then, before he could say a word, she got into her sedan and drove away, leaving him standing there.

Shaking his head, he jumped into his truck and drove home. Crystal was on the phone when he arrived, lying on her back on the couch, one foot in the air. She turned when she saw him and sat up. "I'll call you tomorrow. My dad is back."

"You don't have to hang up on my account," he said, but it was too late. She'd already ended her call.

"How was your date?"

He didn't bother asking how she knew he'd been on a date. She would only smile mysteriously and say she had her sources. He dropped into his recliner. "It started off well. Then it went off the rails so fast my head is still spinning."

"Tell me everything. Then I'll let you know what you did wrong so you can fix it."

"Why are you so sure that I'm in the wrong?"

She narrowed her eyes. "Do you want my help or not?"

Cole bit back a laugh. "I suppose I do."

Crystal smirked and sat cross-legged. She listened intently as he told her about the evening. When he finished, she shook her head. "Really, Dad? You told Andrea you were going to throw a party when she left? That sounds like you're celebrating the fact that she's leaving."

"That wasn't what I meant. I just wanted to show support for her decision. I didn't want her to feel pressured to stay for you."

"You need to stop hiding behind me. I don't want to be the excuse you use in order to avoid having a relationship because you're scared of getting hurt."

"That's not what I'm doing."

"Of course it is. You act like you're being cautious because you don't want to damage my relationship with Andrea, but it's really because you don't want to repeat the past."

"She broke my heart."

"I know. But as you told me, she came back."

"For you."

"Maybe that was the reason at first. But I see the way she looks at you. Just talking about you makes her smile. She actually starts to glow." Crystal leaned forward and looked into his eyes. "I know a lot has happened since I called you guys soulmates, but I think my intuition was right. You belong together. Maybe the time wasn't right before, but it's right now. Be brave, Dad. Tell Andrea how you feel. Or you really will lose her forever."

Without waiting for Cole's reply, Crystal rose, kissed his cheek, bid him good-night, then climbed the stairs.

Cole sat there for a moment, Crystal's words echoing through his mind. She was right. It was time to be brave. He was going to tell Andrea how he felt and let the chips fall where they may.

He grabbed his keys off the table, and then yelled up the stairs to Crystal. "I'm going out. Don't wait up."

Andrea drove back to the cabin, trying to ignore the pain in her heart. She'd had such high hopes for the evening. And it had started out so well, exceeding her expectations. Skating across the ice in Cole's arms while music played in the background had been the most romantic thing she'd ever experienced. There was something special about Cole. He drew emotions out of her in a way that nobody else had been able to do. He touched a part of her heart that was reserved only for him. The simplest moment with him was a joy. Foolishly she'd thought he felt the same. But she'd been deluding herself.

She sighed. They'd made so much progress these past weeks. She had begun to envision a world where they were more than just co-parents. A world where a romantic relationship for the two of them was possible. She'd fallen in love with him, but it was clear that he didn't feel the same.

She knew she should be grateful that he wanted her to be a part of Crystal's life and had worked to make the mother-and-daughter relationship work. He could have stood against her, building a wall between her and Crystal. Instead, he'd been a bridge. But her daughter wasn't the only one she wanted a relationship with.

When she reached the cabin, she forced herself to get out of the car. She didn't have the energy to go inside, so she sat in the rocking chair. Despite her best efforts to dispel them, Cole's words repeated in her mind. *Crystal* would miss her. Not a word about his feelings. *He was going to throw a party.* But why was she hurt or surprised? She knew he was attracted to her. The way he kissed her was proof of that. But she also knew that she'd hurt him too badly in the past for him to risk loving her again. Even so, he wanted them to be on good terms for their daughter's sake. But Crystal would be going away to college in a couple of years, and Andrea and Cole wouldn't have a reason to spend time together.

And she'd been thinking about starting a practice here in Aspen Creek. Thankfully she hadn't mentioned that to Cole. Being the type of man he was, he'd gently tell her to stay where she was. No matter how kindly he phrased it, the humiliation would be crushing. At least she'd been spared that. But she'd wasted enough time thinking about Cole. She needed to focus on herself and her next steps to build a happy future for herself. She'd risen from the ashes before, and she could do it again. If only it didn't hurt so bad.

Andrea sat there for a while. Gradually she became aware of a noise that didn't fit in with the peaceful nature sounds. It grew louder, and she recognized it as a truck engine moments before the headlights came into view. She only knew one person with a truck. *Cole.* Why was he here? That question was still forming when Cole jumped from the truck and practically ran up the stairs.

He must not have seen her sitting in the shadows because he knocked on the door.

"I'm right here," she said, pleased at the way he jerked in surprise.

"Andrea. I came here to talk."

"I figured as much."

He turned the other rocking chair to face hers, and then sat down. Their knees bumped, but he didn't seem to notice. "I think I messed up earlier and said the wrong thing."

"Are you saying you *aren't* going to throw a party to celebrate my leaving town?"

He gave a strangled laugh. "No. I was trying to show my support for you and your decisions."

"Because nothing says support like dancing the night away," she said dryly.

"I see now how it came across. But that is not what I meant. Believe me, I wouldn't be celebrating if you left. But I would—will—celebrate you choosing to do whatever fulfills you. Sixteen years ago I was no better than your parents. We all wanted to dictate your life. I was wrong to join in the arm-twisting. With my offer tonight of a party, I was trying, in my clumsy way, to let you know that I won't try to control your life. There won't be any subtle pressure. You've built a successful medical practice in Chicago. I'm happy for you. I'm *proud* of you. You've told me many times that you sacrificed a lot to get where you are. I don't want you to have to sacrifice another thing in life." He shook his head. "That's not even what I came here to say. I just needed to clear the air."

"Consider it clear."

"Thanks." He exhaled and she realized just how nervous he'd been.

"So what *did* you come here to say?"

He paused and she wished it wasn't so dark. She wanted to see his expressions. She was too wary to even hope, yet hope she did.

"I want you to stay."

"Because of Crystal?"

"She loves having you around."

Andrea's heart plunged.

Cole paused again and swiped his hand across his forehead. Andrea had never seen him so flustered, and that stubborn hope renewed its struggle. "No. I'm not going to hide behind Crystal. I want you to stay for me. I want you to stay because I'm in love with you. I think I've always loved you and I know I'll love you forever."

"I love you, too," Andrea blurted out, unable to contain herself. Her greatest wish was coming true.

"Really?" Cole asked. The shock and hope in his voice did her heart good.

"Yes. I thought you knew." Although since she'd been trying to hide her feelings from him as well as herself she shouldn't be surprised he hadn't caught on.

"I hoped." He sighed. "So where do you we go from here? Do you want to try the long-distance thing for a while?"

"Realistically, I'm going to have to go back to Chicago for a bit. I have patients and partners who are counting on me. I can't just up and leave them in the lurch. I also own a home. But I'll be back. I can open a practice here in Aspen Creek."

Cole smiled. "Do you remember when I said we were family?"

"How could I forget?"

"How do you feel about making it official?"

Her heart skipped a beat. "What are you asking?"

"I'm asking you to marry me. Will you?"

"Yes." She hesitated. "Could we…"

"Could we what?"

"I know that you've spent the past sixteen years being a parent. Your nest is about to become empty. How would you feel about starting over?"

"You mean have another child or two?"

Holding her breath, she nodded.

He cleared his voice. "I would love that."

Andrea sighed. It had taken sixteen years, but Andrea and Cole were finally going to be a family. Life truly didn't get better than this.

Epilogue

"Can you come downstairs a minute?" Cole called when he and Andrea stepped into the living room an hour later. They wanted to let Crystal share in their joy right away. After the role that she'd played in getting them together, it was only right.

Andrea's heart thudded with anticipation.

Cole squeezed her hand. "She's going to be thrilled."

"I know. It's just that everything is so perfect. It's almost too good to be true."

"But it is true," Cole said, brushing a quick kiss on her lips.

"What's up?" Crystal asked as she jogged down the steps.

When she stepped into the room, her eyes immediately widened as she noticed that Cole and Andrea were holding hands. Then she smiled.

"We have something to tell you," Andrea said, her voice trembling with excitement.

"You're staying?" Crystal guessed, a smile brightening her expression.

"Well, yes…but there's more—"

"OMG! You're getting married!" Crystal exclaimed before Andrea could say another word.

"Yes. I hope you're okay with that," Andrea said gently.

Crystal raced over and hugged her. "I'm more than okay with that. I'm the happiest I've ever been."

"So are we," Cole added, wrapping his arms around Crystal and Andrea, holding them in a warm embrace.

After a moment, Crystal spoke. "I know I said before that I didn't need a mom, but that wasn't the truth. I need you. And I love you. I'm so glad that you're my mom."

"So am I," Andrea whispered over the lump in her throat.

"Can I be a bridesmaid?"

"You can be anything you want," Andrea said.

"That's right," Cole added. "After all, we wouldn't be getting married if not for you."

Crystal grinned. "It's like I said. You're soulmates. You two belong together."

"We three belong together," Andrea said, including Crystal in her statement.

"That's right," Cole added. "We belong together. We always have."

* * * * *

Look for the next book in the
Aspen Creek Bachelors miniseries by Kathy Douglass.
Coming soon to Harlequin Special Edition!
And catch up with the previous books in the series

Valentines for the Rancher
The Rancher's Baby
Wrangling a Family
The Cowboy Who Came Home

Available now!